Propose To Me
A Romance Anthology

Charmaine Pauls
Ellyse Roberts
Elena Kane
Tara Fox Hall
Caroline Andrus
Louise Redmann
Katie Stephens

Published by
Satin Romance
An Imprint of Melange Books, LLC
White Bear Lake, MN 55110
www.satinromance.com

ISBN: 978-1-68046-138-1

Cover Art by Caroline Andrus

Propose To Me
A Romance Anthology

Artificial Tears by Charmaine Pauls
Lourdes March has cried enough tears over her dishonest ex. She is moving on. Until she walks into an optometrist's office, and is confronted with the splitting image of the man she's trying to forget.

The Spark by Ellyse Roberts
Anna Claire had everything: money, a fiancé, and a successful job as an architect. Her life was going great until a homeless guy with a grudge decided to set the building she was renovating on fire. Ethan was a firefighter filled with regret from a mistake he made long ago. An inferno brought them back together. But can fate re-ignite the spark they thought was lost forever?

Proposal Unexpected by Elena Kane
Adele had the perfect life, until it all fell apart. She's left alone and bitter after discovering her husband's many transgressions, when she finds herself face to face with a familiar face from the past. Wondering why they ever parted ways to begin with, Adele is faced with the difficult choice of forgetting and forgiving her husband, or starting a life with the man she spent years loving before life got in the way.

One Perfect Moment by Tara Fox Hall
Coriander Hartwell's dream of getting married has almost come true; her longtime lover Stefan VanKellam II has finally popped the question. But the instant she locks eyes with old flame Dustin at her high school reunion, Cori begins to rethink her dream of a perfect wedding…and the man she wishes would make her his wife.

Running Late by Caroline Andrus
On her way to meet with her boyfriend, Will, Paige reflects upon their seven-year relationship and prepares herself to be dumped. Meanwhile, Will has something else in mind.

Cappuccino Dreaming by Louise Redmann

What does it cost to be yourself? She's cooked for her boyfriend, played nice with his friends, and twisted her personality to fit his. He's booked an expensive restaurant for Saturday night. *Surely he's going to propose.* But when she sees her lover kiss her best friend, she flees into a coffee house only to trip up the stairs, spilling her cappuccino over everyone. Out of the angry crowd, one man offers his hand and a fresh drink.

Love Weavers by Katie Stephens

Hannah and Wynter have two things in common: an incredible artistic talent and witchcraft. In order to acquire Wynter's jewelry-making secrets, Hannah finds a way to travel across time and meet her ancestor. However, her novice powers simply amuse Wynter, who is embroiled in a love triangle and has no time for the young witch. When an enchanted necklace disappears, can the two work together or must their men take matters into their own hands?

ARTIFICIAL TEARS

By

Charmaine Pauls

For Marguerite

Lourdes looked up from the Kindle she was reading in the plush white chair of Santiago's Clinica Alemana when the receptionist called her name.

"Ms. March to consulting room two."

Finally. It had taken long enough. Why were doctors always behind schedule? Lourdes shut down her tablet and made her way down the clinic hallway.

Halfway there, her step slowed. It couldn't be. The man waiting for her in the white overcoat looked nothing like his on-line profile photo. Sure, his face was framed by tousled hair and day-old stubble, but it had a red tint instead of blond, and his eyes were blue not gray. On her computer screen, he had looked older. In real life, he was young–and the spitting image of Dirk, her ex-boyfriend.

The strained lines of his mouth slackened, and his eyes warmed a little as he watched her pause. She faltered for only a second, and then moved forward again before it could seem awkward. Lourdes had chosen him for his credentials, despite the lack of reservations on his clinic page. Most optometrists in this clinic booked up six months in advance. She had attributed his unpopularity to his gringo appearance. This was Latino country. But she hadn't expected a carbon copy of Dirk. Minus the freckles. Standing in front of him now, she couldn't help but stare.

His expression softened as he gave her a smile. "I'm Dr. Bouwer."

She held out her hand to shake his, but he bent down and pressed his cheek against hers, the customary Chilean greeting reserved for friends. The act took her aback so much she didn't introduce herself. But then he

1

already knew her name. His gaze was even as he motioned her to the room at the end of the corridor.

Lourdes watched his broad back as he walked around his desk and took a seat. His build was similar to Dirk's, except a bit taller. The resemblance was disconcerting.

Lourdes suddenly became aware of Dr. Bouwer staring at her with a raised eyebrow. "Well?"

She blinked. "Oh. Um, I need an eye test."

"What seems to be the problem?" he said, folding his hands on the desk. She couldn't help but notice those big hands with strong veins and neatly trimmed nails.

"I have trouble reading small text."

He turned his chair to his computer and started typing. "Since when?"

The side profile could have been Dirk: same straight nose, same square chin, and same dimple. "A month or so."

"Any other symptoms? Headaches after reading or watering eyes?"

His fingers moved competently over the keyboard, eyes fixed on the screen.

"Just a lot of redness and burning."

"Right." He turned back to her. "Ms. March…" In the short hesitation that followed, Lourdes noticed the corner of his mouth lift, making his dimple more pronounced. He shifted. "Let's have a look at you." He got up and indicated an examination chair.

Lourdes could have sworn he wanted to say something else. She sat down on the edge of the seat and waited for the right moment to ask him if he was related to Dirk. Then she decided against it. That was ridiculous. She had dated Dirk for two years. He had never mentioned a brother or a cousin. Certainly, nobody who looked *exactly* like him. She had heard once that everyone had a double. It seemed like she had found Dirk's.

After Dr. Bouwer moved the phoropter into place, he touched her shoulders and gently pushed her back. Next, he laid his palm on her head, ever so softly, positioning her so that her right eye aimed through the lens. The contact lingered. It caused a tingling through Lourdes' body, and she clenched her hands together between her knees in an effort to calm her rioting nerves.

"Please read what you see." His breath moved the air. She felt it close to the side of her head, like a warm whisper. He changed his position and sat on the stool in front of her. For some reason, Dr. Bouwer unsettled her, and it was more than just his likeness to Dirk.

She cleared her throat and called out the letters and numbers that appeared in her view. The charts were easy to read. She sprinted through them, while he took notes.

"Very good," he said at the end of the test, sounding surprised. "I've never had a full score before."

She smiled, and then jerked a little as his hand touched hers. "Now the other one."

The left eye did not perform as well. The last two rows were a blur. This time there was no praise from Dr. Bouwer.

"Are your eyes often as red as they are now?" he asked, wheeling the phoropter away.

Lourdes squinted to adjust her focus. "Yes. Light, wind or air conditioners easily irritate them."

"Probably due to dryness." His voice became sympathetic, as if he tried to soften a blow. "Or ageing."

It was on the tip of her tongue to say she wasn't old, but then she remembered Dr. Bouwer had access to her medical records.

"I need to swipe this over your eye," he said, holding up a strip of paper. "It won't hurt." He put his forefinger under her chin. "Lift your head."

Lourdes obeyed, staring anywhere but at him as he gently opened her eye with his index finger and thumb. *Won't hurt?* It felt as if he had cut through her retina with a scalpel. She cried out softly.

"Sorry," he mumbled, keeping the piece of paper in place. "I touched the corner of the phenol to your eye. Are you fine?"

The genuine tone of concern touched her. "Don't worry about it. My eyes are very sensitive."

He removed the strip and handed her a tissue as he peered down at her face. "I'm impressed, Ms. March. You have very good eyes."

"Really?" She dabbed at the tears running down her cheek. The more she tried contain them, the faster they flowed.

"You have the pret—" he cleared his throat, "eh…the best eyes I've seen."

"Then what about the fine print I can't read?"

"Normal part of the degenerative process. They're still incredible for your age." He patted her shoulder. "We're almost done." He lifted a card from the counter and held it toward her. "Read this out loud."

Lourdes took the cardboard and squinted at it. With her eyes tearing up, she found it difficult to focus. On top of that, the text was in Spanish.

She bit her lip and looked at him.

Catching her expression, he frowned. "Read it, please."

Lourdes shrugged. He must have his reasons for requiring the strange test. She stumbled over the pronunciation.

"Stop."

When the next word spilled over her lips, he plucked the card from her hands and glared at it. "My apologies."

He opened a drawer, put the card away and gave her another one in English. This time she managed to read through her blinking.

Dr. Bouwer seemed satisfied when she was done. "You don't need glasses yet. They make the eye muscles lazy. Hold out for another year."

"Thank you." She started to get up.

"Wait." He sat down on the stool again. His voice was soft when he said, "I really irritated your eye. Would you like me to give you some artificial tears?"

"What?" She blinked faster in a futile effort to dispel her weeping.

"Artificial tears," he repeated.

"Yes, thank you."

He gave her a satisfied nod and took a bottle from the shelf next to him. She lifted her head for him, and he stretched her eye open as if it was a delicate crystal bubble that might break. This time she didn't look away and saw him studying her with something like curiosity.

"Truly amazing eyes," he said, his breath warm on her face. "Perfect score."

He smelled of the forest and mountains—fresh and outdoorsy.

"Almost perfect," she corrected.

"It wasn't to the tests I referred, Ms. March."

As she tried to analyze his words, he leaned forward to administer the drop. Their knees touched. A bolt rushed through Lourdes, surprising her as much as the pain the strip had caused in her eye. For all the control she possessed, she couldn't move. Instead, she sat dead still, aware of only the small spot where his body applied pressure to hers. It should have been uncomfortable, but it was strangely comforting. And then a cold drop fell into her eye. It stung for a second before the burning eased. He repeated the process with the other eye before pushing the chair away. If he had been affected by their accidental touch, he didn't show it.

He handed her another tissue. "All better?"

"Thank you."

Dr. Bouwer offered her a hand when she got up. "If there's no emergency, I'll see you next year."

"All right." Lourdes picked up her bag and headed for the door. She contemplated asking about Dirk again, but glancing over her shoulder, she saw he had picked up a file from his desk. Next patient. He didn't even offer a farewell as she quietly closed the door behind her.

What on earth was that about? Lourdes' heart beat fast as she walked back to the car park. He probably only affected her because he looked so much like Dirk. And Dirk was a *bad* mistake, one best left in the past.

Inside her car, she tilted the rearview mirror and uttered a cry of shock. The whites of her eyes were bloodshot, with the left one tainted orange. Both green centers stared back at her surrounded by smeared circles of mascara. She looked like a rabid zombie. No wonder he couldn't look at her.

~ * ~

By the fifteenth of the month, Lourdes couldn't shake her anguish. She should have business lined up until April, but the recession slowed everything down. If something didn't come in soon, her event organization company would be in serious trouble.

"I shouldn't have taken on the city council account," she said to Trudy, her assistant and only other Executive Events employee. "They never pay on time."

"We can hold off our creditors for another few days," Trudy offered.

Lourdes crossed her legs on her desk and chewed the end of her pencil. "I've put out proposals to more than fifty companies in the past two weeks and we've heard nothing back."

"Why don't you ask Dirk?" Trudy said, already looking guilty for the suggestion.

"You know I can't speak to him."

"I know. But he's in the entertainment business. He's always had plenty of contacts."

Lourdes rolled her eyes. "He's a professional gambler. Don't sugarcoat it. Besides—"

The phone cut her off. Trudy replied with her practiced greeting, put her hand over the receiver and said, "It's for you."

"Put it through."

Lourdes took the call, praying for a client who needed a competent event organizer.

"Ms. March?"

"Yes?"

"Hi." There was a small pause. "Dr. Bouwer here."

Lourdes felt herself flush a little. She dropped her feet and sat up straight. Why in the world would he call her? Had he analyzed the strip and found something wrong with her eyes?

"Is something the matter?" she asked in alarm.

"No," he said hastily, "no, nothing's wrong, at least not with you."

His words confused her. "Then how can I help you?"

"I honestly hope you can," he said softly but didn't elaborate.

A nervous laugh bubbled from her throat. "I'm not a mind reader, Dr. Bouwer."

He hesitated again and finally blurted out, "I'd like to talk about Dirk."

It shouldn't have surprised her, but it did. The resemblance was too much of a coincidence. Her throat contracted. "Are you related to Dirk?"

"I think that's obvious."

The evasiveness of his reply didn't please her, but she didn't push the issue. She would not discuss her ex with him or anyone. "I have nothing to say about Dirk."

"You dated him for two years."

"How do you know that? Dirk never mentioned you."

The silence stretched for a few seconds again. "I won't lie to you. Dirk didn't tell me. But I have other sources of information."

"Dr. Bouwer, I don't know what you want or what Dirk is to you, but that subject's not on my topic list. End of discussion."

"We'll have to meet anyway."

Lourdes could hear a smile in his voice. "Not for another year. And I think I'll change doctors."

"That'll make me sad," he said, the amusement thicker now, "but I meant we'll have to meet because I'm employing your company to host my medical seminar."

"What?" She glanced at Trudy, listening in on the call, of course. Trudy only shrugged. "I didn't specify my business in my medical records."

"I looked you up on Google."

"You did a search on me?"

"Doesn't everyone these days?"

"No!"

"You did when you took an appointment with me."

"That doesn't count. That's how the clinic operates."

"And you chose me for what? My empty schedule?" he asked, sounding sarcastic, "or my resemblance to your ex?"

"For your information, your photo looks nothing like you. I chose you because you're well qualified and I felt sorry for you."

He chuckled. "Sorry?"

"Yes. Because nobody else booked you."

"Thanks for your charity, Ms. March. I'm flattered. As much as I'm enjoying this conversation, I have to go. I actually have a patient waiting, believe it or not, so can we please confirm a date for our appointment?"

Lourdes mentally scolded him. *Blackmailing son of an evil doctor.* "I'm afraid my schedule is full. I doubt if I can fit in another event for..." She flipped noisily through her diary. "Ten years."

His soft laugh vibrated through the receiver down to her very bones. "I've checked your schedule, too, Ms. March. It's as dry as a desert. Send me a contract for the sixteenth of August. My secretary will get the details to you. Shall we make it Monday at ten, your office?"

Lourdes opened her mouth to tell him where he could send his details, but Trudy interrupted. "Noted. Thank you Dr. Bouwer. See you Monday," she confirmed and quickly disconnected.

Lourdes gaped at her. "What did you do that for?"

"Because we're dead without the business, and you know it."

"Sadist," Lourdes mumbled, but Trudy only blew her a kiss.

~ * ~

Monday morning found Lourdes a nervous wreck. She didn't want to talk about Dirk. More than that, she didn't want to meet the arrogant Dr. Bouwer again. Just looking at him reminded her of all the reasons she had fallen for Dirk, and why it had been the worst move of her life. True to his word, his secretary had emailed her a list of detailed requirements, down to the kind of music and flowers Dr. Bouwer fancied. She had even included the maximum time his guests should have to wait for a drink. If she didn't need the business so badly…Well, she did. No use pondering the ifs.

At ten minutes before ten, Dr. Bouwer announced himself at the downstairs security desk and was shown up to the small office space Lourdes rented in a prominent business block. In her industry, appearance was everything. Even though not spacious, her office was uncluttered and tidy. A white leather chair faced her Bauhaus wooden desk. An original Francisco Copello print—a gift from her late father–adorned the wall and a white mohair carpet added warmth to the parquet floor.

The image that greeted her when the optometrist walked through her door rendered Lourdes speechless for a second. His copper-colored hair looked as if he'd just tumbled out of bed. For some silly reason, she had pictured him in his white doctor's coat, not in tight, faded jeans and a black T-shirt that hinted at impeccable abs. His broad smile indented the dimple that gave him a boyish appearance.

Lourdes got to her feet behind her desk and pulled on her black jacket. She had chosen the most professional outfit she owned—a linen suit tailored for her by a friend studying fashion design. She extended her hand, but she should have known better from their first encounter. Dr. Look-Alike rounded her desk and pecked her on the cheek.

She didn't miss Trudy's lifted brow, before the traitor scampered from her desk and held out her hand. "Trudy. Lourdes' assistant."

Dr. Bouwer didn't kiss her. He shook her hand jovially. "Pleased to meet you."

Trudy beamed as if he had just praised her for an impeccable job. "Tea?" Her smile was so broad Lourdes worried her face might crack.

"Please. Milk, two sugars."

"Got it." Trudy all but ran to the small kitchen at the back.

Lourdes indicated the chair facing her desk. "Please, have a seat."

Of course, the doctor wheeled the chair around so that it faced her from the corner of the desk, a much more intimate position.

Lourdes pushed her chair back involuntarily. "About the event—"

"I'd like to start with Dirk." He leaned forward and rested his elbows on his knees.

She had to admit, she was curious about how they were related. "Why didn't you say something when I came to your consultation room?"

He tipped his fingers together. "I thought you had realized it when you picked me. Once I saw the shock on your face, it was clear you didn't know. I wanted to tell you but..." He looked at his hands. "I'm sorry. I should have said something."

"You knew who I was beforehand?"

"Of course I knew. I knew the minute I saw your name on my schedule."

"Then why didn't you say something?"

"You were so shocked..." He broke off and looked back up at her. "I realize none of this makes sense, but I need to ask something of you. I wouldn't ask if it didn't mean the world to me."

"Wait." She held up her hands. "How are you related to Dirk?"

He frowned. "You haven't put the pieces together?"

She shook her head as she looked at him expectantly.

"I'm his twin brother."

"Twins?" Her voice came out in a whisper, "No. Dirk didn't... Dirk would have ..."

"He never mentioned me," he said sadly.

Unable to speak, she only stared at him.

"Dirk and I haven't seen each other since the day he left our parents' house."

She blinked rapidly. "But you have different surnames."

"Dirk took my mother's name. It's a long story, and one I don't wish to bore you with, so—"

"Oh no. You opened this can of worms, so you have to spill the beans."

"Let's just say there was a family row with my father, and Dirk blamed me. He left, against my father's wishes, and was disowned."

"That's terrible," Lourdes whispered.

"Yes, and I wish to make amends."

The reason for his call dawned on her. "And you want me to put you in touch with Dirk."

His look was so pleading, she almost faltered. "The answer is yes, again. I want you to talk to him for me. He'll listen to you."

Her laugh sounded hollow in the quiet office. "You don't understand the circumstances under which we broke up. He won't want to listen to anything I have to say."

He tilted his head and studied her. "Oh, but you're wrong. He'll hang on your every word."

"Dr. Bouwer—"

"Please, call me Henk."

"Henk, I–"

His hand lifted and cut off her words when he gently touched his finger to the corner of her left eye. "How's your eye?"

Her lips remained parted. She wanted to say something. Really. If she could only remember... Trudy saved her by bustling through the door with a tray, which she planted on Lourdes' desk. Lourdes' eyes widened when she spotted the plate of biscuits. They didn't keep biscuits. Trudy had run to the store? Seeing Lourdes' expression, Trudy cocked her shoulder, took the seat behind her own desk and leaned her chin on her hand as she studied Henk Bouwer.

Henk gave Lourdes a devilish smile. "I realize your time is precious with so many events lined up. How about if we run through mine, and then I'll pick you up for dinner to discuss the other private issue?"

Trudy's eyes almost popped out of her head. Lourdes shifted uncomfortably. She was about to decline when Trudy said in her sweet secretary voice, "Where shall I make a reservation, Ms. March?"

Lourdes shot her a cutting look, but Henk took charge. "Not to worry. I'll take care of it. Eight sharp? Now, about the event..."

~ * ~

Lourdes stood in front of the mirror, inspecting her reflection. Why did she even care what she looked like? Ten times she had picked up the phone to call off the dinner with Henk, but her curiosity had won out. She had chosen a green sleeveless dress, nothing too formal or too casual, since she did not know what Henk had in mind as a venue. He rang her bell at eight sharp. Taking a deep breath, she opened the door and then held that breath. Henk leaned on the frame, wearing white shorts and a blue T-shirt. Without meaning to, her eyes moved from his biceps to his calves. He definitely worked out. His hair was damp, as if he'd just stepped from the shower.

"Good evening, Lourdes." His eyes traveled over her in turn. "You look lovely. Ready to go?"

She grabbed her purse, locked her door and followed Henk downstairs to a Triumph TR6 parked on the curb.

Lourdes inhaled sharply. She ran her hand over the bonnet.

"Like it?" Henk said, holding the door for her.

"Love it. I have a thing for vintage cars, especially British cars in racing blue."

He gave an appreciative smile, closed her door and went around to get behind the wheel. He patted the dash. "Had her restored down to the original wooden panels and leather seats." He turned to her suddenly. "Would you like to drive?"

Lourdes shook her head. "No, thanks. I know she's a hard drive."

Henk grinned. "Top down okay, or shall I put it up?"

"Down, of course."

His grin widened. "I was hoping you'd say that. Most women worry about their hair."

She pulled her auburn hair into a ponytail at the base of her neck and marveled at the powerful sound as Henk started the engine. The noise made conversation difficult, so Lourdes sat back and enjoyed the ride. They drove in the direction of Las Condes, toward the hill. After ten minutes they left the double carriage way and noisy buses behind to take the residential turn-off. The houses became sparser and the properties bigger as they made their way up the mountain.

At a traffic light, Lourdes studied Henk's profile. His skin was tanned, not pale like Dirk's. While Dirk had model looks, Henk's features were slightly squarer, more masculine. Her awareness of his hand resting on the gearshift, close to where hers lay next to her thigh, was worrisome. The way his fingers folded around the stick was like a gentle, yet firm caress. For a second, she imagined that hand on her leg, his broad palm cupping her knee, and her mouth went dry. She bet he knew exactly when to take and when to give control.

"Taking stock?" he said with a smirk in her direction.

Not wanting him to think she was "taking stock" for the wrong reasons, she said, "Just observing."

"And?"

"You're darker than Dirk."

His smile faded. "I spend time outdoors."

"Are you a sports fanatic like Dirk?"

"I won't say fanatic. I enjoy tennis and weekend hikes."

"Dirk likes hanging out in the gym." Yet, he definitely didn't have the muscle definition of his brother. "Who was the firstborn?"

He sounded wary when he answered. "I was."

The light changed, and he pulled off to take the road to the ski resorts. Just before the mountain pass, he turned in the opposite direction and drove a short distance down a gravel road to a wooden house situated on a large property.

Lourdes regarded him with surprise. "I thought we were going to a restaurant."

Henk cut the engine and turned in his seat to face her. "What I'd like to discuss needs to be done in private. It won't be comfortable in a restaurant." He probably sensed her hesitation because he continued, "The minute you ask me, I'll take you home. Promise."

She believed him. Henk surrounded her with a sense of comfort and protection. Relaxing a bit, she looked at the house and asked, "Is this yours?"

"Yes. Moved in a couple of months ago."

"Where were you before?"

"New York."

Dirk had told her his family was from Amsterdam. "Your accent is stronger than Dirk's, but you don't sound Dutch."

"I studied in the States."

"Dirk hated the States. He always told me how much he missed Europe."

His hands clenched around the steering wheel. "I'm not Dirk, and he's not me. We look the same. That doesn't mean we have to be the same."

She frowned at his sudden animosity. "I didn't mean—"

"Forget it. I know it's hard not to compare." Without giving her a chance to reply, he opened his door. "Come. Let me show you around."

The house consisted of two levels with a deck that overlooked a narrow gorge and river. Like the walls, the floors were wood, giving the spacious rooms a cozy ambience. The interior was decorated with colorful Mapuche tapestries and carpets that accentuated off-white sofas and armchairs, and curtains and lampshades in earth tones. A massive fireplace dominated the open-plan lounge. Henk's house was just like him— understated elegance.

After starting the barbecue grill on the deck, Henk led Lourdes to one of the comfortable chairs surrounding a wooden table and poured her a glass of wine. It was pleasant outside, and she eased back in the chair. With the fire blazing, Henk disappeared into the kitchen and returned with two plates of ceviche.

"Starters," he announced, placing one in front of her.

"You made this?" she said.

"Yes. Why do you sound so surprised?"

"Dirk never cooked…" She trailed off and bit and her lip. "Sorry, I didn't mean to—"

"Compare. It's all right. I guess it's hard not to. That's the mistake my father made. He expected us to be the same."

Even if she didn't know Henk very well, it was obvious that he and Dirk were worlds apart. She sensed the pain in his words. "Have you tried to speak to Dirk?"

He refilled their glasses. "Many times. He never responds to my emails or messages."

"Excuse me for sounding blunt, but if he makes it so clear that he doesn't wish to see you, why force him?"

"Because Dirk is in trouble."

Lourdes didn't have to ask. "It's the gambling."

"He owes the wrong kind of people a lot of money, Lourdes. I wish to help, but he won't let me. If I didn't believe he was in danger of destroying himself, I wouldn't be so assertive. I want to help him. I want to make amends for our past."

"What exactly do you wish me to do?" Lourdes took a bite of the marinated fish. It was one of her favorite dishes, and she almost closed her eyes in ecstasy.

"I need you to talk to Dirk and convince him to accept my help."

She ate some more, contemplating the request. "What happened between the two of you?"

"My dad wanted us to follow in his footsteps and go to medical school. Dirk had no such desire. How much has Dirk told you of his past?"

"Not much. He told me he didn't have family." She gave Henk a compassionate look.

He nodded, his eyes sad. "He was trouble from a young age: getting into fights, sneaking out of the house, smoking and experimenting with alcohol. When I went to med school, Dirk decided to take a year off studying to travel. Only, he was deported back to the Netherlands shortly after for illegal gambling. My dad gave him an ultimatum. He tried to force him to join me at the university, but Dirk wanted to study art. Dad said that wasn't a profession and he wouldn't pay for a degree in fine arts. I believe if Dad hadn't pushed him so hard to be someone he wasn't, things might have been different."

He took a gulp of wine and swirled the liquid in his glass. "I wish Dad hadn't compared us the way he did. I got good grades, but Dirk didn't. He held it like a sword over Dirk's head until Dirk started hating me."

Lourdes leaned over the table to squeeze Henk's hand.

He gave her a faint smile. "After Dirk returned from his interrupted travel, he got involved in on-line gambling and lost a substantial amount of money. Dad paid off the people who came after him, but he had reached the end of his patience. He kicked Dirk out of the house and disowned him. Dad said the day Dirk gave up his gambling habit, he'd welcome him back with open arms. By then, Dirk had already been taken in by a famous player who trained him for the poker table."

He paused. "My mother was heartbroken. My dad spent everything he couldn't give to Dirk on me, both his money and his affections. To Dirk, I was the favorite—the golden child. Dirk had always been the black sheep, but now he was a poor, homeless black sheep. I tried to speak to him, but he pretended I didn't exist. He turned his back on us, and for a while, no one knew where he was or how he survived.

"When we had news of him again, he was in a coma at a London hospital. Someone in the poker scene had accused him of cheating and decided to teach him a lesson. Dad flew out there, rented a car..."

He stared at the bottom of his glass for so long that Lourdes thought he wouldn't finish the sentence. Finally, he said, "On the way, Dad had an accident. He was killed on impact."

Lourdes swallowed. She thought the biggest secret Dirk had hidden from her was his gambling addiction.

"Henk, I'm so sorry."

He looked up. "It's not your fault. Anyway, I did blame Dirk for a long time. I can't deny it. When he came to, I told him it was his fault our father was dead." His voice softened. "I've regretted it ever since, but he's never given me an opportunity to apologize."

Lourdes' heart squeezed painfully for both brothers. "I wish I had known."

His gaze fixed on the horizon for a while, and when he turned back to her, he said, "Why did you and Dirk break up, Lourdes? I know my brother isn't an easy person to live with, but I mean, why did you *really* give him the boot?"

She set her fork on her plate and wiped a hand over her face. It wasn't something she cared to discuss, but after Henk had opened up to her, it seemed unfair to shut him out.

"Dirk is the most important person in his life, I guess," she said, carefully choosing her words. "I didn't matter, and I believed I deserved better."

Henk wasn't going to give up easily. She could tell by the way he kept his eyes expectantly on her. "And?"

"He betrayed my trust."

"How? Did he cheat on you?"

She gave her shoulders a little shake, as if to physically dispel the unpleasant memory. "Does it matter?"

His eyes narrowed. "It does. To me. Tell me what he did, Lourdes." When she didn't reply, he said, "I know you kicked him out, from one day to the next. I know you left his belongings in the street."

Lourdes flinched a little. That had been mean, but she had been livid.

"He had to have done something big to deserve that," Henk continued.

It was her turn to swallow a big mouthful of wine. "He stole from me," she said under her breath.

"Stole from you?" Henk's expression was incredulous. "What did he steal?"

She cleared her throat. "He cleaned out my bank account."

Henk went quiet. He pulled a hand through his hair. "That explains why your business is in trouble."

Flushing, Lourdes shot him a look. "How do you know about that?"

"I told you I did my homework." He leaned forward suddenly and grabbed her hand. "I'll pay it all back, I swear."

She pulled away from his grasp. "You don't have to. It's not your responsibility. I'm managing."

For a second it seemed as if he might argue, but instead he motioned to her plate. "Finish up, the fire's ready. I hope you like fish."

She loved fish. She ate in silence, aware that Henk watched her, feeling uncomfortable under his scrutinizing stare. When she was done, he took their plates and pulled her to her feet.

"Care to give me a hand with the salad?"

"Sure." She followed him into the kitchen.

He placed a chopping board and tomatoes in front of her. "You were right, by the way."

"About what?"

"That you deserve better."

Feeling her cheeks grow warm, she turned to the sink and busied herself with rinsing the tomatoes.

"I forgot to ask you the other day, during the consultation, if you needed a prescription for artificial tears."

"No," she said with her back to him. "I've had enough real ones for a lifetime."

She hadn't heard him move, so when she suddenly felt his hand on her shoulder, she gave a startled jump.

"I appreciate your help, Lourdes. I know you don't have to do this, but it'll mean a lot to me."

She didn't answer.

Henk washed the lettuce and diced the cucumber while she chopped the tomatoes. All the while, she sneaked glances at those strong, capable hands. What was it about Henk's hands? She recalled the gentle way he had touched her during her check-up before quickly dismissing her. The woman who would one day win his exclusive affection, and that gentle, yet commanding touch, would be a lucky girl. That's to say, if he was single. He didn't wear a ring, but that didn't mean there wasn't a Mrs. Bouwer or a girlfriend in New York. Some married men didn't wear rings.

"Are you in a relationship?" She rinsed the cutting board so she didn't have to meet his eyes.

Henk looked up from tossing the salad. "No." He smiled. "Why?"

She shrugged. "Just curious. I thought maybe you had a family and came ahead to prepare a place for them to live."

"If I had a wife, I wouldn't have left her alone in New York. Not even for a minute."

"Oh." *Lucky future wife.*

"You?" He raised an eyebrow.

"I just got out of a relationship. I have no intention of rushing into another."

He took a hand towel from a hook on the wall and walked to her. "Give me your hands."

Lourdes swallowed. His proximity was not good for her heart. It tripped over its own beat as she obediently lifted her palms.

Henk took his time to pat them dry. "There we go." He draped the towel over his shoulder.

"You didn't have to…" she said lamely.

"I don't want the salad bowl to slip from your wet hands." His smile was disarming. "Do you mind?"

"Mind what?"

His eyes moved to the bowl on the table.

"Oh. Of course not." She picked it up quickly and carried it outside where the air was cool against her hot cheeks.

Henk grilled the fish while Lourdes set the table for their main meal. After Henk slid a perfectly cooked fish fillet onto her plate, she said, "Did you work in a hospital in New York, like here?"

He took a seat opposite her and poured them more wine. "I shared a practice with a partner but sold out when I moved."

"Was it hard to give up?"

"Wasn't easy. It took a long time to build."

"But you did it for Dirk?"

"He's the only family I have left."

She rested her chin in her hand. "Do you enjoy working at the clinic?"

"It's not the same, but I'll get used to it."

"So will you stay?"

He lifted his eyes to her. "That's the plan."

"Giving up your practice in New York and moving all the way here was a big sacrifice to make."

"I want Dirk to know how serious I am about fixing things between us. I want to be here for him." He took a sip of wine. "How about you? What brought you here?"

She gave a rueful smile and toyed with her fork. "Dirk. We met in Atlanta two years ago. And then he started playing big in South America, so…" She shrugged.

He studied her from under his copper lashes. "Looks like both of us have made big sacrifices."

"Two years and I still battle with Spanish," she said with an uncomfortable laugh to change the subject.

"Mm." He took a bite of his food. "I've noticed."

She flushed as she remembered the card she couldn't read in his consultation room. "It's just that I've always worked with American or English companies here."

"No need to explain. I know you're a clever woman, Lourdes."

She wanted to ask how he would know, but before she could formulate the question, he said with a glint in his eyes, "I looked you up on LinkedIn, too. Impressive resume. I may have also stalked you a bit on Facebook–from a professional interest, of course."

She buried her face behind her wineglass. The statement shouldn't please her half as much as it did. She had no business noticing Henk's hands, or his broad shoulders, or his tanned arms, or the intenseness of his stare.

After dinner, she helped clear the dishes and watched as Henk prepared Kalúa coffee for dessert. When the night turned cooler, he offered her a throw from the sofa and moved her to the kitchen table, always the attentive gentleman. Maybe it wasn't a good idea to spend too much time in Henk's company. She didn't want to like him too much.

She finished her coffee and checked her watch. "I have to go. Tomorrow's a work day."

He got to his feet without arguing. "Thank you for hearing me out tonight, Lourdes." He rounded the table and took her hand. "Will you help me? Will you speak to Dirk?"

After everything he had sacrificed for Dirk, how could she refuse?

"I'll think about it," she said softly.

He squeezed her hand. "I appreciate it."

She pulled her fingers from his grasp. "Thanks for dinner."

As she pushed the throw from her shoulders, he stopped her. "Better hang on to this for the ride home."

This time he put the hood of the car up. At her house, he walked her to her door and waited until she was safely inside. No peck on the cheek. Her father would have been impressed.

~ * ~

18

Later that night in bed, Lourdes lay in the dark and replayed the evening in her mind. A lot about Dirk made sense to her now, like why he always closed up like a clam when she asked about his past. Admiration for Henk swelled inside her. He had given up his life in New York to come after his estranged brother, to help him out of a dilemma that wasn't his duty to solve. How could she deny Henk's request? Despite the fact that Dirk had caused her heartache and suffering for most of the two years they had been together, they had been happy, too. Sometimes he had been so loving, he had actually convinced her he cared. She had just grown tired of having more tears than laughter. And stealing her money had been the last straw. As she drifted off to sleep, musing about the two brothers, her thoughts dwelled on the one who had offered her artificial tears.

~ * ~

On Tuesday morning when Trudy was at the bank, Lourdes sat down at her desk and stared at the phone. It was now or never. If she was going to call Dirk today, she'd better do it while she had a private moment, or her courage would fail her. It had taken months for Dirk to stop bombarding her voice mail, begging her to take him back, and now she was willingly making contact again. This was for Henk.

Before she could back out, she dialed his number. He picked up on the second ring.

"Baby." His voice was a sigh. "You have no idea how glad I am that you called."

"Don't 'baby' me. I—"

"You're still angry. That's all right. I was an idiot. I swear to God, love, I'll pay you back every—"

"Dirk, this isn't about us."

He paused. "What then?" His voice suddenly became strained. "Did someone call you about me?"

"Yes." She knew he worried about the people who he owed and couldn't pay off, even with all the money he had taken from her.

"Baby, listen to me, you can't tell them where I am. Don't—"

"Dirk, be silent, will you? I've met someone I believe you should see."

He sounded downright anxious now. "Is someone there with you? Are they forcing you to—"

"I met your brother," she said softly.

19

He was quiet for so long she wondered if he had hung up. Finally, he said in a flat, cold tone, "I don't have a brother."

"He wants to help you. Please just—"

The line had gone dead.

Lourdes stared at the phone. She couldn't believe he had hung up on her. Her eyes narrowed in determination. He wouldn't get off the hook that easily, not after everything he had put her through. The least he could do was hear her out.

She pulled on her jacket and grabbed her purse and keys. As she bypassed Trudy in the hallway, her assistant asked, "Where are you going?"

"To see Dirk." She pushed the elevator button.

"What? Lourdes, wait!"

But Lourdes was already in the elevator, the door closing on Trudy's baffled face.

~ * ~

Lourdes drove to the bachelor pad Dirk had moved into after she kicked him out. Never having been there, she used her mobile phone GPS to locate the building near the heart of the city. Always meticulous, she had saved Dirk's email with his address in a file titled, "Do Not Answer." She parked on the street in front of a warehouse revamped into fashionable, expensive loft apartments. There was no reply when she rang Dirk's number, but a second later, a woman opened the security door. Lourdes followed her inside with a smile she hoped seemed confident.

She took the stairs to the third level and moved to the door with Dirk's number. About to knock, she noticed the door was ajar. Dirk had always been pedantic about security and would never leave his door open. Fear gripped her. This didn't feel right. Something was wrong. Should she call the police? Still contemplating the options, the shrill ringtone of her phone echoed in the acoustic hallway. *Oh, crappy, crap, crap.* She dug through her bag for her phone, desperate to locate it, but it took a while before her fingers folded around it. Lourdes pushed the button to reject the call three times before it worked. Trudy's number flashed on her screen. She turned in her tracks to rush back to the lift when a hand closed around her arm.

"Not so fast, lady."

She shrieked, trying to pull out of the grip, but the fingers that held her fastened painfully around her flesh and twisted her around. The man had dark, cold eyes and black hair, his lips pulled back into a satisfied snarl.

"Well, well, what have we here?"

"Let go of me!"

He snickered. "Rod! Look what I've got." He dragged her inside the flat and kicked the door shut. Lourdes inhaled audibly at the sight in front of her. Dirk sat in a chair, tied up and gagged, blood running from his nose. His face was swollen on one side. A bulky man with a headband cracked his knuckles and looked over his shoulder at them.

"Piece of luck," her captor said. "Now, Dirk, who is this *piece of luck*?" He laughed sardonically. "Anyone important to you?"

Rod jerked the gag down. "Mikey asked you a question. Answer him."

"Lourdes," Dirk said through a split lip. It sounded like a cry for help. He was missing a tooth.

"This makes our job so much easier," Rod said. "We'll keep her as insurance."

Lourdes fought Mikey's hold, but her efforts were futile. He easily grabbed her wrists together and held them out to Rod, who picked up a piece of rope from the floor and bound her hands together. Mikey pushed her down on the couch while Rod took a knife from his pocket. Lourdes flinched, starting to tremble. Rod cut Dirk loose and pulled him roughly to his feet. Unstable, he almost tripped, and Lourdes exclaimed when Rod's fist punched into Dirk's stomach. Dirk doubled over, his hands clenching his belly.

"You have two hours to come back with our money," Rod said, "or the chick's dead."

Lourdes wanted to cry, but Dirk was already sobbing enough for both of them as he stumbled to the door. No. Dirk wouldn't come back for her. He'd run as far and as fast as he could. Her breath came in gulps. She was as good as dead.

Frightened, Lourdes watched Dirk's exit. She had to keep her wits about her if she wanted to stay alive.

"Listen," she said to the man named Rod, "he's not coming back, and you know it."

His lips pulled back, revealing a gold tooth. "Then you're dead, honey."

"He won't come back for me," she persisted. "We broke up. I'm not his girlfriend any longer."

"Nice try, sweet cheeks," Mikey said.

She shrugged. "You don't have to believe me, but he won't come back. He doesn't love me, probably never even liked me. May already be halfway to the border."

Mikey cursed.

"Shut up, Cinderella," Rod said through clenched teeth.

"How much does he owe?" she asked, trying to sound brave.

Rod looked at his friend. The two seemed to exchange a silent message.

"A lot," Rod said. "You better hope you can pay back what he owes, plus interest."

"I'll give you the money." She shook as she prayed this would work. "Just let me go."

Rod, who seemed to be the leader, said nothing at first. Then he nodded at his friend. "If she's right, if he doesn't come back for her, we're screwed. Get her a phone." He turned to Lourdes. "A hundred grand. You have five seconds to convince someone to drop off the money. Tell Mikey what number to dial. Make it quick, and if you value your life, honey, don't try anything funny."

"All right." She licked her dry lips. "But no one is making a drop. I don't trust you. I want a transfer."

Rod looked at Mikey again. "Smart chick. Fair enough. But you stay put, honey, until I see the money in my account."

Lourdes prayed to all the angels and gods of good luck to speed to her aid. Please, please let Tomás, her personal banker, get the money.

Mikey hovered above her, going through her bag. After a while, he retrieved the phone. "Who do you want to call?" He grinned. "Hey, Rod, what's that program on the tellie where you can dial a friend?"

"*Who Wants to be a Millionaire.*"

"Yeah." Mikey's stomach shook with a low laugh. "Let's play millionaire, sweet cheeks. Who'd you like to call?"

"Trudy. Check on my contact list."

Mikey scrolled down the list and pressed the dial button. He put the phone on speaker.

Rod held the knife to her throat. "Any funny business and I cut."

Lourdes swallowed. When Trudy took the call, Mikey pressed the phone against her ear.

"Hey, Trudy, it's Lourdes."

"What the heck? I called you. Why didn't you answer? I was worried."

"Trudy, please, just listen." Her tone had the desired effect. Trudy was silent. "Call Tomás. I need him to authorize a transfer of a hundred thousand dollars from my account."

"What?" Trudy's voice was shrill. "You've got to be kidding me."

"Please, don't argue. Just call Tomás. The equity in my house, tell him to take the money against it." She glanced at Rod. "The account details?"

"You'll text it," Rod said.

"I'll text it," Lourdes repeated for Trudy's benefit.

"Lourdes," Trudy's voice wavered like it did when she was about to cry. "Are you safe?"

Mikey brought the phone to his lips. "No, Trudy sweet cakes, she's not. No money, no Lourdes. Get it? Tell Tommy he's got two hours." He ended the call and chucked the phone onto the couch next to Lourdes, far enough away so she couldn't reach it with her bound hands.

"Now what?" Lourdes said.

"Now we wait." Rod walked to the fridge in the corner and took out two beers. He threw one to Mikey and cracked his open. "I'm sure we can find something to pass the time."

~ * ~

Two hours had never felt so long. The minutes ticked by while her captors spoke to someone on the phone. They explained how they had set Dirk free to get the money, and then managed to win a hostage who would also deliver on the money. Double wages, Rod had said. He and Mikey wanted double pay. And if Dirk didn't deliver, he was dead anyway. Lourdes sat with her hands tied together in her lap, trying to act invisible so they would forget about her presence. But after his third beer, Mikey sauntered over to her.

"Thirty minutes left to go, sweet cheeks."

"He'll call," she said with false confidence.

What if Tomás couldn't get the money together? He had told her a month ago it was the only option to get her hands on cash—a last resort to save the business, if push came to shove. This was shove.

As if on cue, her phone rang. Mikey picked it up and checked the screen. "Dr. Henk Bouwer." He looked at Rod. "What now?"

Lourdes' heart sat in her throat.

"Take it," Rod said. "And no funny business." He showed her the knife.

When Mikey pressed the answer dial, Lourdes said, "Hi Henk," her voice a croak.

"Lourdes, are you unharmed?"

Mikey narrowed his eyes and shook his head.

"Yes," she said.

"I've got the money."

Her eyes widened. What the… How did Henk know? Had Dirk somehow gotten hold of him? "How?"

"I'm not doing this by transfer," he said. "I'll hand over the money when I see you in person."

Mikey grabbed the phone.

"Who's this?"

"Dirk's brother. Who are you?"

"None of your business. The only thing you should worry about is your brother's cute little girlfriend."

"I've got what you want. You'll have it if she's unharmed."

"You have thirty minutes," Mikey hissed.

"Then stop playing around and give me the address."

Mikey gave him Dirk's address and cut the call. "Not a bad day, Rod, considering we're getting double what Tony asked for."

"Shut your mouse trap," Rod yelled.

After that, Mikey was quiet until the intercom buzzed on the wall next to the fridge. If she could chew through the cord holding her wrists, she would have done it. She sat on the edge of the seat while Henk announced himself, minutes ticking by like hours as he traversed the distance from the entrance to Dirk's flat. *Please, please.* She rocked forth and back. If Henk got hurt… When the knock came on the door, both fear and relief washed through her. Rod pulled his knife, and Mikey a pistol, before answering the door.

They both did a double take.

"Who are you?" Mikey said. "Dirk's double or something?" He nudged Rod. "Like a stuntman, hey bro?"

"Whatever." Rod waved the knife at Henk. "Step inside."

Henk didn't waver at the weapons aimed at him. He lifted his hands, a sports bag slung over his shoulder. "I'm unarmed." His eyes immediately searched out Lourdes. "Are you okay?"

She could only nod.

Mikey pulled him inside and shut the door while Rod checked the window. Studying Lourdes for a second more, Henk turned to Mikey. "It's half of the money. The other half's our insurance policy."

Rod laughed softly. "Then neither of you two are going home, stuntman."

"The amount in this bag is what your boss asked for." He dropped it to the floor. "The rest of it, I deposited with him. So now, you can go back to your boss and explain why you doubled his price. Doing some backhanded gambling of your own?"

Rod went pale. Mikey raked a hand through his hair.

"Rod," Mikey said, "we're in trouble, man."

"Shut up," Rod said. "It was for the boss. A nice surprise," he said, trying to convince himself.

Henk held his hand out to Lourdes. "Come here."

She didn't hesitate. She scrambled to her feet and ran into his arms.

Henk moved her behind his body and backtracked to the door. "We won't have the pleasure of meeting again. Tony will make sure of that."

Whether he meant Tony would kill them for the betrayal, or Tony had promised that his men wouldn't bother her and Henk again, she didn't know. Apparently, neither did Rob or Mikey. They both stared wide-eyed at Henk, Mikey hitting a fist against his forehead.

As soon as they reached the door, Henk steered her outside and closed it behind them. They didn't linger. He bolted for the lift, pulling her behind him. He didn't even stop to untie her hands until they were in the lobby.

"Here, sweetheart," he said, pushing her up against a wall. "Give me your hands."

She held them up to him. Instead of trying to undo the complicated knot, he took a knife from his pocket and sawed through the rope until it gave way. He bundled it into his jacket pocket and took her arm.

"My car is nearby. So are the cops. I want you out of here before they storm the building."

Outside, a detective in civilian clothes waved his badge at them. "My car's here."

"I'll take her," Henk said in a non-negotiable tone. "She's been

25

through enough."

The man nodded stiffly. "I'll be right behind you."

Henk led her across the street to his Triumph and moved her into the passenger side, swiftly taking the driver's seat. He drove fast, and they didn't speak until he stopped in front of his house.

His jaw was tight as he turned to her. "There's a detective in the house and a doctor who'd like to make sure you're fine."

The shock set in, making her shake. His arms went around her and pulled her close. His nose was in her hair, his mouth on her temple.

"Thank God, you're unharmed." He held her at arm's length. "You are, aren't you? Please tell me they didn't hurt you."

"I'm fine," she said in a shaky voice. "Just scared."

He seemed to pull himself away with difficulty and then came around to help her out of the car. The detective who had parked behind them waited at the door. Once inside, a doctor asked to examine her, but Lourdes assured her the only injury she had sustained was the chaffed skin on her wrists. After the doctor left, she told the detectives everything that had happened. Henk gave the police the rope for forensics. An hour later, she found herself alone with Henk. She sank down on the sofa, exhausted.

He was at her side with a glass of amber liquid. "Here"

"What's this?" She took the tumbler from him.

"Scotch. For the shock."

"How did you know?"

"Trudy called me. She told me where you were and what you had asked for, and I knew what had happened. I managed to get hold of Dirk on his mobile phone. He only took the call because of his predicament, not knowing what to do and how to save you. He told me he owed them fifty grand and gave me the number of the loan shark. Realizing the schmucks who held you were overcharging, I called Tony and cut a deal. I left fifty grand with him and fifty with his men."

"Henk, these people are dangerous. I'm afraid we won't be safe, ever again."

He took the untouched drink and left it on the coffee table, pulling her close. "The money is marked. The police have been after Tony and his gang for a while, and this will help to put them behind bars."

His arms were soothing. She leaned closer and rested her head on his chest. "Dirk?"

"I booked him into a hotel. He didn't want to come here."

"I suppose he doesn't want to face me," she said bitterly, knowing Dirk would have deserted her.

He pushed away to look at her. "I'm sorry for the position I've put you in. I had no idea." His hand smoothed over her shoulder, down her arm. "If they had harmed you … I wouldn't be able to live with myself."

"You couldn't have known," she said, staring up at his blue eyes, so similar and yet so different from Dirk's.

His hands moved up to cup her face. "If you were mine Lourdes, I would never have let you go."

His thumb brushed over her bottom lip. Her heart raced to a crescendo as his lips came down to gently brush over hers. This was so wrong, but it felt so right. The light pressure of his caress stirred intense feelings within her. She wanted to melt into his arms and stay there, safe, even if only for tonight.

Abruptly he pulled away. "I should take you home."

"No, please. I don't want to be alone. Can I stay here? Just for the night? I can sleep on the couch."

"Of course." He stroked his hand over her hair, pulling her head back to his broad chest. "You can stay as long as you like."

They sat like that until her body relaxed, the tenseness easing from her muscles.

Henk lifted her chin. "Let's go make you some dinner."

Her tummy grumbled, reminding her that she hadn't eaten since breakfast. "Thank you."

She sat at the kitchen table, sipping the Scotch, while Henk whipped omelets together. They ate in the kitchen in companionable silence. When they were done, he said, "Would you like to take a warm bath, or a shower? We could go back to your place and fetch your clothes if you'll feel more comfortable in your own things, or I could lend you some of mine."

It was a long drive back to her place, and right now, all she wanted to do was collapse in the aftermath of the earlier adrenalin. "Your stuff will do just fine." She smiled at his consideration.

After showing her to his guest bathroom, Henk gave her one of his T-shirts, a pair of boxer shorts and sweat pants. Lourdes filled the bath to the brim and lay back in the soothing water. She blamed herself for having been blind to Dirk's addiction. How could she not have known he was mixed up in a dangerous mess? She realized with some guilt that she had never called Trudy back. She would be worried. As soon as she was done, she'd let her know what had happened.

When the water had cooled, she got out, dried herself and pulled on Henk's clothes. It smelled of him–of pine forest and mountain air. She rolled the pants up several times so as not to trip. Padding barefoot to the lounge, she found Henk in front of the television, watching the news.

"Come here." He moved over, making space for her on the couch. "What would you like to do? Watch a movie? Or are you tired?"

She didn't want to close her eyes, not just yet. Frightened that the nightmare would play itself over again in her mind, she said, "A movie would be great."

"What do you like?" He switched from the news to the movie menu. "Action, thriller, comedy, or classic?"

"No thrillers. A classic."

"Here." He handed her the remote. "You choose."

She scrolled down the list and paused on 'Gone with the Wind'.

"Seriously?" he said, grinning.

She shrugged. "Sorry." She knew guys hated that movie, but it was a long one. She could put off going to sleep.

"I love this one," he said with approval. "I do a pretty good Clark Gable imitation. Want to see?"

She laughed. "No, please. I'll take your word for it."

"All right," he said with a mock serious face. "But you don't know what you're missing." He took back the remote and pressed the rent option. Lourdes watched him get up and disappear into the kitchen. For a minute, she worried that he would let her watch it on her own, but he returned with a bottle of wine and two glasses. He had changed from his formal pants and shirt into faded jeans and a gray sweatshirt. Like her, he was barefoot. He poured two glasses, offered her one, and then settled back on the couch with one arm casually around the back.

For the first hour, Lourdes was stuck to the screen. By the time her glass was empty, she felt warm and fuzzy and leaned into him. Henk took their empty glasses and left them on the table, his arm moving from the backrest of the couch around her shoulders. His fingers played up and down her arm in a comforting tune. Lourdes realized with a little jerk of her heart that this was what she had always wanted with Dirk, but never had.

They had never shared a quiet moment in front of a movie, doing nothing. It was not a useless moment or a waste of time, but beautiful and precious, because Henk was giving her what she needed most–comfort. Feeling indebted to him, she rested her head on his shoulder and allowed his warmth to seep through her body and into her soul.

A long time later, Lourdes awoke with her head in Henk's lap. The movie was close to the end. Henk played with her hair, brushing his fingers over her scalp. She wanted to stay like that forever and pretend there was no company to take care of, no business on the brink of bankruptcy. But then she remembered Trudy and shot upright.

"What is it?" he said gently.

"Trudy! I never called her to tell her I was all right."

He touched the tip of her nose. "Done."

"You called her? When?"

"While you were in the bath. I figured you had enough to deal with for one day."

"Thanks." She breathed a sigh of relief and settled her head in his lap again.

Too soon, the credits rolled over the screen. She turned her face to look up at Henk. "Thanks for saving me. The money ..."

"I don't want you to think about the money. If it wasn't for me, you'd never be there. It's over now. Forget about it."

"Dirk?"

"I'm seeing him tomorrow."

His expression seemed so vulnerable; she wanted to wrap her arms around him. "Then you've accomplished what you've set out to achieve?"

"Not yet, but I hope to."

She nodded.

"Time for bed," he said, sounding reluctant. "You've been through an ordeal."

He took her hand and led her to a room down the hallway. "Guest room." He opened the door for her. "I'm upstairs. Just shout if you need anything."

"Thanks. For everything. For letting me stay." She went on tiptoe and kissed his cheek. His stubble pricked her lips, but it was a masculine, welcome feeling.

Emotions played across his face as he looked down at her. Without warning, he took her face between his hands, his lips meeting hers for a tender kiss. It was a slow, undemanding kiss, but one that melted her insides and made her knees shake. When he pulled away with a final peck on her nose, his gaze was serious.

"Your eyes are the color of a forest," he said. "Deep green, like moss. Except when you cry. After your tears, they shine like emeralds. You have the most perfect eyes I have ever seen."

Her heart swelled with something she couldn't explain.

"And despite how beautiful they are when you cry," he continued softly, "I don't ever want to see real tears in them."

There were no words in her mind, nothing to form a sentence with.

"Good night, Lourdes March." He turned and walked away.

Lourdes watched him until he turned the corner, wanting him to stop, but feeling like she couldn't ask him to stay. She went to bed and lay awake for a long time. What was happening to her? Was it wrong to fall for Dirk's brother? It was over between Dirk and her. She was free. But how would Dirk feel about a relationship between her and the brother he believed had taken everything away from him?

~ * ~

The smell of bacon hung in the air when she woke up. She sniffed with appreciation, threw the covers back and followed the odor to the kitchen. Henk stood in front of the stove, flipping pancakes. He looked all showered and fresh in dark jeans and a white T-shirt, his curly hair damp.

"Good morning," she said, pulling at the hem of the over-sized T-shirt.

When he turned to look at her, she almost faltered at the heat in his eyes. "Morning." He grinned as his eyes traveled over her. "Sleep well?"

Instead of replying, she took a seat by the table. She wasn't sure where last night's kiss left them. Maybe she was making a big deal out of it. Henk removed a plate from the hot drawer stacked with bacon.

"Hungry?" He served her some pancakes without waiting for her answer. After pouring them each a cup of coffee, he took the chair next to her.

Definitely nothing, she decided, or he would have said something or kissed her good morning. Probably one of those weird kisses guys dished out after a girl had been held hostage.

For now, the food dominated her attention. It had been a while since she'd had pancakes and bacon for breakfast. She added a few strips of bacon to her plate and dribbled syrup over everything. She became aware of Henk staring at her after she had taken a few enthusiastic bites.

"What?" she said, taking a big gulp of coffee.

"Nothing. I just enjoy watching you eat."

She shrugged. "I'm a breakfast person."

"That's good to know. So am I." He tugged a strand of hair behind her ear.

The intimacy of the act made her freeze with her fork halfway to her mouth. Or was his cuddling meant to soothe her? Her heartbeat picked up, and in a second, the atmosphere between them became charged.

As if sensing the change in mood, Henk swiped his thumb over the corner of her mouth. "You look cute when you wake up."

A flush of heat crept up her neck. She hadn't looked in the mirror, but she knew her hair had to be a tangled bird's nest.

"You have an unfair advantage," she said. "You showered and brushed your hair."

His eyes turned a darker shade of blue. "We can remedy that."

Before she could contemplate the meaning of his words, the intercom buzzed. Immediately his expression turned apologetic. "I didn't have time to tell you, but that will be Dirk."

She almost choked on her coffee. "Dirk is coming here? Now?"

"He called early this morning and said he needed to see me."

She got up so quickly she almost knocked his mug over. "I'd better give the two of you some privacy."

"Please," he laid his hand on her arm, "sit. Finish your breakfast. I'm sure Dirk has a lot to say to you."

The food got stuck in her throat. She sat down again slowly, not sure she was ready to face Dirk after the coward had left her to the mercy of those bastards yesterday.

Henk answered the intercom, opened the gate for Dirk, and then left to wait by the door for his brother. A short while later, the two men entered the kitchen, Dirk with hunched shoulders, Henk tense.

When Dirk spotted her at the table, he dashed forward and grabbed her into his arms. "Lourdes, baby, thank God you're safe. If anything had happened … I'm so sorry. I'll make it all up to you. I promise. I love you so much."

From over Dirk's shoulder, she saw Henk turn his face away, his jaw clenched.

She pulled away. "This changes nothing."

"You're right," Dirk said quickly. "Nothing has changed. I still love you."

Glancing at Henk, she said, "You two have a lot to talk about. I'll get dressed."

Dirk seemed to register her appearance then. He looked from her clothes to Henk, his face tight. "You spent the night?"

"I was scared," Lourdes said, mentally kicking herself for sounding defensive. She didn't owe Dirk any explanations. "I slept in the spare room."

Relief washed over Dirk's face. "Of course." When she got up, Dirk held her back with a hand on her arm. "I just want you to know that I wouldn't have left you there. I was looking for the money."

This wasn't about her. It was about Henk and his brother, and she didn't feel like getting into an argument. Without another word, she left the kitchen, went back to the spare room, called a taxi, made the bed and changed back into her own clothes. Shortly before the taxi was due to arrive, she made her way back to the kitchen. The heated discussion stopped her in her tracks. She didn't want to eavesdrop, so she called out to Henk before she got to the door. Both men fell silent at the sound of her voice.

"Um, thanks for letting me stay," she said to Henk.

He took in her crumpled garments. "I'll take you home if you're in a hurry. But you're welcome to stay as long as you like."

"My taxi will be here any minute."

Henk looked like he wanted to argue, but the intercom buzzed.

"That'll be my taxi."

"I'll walk you out," Henk said resignedly, pushing the button to open the gates.

Dirk moved forward, blocking her path. "Can I call you?"

"Dirk, please, we've been through that."

"Just to talk about yesterday," he said, his eyes pleading.

"Fine." She turned to Henk. "Thanks again. For everything."

"I love you, baby," Dirk said.

Henk went rigid. Instead of kissing her goodbye like she expected him to, he suddenly took on a formal pose.

"Goodbye, Lourdes." He extended his hand, shaking hers. "Call if you need anything."

Thoroughly confused, she took her purse and made her way to the waiting taxi.

~ * ~

Lourdes needed the distraction of work, but it was Henk's event; she couldn't stop thinking about him or the events of the day before. On top of that, Trudy bustled around her like a mother hen, until she couldn't take it any longer.

"Trudy, I appreciate your concern, but can we drop it now?"

Understanding as always, Trudy lifted her hands. "Sure. Sorry. I just freaked out about what could have happened."

Lourdes gave her a stern look. "Drop it."

"Okay. Okay." She squared the papers on her desk. "I hope you're not angry that I called Henk."

Lourdes rolled her eyes. "No. Thanks for that." In an effort to change the subject, she said, "I'd like to do sight checks for the venues we've narrowed down. The university can take five hundred people, but I don't like the ambience."

"Has Dirk been arrested?"

Sighing, Lourdes gave in, knowing Trudy would not give up. "No. He's working with the police. They cut a deal."

"Is he going to give it up? I mean the gambling?"

"I don't know." Frankly, she didn't care. Dirk wasn't her responsibility any longer. And she definitely didn't want that problem back in her life.

The 'Do not Answer' ringtone sounded from her bag. *Speak of the devil* ... As she reached for her mobile, Trudy muttered, "I guess you're about to find out."

Lourdes contemplated cutting the call, but it would only make him try again. And again. Pressing the green button with a sigh, she braced herself.

"What is it, Dirk?"

"That's not a nice way to greet me."

She wanted to say something snarky but held her tongue. "What can I do for you?"

"Meet me for lunch."

"No."

"It's not a date or anything," he said quickly. "I only want to talk to you. There are things I need to say."

"So say them."

"Not like this. Please."

She held her breath and let it out shakily. "Fine. But don't get any ideas. There's no 'us' any longer. There never will be again. I only called for Henk."

"I know," he said softly.

"Where and when?"

The landline rang sharply. While Dirk seemed to make up his mind about a meeting place, Lourdes heard Trudy take the call. "Oh, Henk, hi."

"Today. At the sandwich bar downstairs," Dirk said.

"Hold on," Trudy said. "She's on the line with Dirk." A little pause. "No, she's setting up a lunch date with him right now. Her schedule is open for tomorrow, though."

"See you there at one." Lourdes ended the call and picked up the receiver on her desk. "Henk?" Her tummy did a funny tap dance.

His voice was strangely formal. "I just wanted to make sure you were fine. I didn't expect you back at work so soon. I tried your mobile, but ..."

"That was Dirk," she said. "How did it go with the two of you yesterday?"

"That's the other reason for my call, to thank you."

"Does that mean you've sorted out your differences?"

"Not quite. But we'll get there. Eventually. There are a lot of issues. It'll take some time."

"Good. I'm glad."

Silence stretched between them. Lourdes wracked her brain for something else to say, but the things that came to mind weren't things she should bring up. Certainly not how much she enjoyed falling asleep on his lap.

Just when she thought she would have to say goodbye to end the awkward pause, he said, "About the event, I got your email about the budget. I won't have time to deal with this, so liaise directly with my secretary about the arrangements. I trust her. She'll be the decision maker, so you don't need my input."

They both knew he was far from being the most popular optometrist in the city. Not because he wasn't good, she thought in his defense. This was a diplomatic way of telling her he didn't want to see her.

Feeling her pride armor dent, she said, "If you'd prefer to take your business elsewhere, I'll understand."

"No. We signed a contract, and I honor what I've signed. Just deal with Claudia. She knows what I want."

"Thanks, I guess."

He mumbled some impersonal greeting, and the line went dead. Lourdes stared at the phone in astonishment. The tap dance stilled to a pathetic little thump that left a painful ache in her throat. It was nothing, after all. Just a kiss.

"Do you want some tea?" Trudy said, her gaze sympathetic.

Lourdes agreed, but only because it would mean she'd escape Trudy's well-intended attention for a short while. Trudy returned with a tray stacked with her favorite choc-chip biscuits.

~ * ~

At one, she made her way downstairs to meet Dirk at the small deli in her building. At least he was considerate to meet her on her own territory instead of asking her to take a cab somewhere.

He sat waiting at the window counter, two paper cups of coffee and chicken-mayo sandwiches in front of him. Dirk had always been handsome to her but now in the wake of Henk's memory, he seemed lacking. It was as if she saw him in a different light. Ashamed at her thoughts, she gave him an overly cheerful greeting. She took the high stool next to him and reprimanded herself for the comparison.

"Hey." He raked his fingers through his hair. "Thanks for coming."

She had an hour, but she preferred not to spend it all with him, so she got to the point. "What did you want to talk about?"

He pushed the cup and plate her way. "I wanted to say thank you for setting me up with Henk." He stared at his hands. "If it wasn't for you, I would have never agreed to see him again, to hear his side of the story."

"He told me about your father. I'm sorry."

"I am, too. I guess I've just always been a selfish bastard."

It pained her to see the hurt in his eyes. "Don't be too hard on yourself."

"Henk always tried to protect me. But what I wanted was my father's love."

"He loved you." She squeezed his shoulder.

"I'm going to pay Henk back. As soon as I find a job."

She stared at him. He never wanted to do anything other than play cards and throw dice. "You're not going to gamble professionally anymore?"

"That's over. I've joined a group for addicts." He smiled grimly. "And Henk's giving me a loan to study art. I'll find a part-time job, and I'll pay you both back, a small installment every month."

"Forget about it. It's in the past."

"No. I need to do this. I'm paying you back, every cent I stole from you, with interest."

She sensed his need to do this, as part of his healing. "There's no rush. I'm getting by."

He played with his paper napkin. "And I wanted to know if we could go on a date. A proper, first date."

This was the part she had hoped he wouldn't bring up. She shook her head slowly. "It's over, Dirk."

He sat with his head bowed for a while, and then got up, leaving his coffee and sandwich untouched. "Thanks for hearing me out." He walked out of the shop, never glancing back her way.

Lourdes sighed. Her only consolation was that Henk and his brother were on a path of reconciliation.

~ * ~

The event was a major success. Lourdes blew out a long, slow breath. It had been a stressful three months ensuring that everything ran smoothly. She and Trudy had worked around the clock, and she had sent Trudy home after the dinner had been served. The last guests filed from the reception hall slowly. She was beat. If she hit her bed, she would sleep for twenty-four hours. For the duration of the evening, she had lurked in the shadows, overseeing but staying out of sight. Avoiding Henk.

Seeing him had done something to her, something she wished to not analyze. His speech was short but perfect, his stance self-confident, like the time he had rescued her from Dirk's debt collectors. No, it was best not to think of that. It always led to one memory–the kiss. She had watched him closely. He had not looked around the room, had not searched the crowd for her.

It was way past midnight when the hall was finally empty. After seeing to the cleanup, she signed off the bar bill, grabbed her bag and headed to the underground parking. She scanned the lot, but except for her car, it was empty. No Triumph parked out there. Her tummy dropped. That part of her autonomy was too closely connected to her feelings. It had to stop doing these things to her. The hurt was too overwhelming. For the first time since the horrible incident, she wept. She got behind the wheel, shut and locked the door, and shed big, uncontrollable tears. Her head bumped on the steering wheel as she let it all out. By the time she had finished, the dash and her lap were soaked, but she felt slightly better. Henk had caused what he said he didn't want to see—very real, very hurtful tears.

~ * ~

The next few months passed uneventfully until Trudy slammed her hand down on Lourdes' desk one morning, making her jump.

"What was that for?" Lourdes called out.

"You're living dead."

"I am not," she said with as much conviction as she could muster.

"When was the last time you went out?"

"This morning." Lourdes picked up her mug and pretended to drink, hiding her face behind it.

Trudy cocked her hip. "That was a site check."

Lourdes only lifted a brow. So? She was out. Not with a guy. But she was out and about a lot. Since the medical convention she had managed for Henk, she had received a lot of business from the clinic, all referrals from Henk.

"I meant with a man," Trudy persisted.

"I don't need a man." Lourdes put her mug down and started typing on her laptop, a cue that the discussion was closed.

Trudy surprised her by giving up easily, walking back to her own desk with a shrug.

Did she honestly not need a man? She didn't before Henk. Unfortunately, for her, she was the type who believed in love at first sight. Totally. It had happened for her grandmother and she was married for a blissful sixty-something years to Lourdes' wonderful grandfather. It worked

37

for her mom, who had known her dad a week before he popped the big question. They had been happy every day of their lives. Sure, they had fights like everyone, but their relationship was always respectful, understanding. She realized that she had given up on finding what her mother and grandmother had. Not even with Dirk, who she had been with the longest, had she felt that. Only with… No. She wasn't going there. Not again. Enough.

Trudy interrupted her thoughts. "Your meeting with Dr. Hayes is for one, at a restaurant."

Lourdes wanted to argue. Trudy knew she didn't like having meetings outside of her office, but after Trudy's earlier speech, she decided to let it slide. See? She did get out. Lots.

~ * ~

Dr. Hayes was a gynecologist who worked in the same clinic as Henk. When he contacted her for a quote for his wife's fiftieth birthday party, he said someone who attended Henk's convention had recommended her. It was a surprise party with two hundred guests.

The doctor waited outside instead of at a table, and Lourdes warmed at his consideration. He held the door for her, and she stepped inside the Italian restaurant which had pleasant fragrances of garlic and fried onions hanging in the air. The hostess asked if they had a reservation. Lourdes automatically turned to Dr. Hayes, who instead waited for her to speak.

"Go on," he said with a smile. "You made the booking."

She frowned. She was about to question that when the hostess said, "Yes, table for two. Ms. March?" Lourdes nodded. "Follow me."

She walked them down a path that led to the tables at the back. Lourdes headed toward the only unoccupied table and then halted abruptly. At the next table sat two copper-haired men, one with a playful expression, the other serious. No way. Escape. She had to get out of here. Backtracking, she bumped into Dr. Hayes, who uttered a puff of air. The noise attracted the twins' attention, and they looked up and froze. Dirk had his glass of wine halfway to his mouth, and Henk's fork hung in midair. Too late. *Crappy, crap, crap.* Lourdes took a deep breath and plastered a smile on her face. It was Dirk who came to his senses first.

He got to his feet, his face lighting up. "Lourdes!" He took hold of her shoulders. "You look good."

Something was off. Dirk seemed more mature. The boyishness she had known was gone.

"You don't look too bad yourself," she said. It was hard not to return his smile. He seemed so genuine.

Noticing that Henk had gotten to his feet stiffly, too, she nodded briefly in his direction. "Thank you for the business. I'm much obliged."

Henk's eyes were fixed on Dr. Hayes, so Lourdes turned to introduce them. "Um, this is Dr. Hayes. He works at the same clinic. These are ..." She was going to say friends of hers, but they weren't really. Dirk was an ex. Henk was even less than that. At the end of the day, he was nothing more than her optometrist. "This is Mr. and Dr. Bouwer."

It was a huge clinic, so not everyone who worked there knew each other. Gynecology was on a different floor. Lourdes had expected the colleagues to be polite, if nothing more. Dr. Hayes was jovial enough, extending his hand. Though Dirk shook hands with him, Henk glared at him in a way that made her uncomfortable, and Dr. Hayes frown.

"Well," she said, "nice running into you. Bon appetit."

The hostess seated them at their table and handed them menus. Dr. Hayes leaned over the table then, whispering, "Don't tell a soul about the party, not even my colleagues. Some of them may slip it to the receptionists, and I don't want Mrs. Hayes to smell a rat."

Lourdes patted his hand. "Of course. Don't worry." She inclined her head conspiratorially. "You can count on my discretion."

When her eyes lifted, she saw Henk looking at her in a way that made her feel like a worm that should wiggle into the earth. Instead, she squared her shoulders and studied the menu. She was starving.

~ * ~

Back at the office, Lourdes flung her handbag on her desk and regarded Trudy, her hands propped on her hips. "I know you orchestrated the 'accidental' meeting."

Trudy chewed her lip. "Don't be mad. Anyone can see you're crazy about him. You're just too pig-headed to admit it."

"I'm not crazy about anyone."

"Yeah." Trudy rested her head on her hands. "So you say. Did it work?"

Lourdes shed her jacket and draped it over her chair back. "Did what work?"

"Did he fall at your feet and tell you he loved you?"

"I'm never getting back with Dirk."

"Not Dirk. *Henk.*"

Lourdes decided to ignore the question.

"Well?" Trudy lifted her eyebrows.

"I should fire you for that piece of manipulative work. And the lunch bill is coming off your salary."

Trudy sighed deeply. "If it worked, it would have been worth the expense."

"How did you even know?" Lourdes fell into her chair, suddenly feeling emotionally exhausted from keeping up appearances during lunch, while Henk's eyes had drilled holes in her skull.

"Henk's secretary told me they'd be there, and I just thought ..." She crossed her arms and pouted.

"You're not even friends with her. You mean you called Claudia to ask her when and where he was going out for lunch?"

"I just thought the two of you needed an extra push."

Lourdes opened her laptop and fixed Trudy with a stare. "No more pushing."

"Fine." Trudy shrugged. "I give up."

Hearing Trudy say the words Lourdes had been so afraid to utter herself was almost too much to bear. Was she truly prepared to give up? Didn't Henk deserve another chance? Didn't she deserve a chance? And what about Dirk? Dirk and Henk finally seemed to be picking up the pieces of their broken relationship. They looked so at ease over lunch. Happy. Did they honestly deserve her meddling in their newly found relationship?

Opening her drawer, she pulled out a peanut bar. She removed the wrapper with force and crunched down on a quarter of it.

"I thought you just had lunch," Trudy said.

"I was too nervous to eat. I hope you're happy paying for nothing."

Trudy just smiled.

~ * ~

A week later, Lourdes had convinced herself that she was letting go of her silly infatuation, her unhealthy obsession. She had all kinds of clever catch phrases that she pulled from her mind and threw at her heart, like a rope catching a horse or a cow. Whenever her tummy bucked at a thought or memory of copper hair and sky-blue eyes, she roped it and strangled it with one of those lines, until she had convinced herself it was for the best. Henk and Dirk had reconciled. Dirk was out of her life for good. No more messages. No begging. Small amounts of money found its way to her account on a regular basis, and she didn't act on it. If that was what Dirk needed to shed his guilt, she'd let it be.

The problem was Henk. He didn't return to New York as she believed, hoped, he would. He stayed. Sometimes she found herself wanting to drive out to his house, not to ring his bell or anything assertive like that, but just to see it. Those thoughts scared her so much, she decided it was time she relocated. She had only moved to Chile for Dirk, after all. There was no reason left to stay.

"But I don't understand," Trudy had said.

"I want to go somewhere less Dutch."

"Dutch?" Trudy had given her a baffled look. "This is Santiago, babes. You can't get more Latino than this."

Her mind made up, she started looking into options. Europe. England, maybe? She had promised Trudy she would pay her until she found another job. She sure would miss her, despite her interfering ways.

~ * ~

Both women had been downstairs for coffee at the deli, so Trudy went through the messages on the answering machine when they got back. Thanks to Henk's good reference, business was booming again. Executive Events was the sole event organizer for the clinic, now.

Lourdes stared at the map of Europe on her laptop screen.

"You're not going to like this," Trudy said.

"What?" Lourdes looked up.

"Message from Dr. Bouwer's office."

Her spine went so stiff she thought it would snap. "He needs another event?"

"No. Says you have to come in for a retina scan."

"What?" Lourdes said again, her voice a shriek.

"Gosh, I mean, is that something serious? Does it mean there's something wrong with your eyes?"

"Cut the crap," Lourdes said, not feeling so calm. "Make an

appointment with another optometrist."

"Which one?"

"Any one. I don't care. Go through the list on the computer and take the first opening available."

Lourdes went back to her map. Maybe Chez Republic would be a welcome break. Learning a new language should keep her mind off the Netherlands.

Trudy cleared her throat. "Lourdeeeeees?"

"What now?" she snapped. All she wanted to do was to pick a country and move on.

"Everything is full, except for Dr. Bouwer. Tomorrow, nine."

"Impossible." Lourdes typed in the name of the clinic domain and selected the appointment page. Her eyes widened. Just as Trudy had said, all the slots were marked in red, except for that one. It said 'pending' and her name written in yellow over the bar.

"I don't want to play devil's advocate or anything," Trudy said, "but what if he found something serious in your tests? What if you're going blind?"

"For crying out loud, Trudy, don't be so dramatic."

"Why do you need a retina scan then? Cataracts?"

She didn't know. Lourdes typed "retina scan" in Google and read for a while, but no meaning sunk in. She shut her laptop screen.

"I'm not scared to face him," Lourdes said, more to herself than to Trudy.

"Good, because I've just booked you for nine tomorrow morning."

~ * ~

There was no waiting this time because Lourdes' appointment was the first of the day. The minute she walked into the reception area, Claudia waved her through.

"Dr. Bouwer's waiting, ma'am. You can go through."

She knocked once and pushed open his door. He sat behind his desk but immediately got to his feet when she entered.

"Lourdes. I'm glad you could make it."

She blinked at the warm smile he gave her. Was that his doctor-patient smile?

"What's this about, Henk? Why do I need a retina scan?"

"Procedure," he said. "Nothing to be alarmed about. As your optometrist, I need to ensure that you do all the preventative tests needed on an annual basis. In another few months, I'll have to test you for glasses."

She decided not to tell him she had to change doctors since she was moving. In six months' time, someone else would peer into her eyes, offering her artificial tears.

"Please." He indicated the examination chair. After she had installed herself, he sat on the small stool in front of her and cupped her face to move it into a frame of some kind. The intimacy of the touch confused her, and then she realized that what she had felt with him that first time, here in this very room, was probably not special. This is what he did with all his patients. He was only being an incredibly gentle doctor. She swallowed the poisonous piece of hurt at the realization. It dropped into her belly like a lump of sour bread, causing her stomach to cramp. With her chin resting on a rubber band, he placed a slit lamp in front of her face and aimed through it.

"The light may irritate your eyes," he said. "Try to keep them open for me."

A few months ago, she would have done anything for him. Even now, she could barely calm the erratic beating of her traitorous heart.

A ray of light pierced her left pupil. Her instinct was to pinch her eye shut, but she managed to do as he had asked. She finished the exam with her eyes intact. Only her heart reminded her that it was still seriously damaged. Maybe she hadn't let go. Maybe she wasn't moving; maybe she was running.

"Lourdes?" Henk said gently, regarding her with a raised eyebrow.

"Sorry, what was that?"

"Can you please read this for me?" He held a card to her, one with fine print.

"Is it in English?"

He responded with the indent of his dimple. "Read," he repeated.

She took the card and started, "Lourdes March, you have …" She jerked her head up to stare at him.

"Continue," he said patiently.

She should refuse, but he had that look in his eyes, that gentleness she had glimpsed when he had kissed her. She had seen it again when he had looked at her that morning in his kitchen.

She took a deep breath. "Lourdes March, you have the most perfect eyes in the world. When I look into them, I forget everything else, even myself. I have wanted to make those eyes mine from the minute I first looked into them, and for every second since. I promise to make you happy …" Lourdes looked up quickly and swallowed. Her throat choked up with emotion.

"Continue," he said softly, his eyes holding hers.

"I promise to make you happy if you give me the chance. I don't need time to know I love you." Tears burned behind her eyes. She had to swallow again. "But I will give you as much time as you need to say you'll marry me."

No longer able to contain them, the tears fell in big blobs on the card she held, blurring the words.

He lifted her chin with his fingers. His thumbs caressed the soft skin under her eyes. "I said I never wanted to cause you tears."

"But these are happy tears," she said, blinking.

"Are they?" He seemed so vulnerable, so hopeful, right then.

"I don't understand," she said.

"What don't you understand?"

"You made it clear you weren't interested."

"Not interested?" His gaze widened. "I stepped aside, to give you and Dirk a chance."

"You knew how I felt about Dirk. It was over."

"But I didn't know how Dirk felt. When I saw how much he loved you …"

"And what changed your mind?"

"That day when we ran into each other in the restaurant, Dirk told me he could see in my face how much I care, how angry I was. He said he realized it would never work between the two of you, and he had set you free."

"Angry?"

"With Hayes, for taking you out for lunch. I thought …"

"I'm organizing his wife's birthday party."

"I know that now. I confronted him."

"You confronted him? Oh, no. I'm so embarrassed."

"You'll have to get used to that feeling. The whole clinic now knows how I feel about you."

"What do you mean?"

He took the card and set it aside, taking her fingers in his big hands. "It took a memo to the whole building to get all the optometrists to block out their appointment slots."

She felt a flush creep up her neck. "So that's how you did it."

He squeezed her hands gently. "You haven't answered yet."

"Answered what?"

"Will you marry me, Lourdes? Will you make me the happiest man alive?"

She pulled from his grip to fold her arms around his neck. "Yes."

"Yes what?"

"Yes, I will marry you."

"Yes, who?"

"Yes, I will marry you, Henk Bouwer."

He closed his eyes and rested his forehead against hers. Letting go of her, he delved in his pocket and pulled out a ring. It was a brilliant emerald surrounded by diamonds. As he slipped it over her ring finger, he said, "I love you Lourdes. I always will."

She was going to say she loved him too, but his lips covered hers, stealing her words and causing new tears of happiness.

THE END

About the Author

Charmaine Pauls was born in Bloemfontein, South Africa. She obtained a degree in Communication at the University of Potchestroom, and followed a diverse career path in journalism, public relations, advertising, communications, photography, graphic design, and brand marketing. Her writing has always been an integral part of her professions.

After relocating to France with her French husband, she fulfilled her passion to write creatively full-time. Charmaine has published six novels since 2011, as well as several short stories and articles.

When she is not writing, she likes to travel, read, and rescue cats. Charmaine currently lives in Chile with her husband and children. Their household is a linguistic mélange of Afrikaans, English, French and Spanish.

Works by the author with Melange Books, LLC

The Seven Forbidden Arts Series:
Pyromancist (Book 1)
Aeromancist, the Beginning (Prequel to Book 2)

Books by Charmaine Pauls:
Between Fire & Ice
The Winemaker
Second Best
The Astronomer

Connect with Charmaine at:
www.charmainepauls.com
http://bit.ly/Charmaine-Pauls-Facebook
http://bit.ly/Charmaine-Pauls-Amazon
http://bit.ly/Charmaine-Pauls-Goodreads
https://twitter.com/CharmainePauls

THE SPARK

By

Ellyse Roberts

Chapter One

The bedraggled old man shuffles over to the side of the building, cigarette in hand, to find the matches he hides in the corner from thieves. The air is muggy and stale, making it hard to breathe as he labors away at the trash collected in his old home. The building is so full of discarded items and debris that no one notices the older, grungy homeless man roaming around the shadows. He picks up the discarded heaps of wood and cloth to find his one precious possession in this world. After many grueling minutes, his hard work is rewarded. He picks up the small black box full of salvation and shoves the cigarette into his mouth. He takes out a stick and strikes the red tip against the hard back. The match ignites and for a brief moment, he is mesmerized by the yellow flame dances before his eyes. Not able to wait one moment longer, he lights his cigarette and takes a deep drag from it, his lungs filled with grey sustenance. He leans against the old dilapidated building and sighs with happiness.

Suddenly, a loud noise breaks the silence around him. From the other side of the building, a loud metal object dropped. The high ceilings echo the effect, making it sound even louder. Somehow, people have invaded his domain. It doesn't matter that he doesn't own it; he's lived here for years. He snorts at the disrespect of others daring to take over his home. He already has to endure the looks of pity on every idiot's face as they pass by his makeshift home.

He inhales deeply from the cigarette as the rage grows. They have no idea that he was a brilliant stockbroker with millions in the bank before the toxic loans of 2008 bankrupted everyone. He takes another long drag from his cigarette to ease the pain brought on by memories. They all think he's invisible. They have no idea the power he once held in his hands. One day, he will make them all pay. He just needs one moment to make them regret that they ever saw him as human trash.

As he brings the cigarette up to his mouth, he sees the beautiful yellow flame sparkle again as it burns from his need to breathe in the smoke.

Then it hits him. An idea so simple, he wonders why he hadn't thought of it before. The invaders must be forced out from this place. They must be eradicated for daring to invade his domain.

They must burn for their treachery.

He looks at the pile of vodka and urine soaked wood that has long since been discarded and tosses his butt down, watching as the wood takes the cigarette beneath its inflexible fingers. It disappears but isn't lost. Within seconds, the yellow flame grows and engulfs the entire pile. He watches in fascination as the flames move closer to him, but he does not move. He doesn't even flinch as he watches the flame lick at his legs, moving upwards until they take hold of his filthy jacket, finding the fuel it needs to thrive. He just inhales the smoke deeply and relishes in the fact that these intruders will regret the day they ever stepped foot into his home.

~ * ~

"When I said 'just drop that anywhere', Martin, I didn't mean on my foot!" I yell as I tend to my bruised toe.

"Sorry, Anna Claire. I guess I had one more than I could carry," Martin says sheepishly.

"Ya think?" I bite out at him before I instantly regret my anger. I look up at Martin as he rings his hands together in front of me. My foot may be bruised but not as much as his ego. "It's okay, really. That bar was heavy as hell and I know it was an accident. Don't worry about it."

Martin stops rubbing his hands together in worry and smiles. "Thanks."

I look up at Martin to ask him if he needs help carrying the bars to the other room. We need them to redecorate for the event, but the words never come out. The smoke rising up in the distance, near the front of the high ceiling warehouse, catches my attention first.

"What in the world is that?" I ask to no one in particular.

Martin, Julia and two others on my team all look in the same direction.

"Is that *smoke*?" asks Julia, the fear clear in her voice.

48

As we all watch, the smoke slowly curls up into the ceiling. We watch it fan out when it reaches the highest point, desperate to find an escape. Before long, we see the flames licking the sides of the building across the big room.

"Do you smell that?" asks Martin, his voice rising in panic with every syllable.

"We need to get out of here. *Now*," I state calmly, doing my best to keep everyone from panicking. I start barking orders and hope that a task will help keep them from freaking out. "Julia, call 911. Martin, go to the front and see if the flames have reached the door yet. If luck holds out, we can still make it out that exit."

As Martin runs off towards the front of the building, I put back on my discarded shoe, the pain in my foot forgotten. Desperate for an escape, I take a second to look around the building. Fear wells within me as my eyes fall upon wall after wall full of locked doors. I look up, hoping to see a stairwell or scaffolding that could help us get out, but all I see are windows that are way too high to reach. The building used to be full of offices and is a labyrinth of rooms. It was supposed to be locked down tight and took an act of congress for me to get a key to the front door.

Martin runs back, his face a mask of disappointment. "The fire is everywhere. It's a big wall of flames blocking the front door and moving this way. We can't get out that way."

"Okay, that's disappointing but not unexpected since the fire started up there. Let's go to the back and see if we can find another door."

The five of us start to walk quickly towards the back of the abandoned building, trying to find a way out and simultaneously avoid the ever-growing flames. Julia had called the 911 a few minutes ago, but I have yet to hear the sirens. The smoke blankets the air within the building, so we all crouch lower to the ground to breathe the precious air not yet tainted by the flames. Pure adrenaline makes my heart beat overtime, but it does little to drown out the roar and crackling of the flames. We move from room to room and try each door as we go, but each one is locked up tight. We turn left and then right with no idea where we are going; we're just running on faith.

I watch as the arms of the blaze crawl up the sides of the building and spread out in a fan-like pattern on the ceiling. It skips the second-story, beautiful stained glass windows too high for us to reach. The fire feeds off the oxygen that remains above, letting it seep into its body as it gorges itself upon what remains of our lifeline. The oxygen acts like a drug; nourishing the fire as it moves along the ceiling menacingly. Is it my imagination or is it moving straight towards us?

I yell to the others, "Run!" We move further into the bowels of this building, discarded so long ago. The halls are like mazes and we are the rats as we run without direction. Our only goal is to escape. But the fire is a living thing and it is has us within its sights. We are the prey running away from a violent predator. Yet, I know in my heart we will lose. Fire consumes all until there is nothing left. It may be futile to outrun the inevitable, but that doesn't mean you give up. I'll be damned if I let that yellow beast devour me. We turn left at the end of the hall and see a door. Salvation at last! I'm the first to get to the door; Martin pushes me aside, grabs hold of the knob and tries to turn it but to no avail. It's locked.

"What the hell?" yells Martin, clearly as frustrated as I am with the lack of exits. "Why do they bother locking a door to an abandoned building?" he asks frustrated.

"See if you can break the lock or the door. Its hinges look old," I say, forcefully trying not to panic as well. Martin nods his head and begins to rattle the knob with all of his 145 pounds of brute strength. Unsurprisingly, it doesn't move. Clearly more panicked by his failed attempt at the knob, Martin begins to throw himself wildly at the door. The sound reverberates off the old walls, making the sound even that much more disturbing to hear. I try to tell Martin that it's no use--the door won't budge--but he doesn't hear me.

"Let's just go back and try to find another door quickly," I suggest, hoping to still be ahead of the fire. The words no sooner left my mouth when around the corner comes the yellow devil, snaking its way toward us, as if saying 'found you!' My heart sinks.

"We're trapped!" yells Julia from in front of me. She grabs her long, straight blonde hair with her hands, in obvious agitation, and her blue eyes are round and full of tears. I want to comfort her but there is nothing to say. We are trapped. Tears fill my brown eyes, as well, but more from the smoke that envelops us. I cough loudly in unison with the others in my group, most of whom I just met today after volunteering for this cleanup project. I refuse to give up and wrack my brain to find another way out. But the more I think, the more the fire advances and the more hopeless things become. The thick, black smoke surrounds us now as the yellow devil hunts us from above and below. I fall to the floor next to Julia, and we hug as we cough, desperate for air and for hope.

Suddenly, I hear a loud thud from the locked door behind us. I look around but the smoke is so thick that I can't see a damn thing. I can hear Martin coughing up a lung, as we all are, but I can't see anything else beyond Julia and me. The air is getting thinner and thinner by the second. My lungs burn from lack of oxygen as vertigo overwhelms me. Beside me, Julia goes limp and it's all I can do to keep her head from hitting the floor. I'm so sleepy I can barely hang on but the fear of falling into the abyss with a yellow monster on my tail keeps me awake. I don't want to die here. I want to make it back to that villa in Spain where the sun was so huge in the sky at dusk that you could almost touch it. Or back to Italy where I tasted the best blend of red wine in the entire world. Not to mention I still haven't hiked up to the Incan ruins at Macchu Picchu in Peru. There's so much I still want to do in my life. It can't end here in a rotting building in the middle of Atlanta, Ga.

Without warning, I hear another thud but this one much louder than the first. I slowly turn my head to the direction of the door, and it blinds me when it gives way. Daylight fills the small hall in which we are all crouched—some of us conscious, some not. I look up through the clearing smoke and see a tall man in a yellow suit enter through the haze. The light behind him gives off an angelic glow as I watch him move forward and kneel beside me. I see his beautiful blue eyes shine through the mask and know he's asking me something, but I can't seem to move; his eyes have me transfixed. Words escape me as time freezes in this one moment. Is this what it's like to die? Am I already seeing an angel from heaven? I want to ask, but my throat is scratchy, and I can't get enough air into my lungs to form the words. Behind my angel, more men in yellow suits enter quickly and scatter to save everyone else.

Though my salvation lies within the blue eyes of the man staring back at me, I can't stay with him. My eyes sting and my lungs burn; I feel dizzy and can't quite keep my eyes open. The cloud of smoke that surrounds us is so thick that the small bits of light created by the blown open door can't penetrate it. The darkness is all consuming. I cough, desperate to clear my lungs of the poison I can't help but breath. I lie down on the floor, feel my cheek against the cool concrete and wait for the blessed darkness to take me to a place where nothing hurts and fresh air is abundant.

In the next moment, my face is lifted gently off the floor and I'm weightless. All I can think of is that my descent into the afterlife must be beginning because there's no other way I would be able to boost myself up off the cool, damp floor. Nor would I want to. My body is numb. All I want to do is sleep. I rise, nonetheless, as strong arms cradle me. I feel the scratchiness of the plastic suit against my face so I know this isn't a dream and I'm not dead. At least, not yet. I swear I hear the flames hiss at us, clearly upset at having been denied its prey.

A murmur reaches my ears, it sounds so far off, muffled. I'm having trouble making out what it's saying. After a minute or so, the same words are thrown around in my brain: "You're going to be alright." Suddenly, a blinding light penetrates the haze and my world is once again illuminated. I turn my head further into the yellow plastic suit to shield my eyes. Once the small silver lights stop flashing behind my eyes, I look around and see that we are outside the burning building. I'm being carried to a stretcher. Again, I hear the words closely resembling 'all right.' I sigh and cuddle closer to the man carrying me to a stretcher beside an ambulance. He lays me down, and I cough anew as the fresh air works hard to get the poison from my lungs.

Above me, the sun is blocked as my blue-eyed savior in yellow leans down and unlatches his helmet. I watch as the he removes his tarnished makeshift head and places it onto the ground. I look up into the face of my angel, a face with sparkling blue eyes that brighten the heavens and short dirty blonde hair that accentuates his face just right. It's a face I knew from long ago. He smiles at me; a smile that lights up the darkness and smoke billowing all around us. I smile back, sure that I will never see my angel again. I open my mouth to give him my thanks, only to be stopped cold by fierce coughing. He lifts me up and gently pats my back to help me replace the smoke with air into my lungs. I want to say how grateful I am but nothing comes out. He slowly lowers me back onto the stretcher. Once I'm back in place, I see him staring at me with a strange look upon his face. He gently removes a stray hair that fell in my eyes and pushes my long hair behind my ear. I smile back at him, the only way to tell him how grateful I am that he saved me.

"Everything will be okay now. Right, Anna Claire?" asks my angel. I smile; his voice is like smooth silk against my ears. I open my mouth to verify his name but I'm so sleepy. All I want to do is close my eyes. I have no idea how long I was out but when I opened my eyes again, my angel was gone. And so, I feared, was my heart.

Chapter Two

~ Budding Flame ~

The constant beeping of the machines in the hospital room awakens me. I open my eyes to the harsh white light above and blink a few times to orientate myself. I move to sit up, but vertigo hits me so I lie back down, groaning. Will this incessant feeling ever end?

"Finally, you're awake," states a deep, masculine voice from beside me. I look around and see Steve pacing beside the hospital bed. I don't even get to see if his grey eyes are concerned since they are always looking at his phone. The phone gets to see more of him than I do. He's decked out in his usual crisp, clean, double-breasted suit and conservative tie. Not a speck of dust blemishes the fabric. I'm not surprised that he isn't sitting in the chair right beside the bed, since he hardly ever sits down. He doesn't like to do anything that might make his suit wrinkle.

I try to sit up but weakness forces me back down onto the pillow. I groan, which solicits a sigh from the man still pacing the room.

"I'm glad you're safe, Anna Claire, but can we please dispense with the dramatics? You know how I dislike that," Steve points out.

I cover my face with my hand, resisting the urge to groan again so as not to bother my fiancé Just then, the nurse comes in to check my vitals and smiles at me. Her grayish hair is in a bun and her aging face is kind.

"How are you feeling my dear?" the nurse asks genuinely concerned.

"I'm still dizzy but okay, I think," I answer, realizing I mean it. I am definitely feeling better than I did after leaving the smoke but also weak, as if I've run a short marathon. How long ago was I rescued anyway? If the increasing darkness descending upon my hospital room is any indication, it has been a few hours.

"How long have I been here?" I ask the nurse.

"About three hours, my dear," states the nurse as she takes my wrist to check my pulse. Satisfied by my progression, the nurse proceeds to take other vitals. I turn my attention to Steve again, intending to tell him to go home. First, I have to peel his attention away from his work.

"Um, sweetie?" I begin but stop abruptly. I'm now acutely aware of how much the effort to speak hurts my throat. But I push on in the hopes that I don't have to say much to get his attention. No such luck. Steve is busy typing something. "Thank you for coming, but honestly I'm feeling better. If you need to work, then by all means go back to the office. I'll be fine. I promise."

Steve looks up from his phone, a strange mix of skepticism and relief written all over his face. He studies me for a minute before he answers. I can practically hear the inner debate going on in his mind right now. Courtesy and societal rules demand that he stay, pressing matters of law demand that he leave. You don't get to be partner in one of the biggest law firms in Atlanta without ambition. And winning a big case doesn't hurt either. Steve is a simple creature and a very predictable one. That's part of what my father likes best in him. I wish I shared my father's preferences. I never had a doubt which option Steve would choose.

Steve straightens his tie and buttons his jacket as he approaches the bed, a smile on his face. I swallow the bitterness as he comes near the edge of the bed, ready for him to be gone.

"Well, if that's what you want, my love, then I'll go back to work. I'm just glad that you're okay."

"Me too," I answer because let's face it; what else is there to say? I hold my breath as Steve kisses my forehead before quickly leaving the room, his phone still buzzing.

The nurse clears her throat beside me as she changes my IV fluid bag. I put my head back down onto the pillow, hoping to avoid any questions. Today obviously wasn't my day. "Well," began the nurse carefully, "he seemed to be in quite a hurry to leave. Was he all right, my dear?

I cringe, not sure how to explain the man I plan to marry. We aren't exactly the most conventional couple. "Steve is a good guy, just a very busy lawyer who wants to be partner. That doesn't leave much time for anything else, including me." The nurse gives me that sympathetic look that I have begun to hate with all my soul. Marriage isn't always about love. I turn away, feigning sleep until the nurse finishes her checkup and leaves. Alone in the darkened hospital room, my mind wanders back to the man that saved me, and the blue eyes I can't seem to stop thinking about. Tears spring to my eyes as I think of how pathetic my life has become. If I were truly happy, I wouldn't pine over a stranger with eyes like the sea after a storm. If I were happy, I would never have taken that stupid ass job to design a new front for that abandoned building my father bought on a whim. I'm a good architect with a small firm of my own. I didn't need or want his help. But who am I kidding? Years of walking on eggshells around my successful father, while at the same time trying to gain his approval, takes a toll. I would have accepted any job just to show him I could succeed. That's the only love my father knows.

Peeling myself from my own melancholy, I try to sit up again in the hospital bed and am happy to see that I don't feel like vomiting from the vertigo. I attempt to focus on happy things I still want to do with my life and be grateful for the second chance. But as I sit lonely in my hospital room, I wonder: am I destined to be alone as I experience all these things? A tear runs silently down my face, my mood as dark and sad as the room. I mentally shake myself as I wipe the tears away. I'll be damned if I'll let that stand in my way. I have a guardian angel and I sure as hell won't waste the second chance he gave me at life. It's time for me to start living.

Chapter Three

~ Smoking Embers ~

The hospital released me the next day. My father's assistant came to pick me up in the company limo to take me back to my father's house. It's times like these that I miss my mother the most. She died when I was five so I have little to no memories of her, save the picture I keep in my room at my father's house. My father tells me stories of how she was a gentle soul taken too early by breast cancer. He doesn't speak of her often, but when he does it's evident how much he loved her. Most memories I have of her are like mist; they come and go and I can't quite grasp onto any of them. I remember her perfume. She loved Sweet Pea from Victoria's Secret. I keep that in my drawer for days I feel down.

The limo pulls up to the cozy eighteen-bedroom house in Sandy Springs, Georgia. The driver runs to the side to help me out of the car. The housekeeper, Alissa, runs out of the front door and wraps me in a big bear hug. "Oh, Anna Claire, sweetie, I'm so glad you're okay!" she says as she pulls me closer.

"Can't breathe, "I say through a scratched throat in a raspy voice. It is obviously too low to hear since Alissa won't let go. I decide a tap on her shoulder might be the best course of action. "Please! Air," I wisp out, hoping that this time she hears.

"Oh! Sorry, baby girl," apologizes the only mother I've ever known. She releases me and I instantly draw a few big breaths of air. It's like my lungs are afraid to let any air go for fear they might never get anymore again.

I smile at Alissa to let her know that I'm not mad. "It's okay, I'm fine," I say, but it comes out as more of a croak than a voice. Alissa's face darkens instantly, and she puts her hands on her hips.

"No thanks to that worthless, absent father of yours," she blares out. "If he cared about you half as much as he does that damn law firm of his, he would have never sent you into that condemned building to work!"

"It wasn't condemned Alissa, just abandoned and unkempt," I point out.

"Well, it should have been condemned from the looks of it, and stop defending that father of yours to me. I have his number already."

I shake my head and say nothing else. History has taught me that Alissa doesn't like my father, and nothing I say will change her mind. Truthfully, I don't want to change it because I know she's right. I follow Alissa into the den and am immediately struck with memories of my mother.

I can see her sitting in the overstuffed leather chair by the fireplace that dominates the room. She watches over me as I play on the soft rug in front of the fire. My mother wanted this one room for herself, and she picked out every piece of furniture and artwork. I never knew why this was her special place, but it's the most welcoming of all the rooms in the house. Since she burned everything she tried to cook, Alissa kicked her out of the oversized, marble dominated kitchen years ago. The two of them were best friends and did what they could to make this stark museum a home. But my version of home was destroyed when she died.

The weakness jars me back from my memories, and I almost collapse. From behind me, Alissa huffs as I allow her to help me onto the couch. Though I'm better, I still feel like I've been run over by a truck and very weak. Lack of oxygen will do that to you, I guess. I lie back and relish the feeling of the soft leather against my cheek. The older couch has always been one of my favorite pieces, since it smells like history and feels as soft as a teddy bear. I used to fall asleep in my mother's arms on this couch. It's the only thing in this mausoleum of a house that actually feels like home.

Alissa disappears into the kitchen and brings me back my favorite red wine blend. "I figured you could use this after the day you've had, sweetie. Drink up."

I smile as she hands me the crystal glass full of 2007 Montevertine Italian wine with some charcuterie and cheese. It's been my favorite since I traveled in Italy years ago. I take a deep sip and visibly relax; it's just what I needed. "Thank you so much. It's perfect."

Alissa simply pats my head and says she'll see about dinner as she leaves me alone with my thoughts. It's a state I find myself in a bit too much lately. Having gone through a crisis, and come out the other side relatively untouched, puts things into perspective. The life I have let my father build for me isn't what I want. Back in the old, abandoned building, with the engulfing smoke and the fire coming for me, I was sure that I was going to die. All I could think of was what a shame that I have never really lived the life I chose. Now that I have a second chance, I need to set things right. First, I need to thank Ethan for saving me.

Chapter Four

~ Budding Flame ~

The firehouse on 5th street and Main is like any other firehouse I've seen before: a square building that houses large fire trucks and mini rooms off to the side for working out and meetings. I walk into the front door, my hands clasping my purse a bit too tight. I start to bite my nails but then force myself to stop. I don't want to seem like the basket case that I am. I look around for someone but the place seems deserted.

"Hello?" I call out, unsure as ever about what I'm doing here. Above me, I hear a noise. I look up and see my angel on top of the nearest fire truck. So, he's real after all. He smiles when he sees me, and I can't help but notice the dimple that shows up on his right cheek.

"Hi," begins Ethan with that adorable smile, "To what do I owe this honor?"

His voice is exactly how I remember it, complete with that irresistible southern accent. Damn, I'm in big trouble. "Um, hi," I begin, unsure. "Is that really you, Ethan?"

He nods his head, the smile still all over his face. "One sec, I'll come down there. Just let me clean up a bit up here from working on the exhaust pipe." He disappears for a few minutes while I hear clanking and clattering from above. I take the extra time to look around the firehouse. There is a distinct smell of sweat and leather in the air. It's a strange mixture but not altogether unpleasant.

The walls are adorned with safety signs and instructional posters, nothing out of the ordinary for a firehouse. I move along the wall towards the office that sits in the corner, and I see his picture beneath the 'Fireman of the Month' sign. There's that cute dimple again. It's almost as if it taunts me. I need to get ahold of myself. He's just a man, albeit a gorgeous man with a gallant nature, who likes to save damsels in distress but a man nonetheless. I take a closer look at the picture. He's in the usual firefighter outfit that fits him so snuggly you can see the bulging of his muscles through his shirt. His wavy blonde hair is combed nicely and his blue eyes sparkle. It's clear from his expression that he's proud.

"I really don't like that picture," a deep voice says from behind me. Startled, I gasp and turn around almost bumping into Ethan. He's right behind me, looking at the same fireman-of-the-month picture.

"Oh?" I say unceremoniously. Seriously? Oh? That's all I've got? I may not be the most debonair woman on earth but I'm sure I can do a hell of a lot better than oh. I take a couple of steps back to distance myself from him and regain some semblance of a brain. What is it about this man that makes me so unsteady? I've always felt more comfortable around old buildings than people, but my dad taught me to mingle with the rich and powerful and I do it well. But for some reason, I've always had some trouble with this man in particular.

I take a deep, steadying breath and get on with what I came here to do. "So I didn't imagine you? You were the one that saved me from a fire down on Main Street a few days ago?" I ask as I try not to stare into those beautiful blue eyes.

"Guilty as charged," he returns, smiling. The years have been kind to him; he's cuter than ever. I smile back, an involuntary reaction around someone so charming and obviously happy with this life. A small part of me envies him for his freedom. Before I get lost again in self-pity, I squash the feeling down and continue with the conversation.

"Well, I wanted to thank you for saving my life."

"You're welcome. But honestly, it's part of my job," he states nonchalantly. It's obvious he isn't comfortable with being the hero or being given gratitude.

"Your job, huh?" I ask a bit miffed. "Well, even if it is your job, I wouldn't be here without you. I wanted to come by personally and offer my gratitude and a donation to your station."

"Thank you but that isn't necessary."

"Nonsense, Ethan. I want to." I'm determined to get this chore done before I make a complete fool of myself over a man I haven't seen in a decade.

Ethan looks at me pensively. "Then our chief will be very happy for extra money for supplies around here," he says, again deflecting the attention off himself. For a moment, I'm lost in those blue eyes as he stares at me. He rubs his hands together with a white cloth to remove the stains from working on the truck. It's unsettling, but I can't seem to break his gaze. For what seems like forever, we just stand there regarding each other. I have no idea how much time has passed, just that I have no will or reason to care. The spell isn't broken until we hear someone cough politely beside us. Startled, I turn and see another firefighter in the doorway that leads to the front. He's dressed in full gear and covered in soot.

"Um, am I interrupting something? A standoff perhaps? Cause I've been standing here for a good minute and ya'll haven't said a word to each other. I wouldn't bother you, but I kind of need to get by so I can head to the locker room and take off my gear."

Embarrassed to the core at being caught gawking, I look only at the ground as I back away to give the man room to pass. He mumbles a thank you before he bolts past us and disappears behind the fire truck that Ethan worked on just a short time ago.

"Well, thanks again for … everything, and please give this to your chief for me," I manage to stammer through as I shove the check into his hand. I made it out to the local firefighter's foundation in honor of Ethan at Station 21. As I turn to leave and walk briskly down the hall, I grip my handbag, wishing it were Ethan's neck for embarrassing me. I'm absolutely positive this was the worst idea ever—to come here and seek out the man I knew and loved long ago. Who cares if he did give me a second chance at life? It isn't worth the vulnerability I feel. It seems that second chance was just something I made up in my own mind. I guess the smoke did more than just hurt my voice; it took my common sense, as well.

I walk fast on my heels, doing my best to get out of here without a full out run. As I near the front door, a strong arm gently grabs me from behind and effectively stops me in my tracks. But it honestly wasn't necessary. His next words would have stopped me cold anyway.

"But just so you know, even if it wasn't my job, I still would have risked everything and gone in that burning building to save you. And it would be my honor if you would have dinner with me Friday night," he asks sheepishly. His eyes are downcast as he shuffles on his feet as if expecting a quick denial.

"No, Ethan," I begin and his entire body tenses, preparing for what he believes is coming. The moment before I tell him that I can't because I have a fiancé. But I realize I don't really want to say no. In fact, every fiber of my being is screaming yes. "The honor would be all mine." And just like that, the walls I've built around my heart begin to melt.

Chapter Five

~ Flames Abound ~

I spent most of the week in a guilt-ridden daze after seeing Ethan at the fire station. It's now Friday night and I'm standing in the middle of my huge walk in closet, looking at every dress I own. I wonder which color a cheating fiancé wears? I try to tell myself that it's only dinner; it doesn't mean anything. But if that were correct, I wouldn't have hidden it from Steve. Despite my misgivings, here I stand still sifting through my closet for the perfect dress to don for dinner, with a man I can't seem to get out of my head.

Behind me, my phone buzzes. I walk over to the bed. It's from Steve, hoping that I'm rested and feeling better. I shoot off a quick text back, knowing he only checks in because he feels he has to, not because he really wants to be here with me. Friday nights are sacred for him since he takes time off to go out with his buddies. I don't blame him really; he works very hard and deserves a break. It's just that I wish I were more of a central part of his life rather than an afterthought. I learned long ago that money can make you comfortable, but it always comes at a price. A price that was long ago paid for me and without my consent.

I walk around my closet, touching the different gowns I own. There is one for just about every occasion a rich girl from old Atlanta money would need: ball gowns, summer dresses, long winter garments, elegant evening wear and everyday dresses made from the finest materials around the world. Names like Prada, Guess, Versace and Gucci are the only acceptable items to wear in my world. And none of it is good for an evening with my savior. It all screams of money and a life that I don't want to rub in Ethan's face. None of it seems right for a date to say thanks for saving a life. Then I spot the perfect dress hiding behind the Versace I wore to the Gala last week.

It's a simple, yellow dress with quarter-length sleeves that hug my every curve. I chose this one specifically since it only goes down to my knees. Add my six-inch high heels and voilà … my insanely long legs, which my father demands I always hide, are highlighted. Well, not tonight, dear father.

I leave my long brown hair down and finish it off with silver jewelry and high heels. I look at myself in the full-length mirror. I'm pleased to see that I look normal, not overly and obnoxiously rich. I try so hard to have my own life that doesn't mix with my Dad's. Tonight is no different.

I check the time on my phone as I head out; I have a half hour to get to the restaurant downtown where I'm meeting Ethan. He wanted to come to my house to pick me up but I insisted we meet at the restaurant. I was pleasantly surprised that Ethan chose Fogo de Chao in Buckhead. It's popular, here in Atlanta, yet not too expensive. I hop in my blue Infiniti and start the trek down 85, battling traffic and my nerves. The closer I get to the restaurant, the greater the feeling to turn the car around and run. Yet, I stay the course; the guilt may guide my thoughts but my heart is guiding the car.

I pull into the parking lot and see Ethan waiting for me by the front door. I park and he's instantly there to open my door and extend his hand to help me out of the car. I smile as I take it, giddy over the gentlemanly gesture.

"Well hello, Ms. Anna Claire Hopkins. You look beautiful," he says before moving my hand towards his lips for a light kiss.

My heart skips a beat the moment his warm lips touch my hand. A jolt of electricity runs through me. I feel like a teenager again. I wish I knew how this man manages to make me feel this way. It isn't as if I've never played this game. In fact, I've played it a bit too often with men who bathe in money and crave the excitement. I've been a conquest and had my fair share of meaningless relationships but this is different. There's something in those blue eyes that I can't seem to resist. And it scares the hell out of me.

I break away from his gaze and busy myself with smoothing out my dress. I close the door and lock my car, happy to have something so normal to concentrate on. Anything to take my mind off the blue-eyed angel bound and determined to charm me to death tonight. At some point, I'll have to tell him about Steve, and I dread every second of it. We make our way into Fogo de Chao and are seated rather quickly. Ever the gentleman, he pulls out the chair for me and makes sure I'm comfortable before he sits down across from me. We are in a secluded spot with candles illuminating the darkness around us. Servers quickly see to our drinks before they quietly and succinctly disappear back into the depths of darkness where they won't be a distraction. It's all like a romantic movie and I wonder exactly what lengths he went to in order to make this all happen. Does he know who I really am? That I'm engaged? I wonder if I should go ahead and tell him about Steve? I hesitate, not wanting to ruin our night before it even begins. So, I'll delude myself as much as possible until the thought goes away. Unable to avoid his gaze any longer, I look up and stare straight into those beautiful blue eyes.

"Are you done avoiding me now?" he asks, smirking.

"Was it that obvious?" I ask, laughing, grateful to move past the darkness lurking in my thoughts.

"Only to the untrained eye," he teases. "We firemen are trained to know when someone is avoiding us. It makes it easier when we have to hose them down."

I laugh loudly, happy to be past the awkward part of the night. "Do you have to do that often then?"

"Only when they misbehave."

I chuckle and instantly relax; the euphoria of being myself around someone engulfs me. With Ethan, I don't have to be proper or be careful with what I say. I can just be me.

"Well then, I'll be sure to behave myself. I'd hate for you to have to hose me down during such a lovely dinner. I prefer other forms of liquid. Like maybe a dirty martini?"

"Nice choice, Anna Claire," says Ethan approvingly as he flags down the waiter and orders for us. While he's occupied with the waiter, I take a moment to look at him. He's wearing a dark blue polo that brings out the blue in his eyes and matching khakis. The shirt isn't too tight but snug enough to see that he's well cut and full of muscle. I imagine running my hand up and down his chest, wondering what those muscles would feel like beneath my fingertips. I look up at his clean-shaven face and notice how his short wavy hair falls just right to accentuate his features. He's gorgeous. Dammit, I'm in so much trouble.

All too soon, his attention is back on me and I'm caught staring again. This time he calls me out on it. "What?" he asks, clearly wondering what I was thinking.

"Sorry, nothing." I grab the menu nearby and bury my blush within its folds. No way in hell I'm telling him that I just imagined him half naked. "So, what are you ordering?" I ask, hoping to change the subject.

"This is a Brazilian restaurant which means any meat they serve is amazing. You can't go wrong with any of it."

Oh shit, I think as I look up from my menu. "Um, I guess this isn't a good time to tell you that I'm a vegetarian?"

His mouth drops open and the color drains from his face. "I'm so sorry," he stammers, unsure what else to say.

"I'm just messing with you. I still love steak!" I tease as I playfully hit him with the menu across his shoulder. He visibly relaxes and smiles at me. Not just any smile, but a grin mixed with a dash of 'color him impressed'.

Our drinks make it to the table and I drink the martini heartily, letting the cool saltiness of the olives mixed with vodka wash over me. I can't remember the last time I've felt more relaxed.

"So, tell me," he begins, "what were you doing in that old building downtown? I thought it was abandoned."

Finally, a safe topic I can talk about all night. "I'm an architect now. A friend of my father's bought that building and asked me to reinvent it. I was down there with my team, making sure all was well before the renovations began tomorrow. I was dealing with one of my worthless interns when I saw the smoke. I have no idea what started it, but the flames blocked our only exit. I didn't panic until I realized every door was locked. It was only then that I understood I was going to know what it feels like to be a turkey on Thanksgiving."

Ethan laughs—a very masculine sound that makes my heart jump a little. Suddenly, memories flood back into my mind. His laugh always drew me to him as a teenager. Coming from a home with little to no laughter, it was comforting and contagious. Even back then, he had one hell of a funny personality. I assume it only got better.

"Well, as it turns out, a stinky man with a tobacco problem was the reason a simple trip turned into an inferno. Well, at least it makes for a good story," he adds.

"My cheating death is a good story? What kind of television shows do you watch Ethan, where *that* is a good story?"

"Oh, you know, the kind where somebody dies at the beginning and it's up to a select intelligent few to solve the mystery. Those are the stories that keep me alive, that make me want to keep saving people despite the misery and heartbreak I see daily."

The smile fades from my face. "I'm so sorry, I should have known."

Ethan smiles. "It's not a bad thing, Anna Claire. I get to save people; make a difference in a life. Kind of like I did for you when I pulled you out of that burning building. That's what makes the job worth it. Even on those days when I'm too late." We look at each other. I have no idea what to say. Luckily, he does. "But luckily, I wasn't too late on your day. I was able to get to you before the fire did and I count that as a win." Ethan picks up his drink and holds it up for a toast. "To a win," he states, his tone solemn as his eyes pierce mine. What is it that he's trying to see?

"To a win," I repeat with a smile, genuinely proud of the work he does.

Soon after the food comes, and we eat heartily from all the different meats and sides that the Brazilian steakhouse offers. We chat about our work and our lives but noticeably avoid the past we left behind a decade ago. So many times, it's on the tip of my tongue to ask him why he left ten years ago, but my pride won't let me.

We finish our dessert of Papaya Cream and pay the bill, but we weren't quite ready to leave. We sit comfortable in the silence and occasional comment as we drink our wine. We talk about anything and everything in life. Ethan didn't once take out his phone during dinner or make me feel like there was somewhere more important he needed to be. Though I know I shouldn't compare him to Steve, it still felt nice to be noticed. Part of me never wants this night to end. I look up from my wine glass, mentally hitting myself for comparing the two men and notice that Ethan is staring at me.

"What?" I ask, my mind buzzing with questions and alcohol.

"I didn't think it was possible, but you got even more beautiful with time."

Uncomfortable with the turn of events, I drink my wine and say nothing. I don't want to be coy; I simply I have nothing to say. Apparently, my silence is Ethan's cue to continue.

"I mean it, Anna Claire, you're stunning."

"Thank you," I say more out of courtesy than flattery. I don't trust myself to say anything more.

"I'm sorry that made you uncomfortable. I didn't mean to make you feel that way."

"I'm not uncomfortable," I respond, though it couldn't be further from the truth. There was only one other time a man called me stunning. It's very disconcerting to hear the same man say it again now. It makes me wonder what he's up to, and if all of this romance was simply a ruse. Immediately, my distrust he earned all those years ago comes back up to the surface full force.

"Okay then, why are your cheeks all flushed now? You seem mad that I called you stunning. Most women would like that."

"The last time you called me stunning, you were running full force out of my life." Stunned by my ire, Ethan couldn't do anything but sit there open mouthed.

Fuming, I continue. "Exactly how did you want to make me feel then, Ethan? Flattered? Beautiful? Do you expect me to just fall back into your arms after all these years because of a little bit of flattery? Is that what this whole night was about? Well, to hell with that. I've grown up, and I have no intention of letting you into my heart again. I have to go," I say as I pick up my coat and purse and practically run out of the restaurant.

I fly through the door and walk briskly to my car, determined to get away from him as fast as possible before I cry or do something else that I will regret. I take my keys out of my purse and fumble with the button to open the door. Suddenly, from behind, a hand covers mine. The warmth of it shoots right through me. I know then and there that I never had a chance. I turn to look at him, and all the feelings from ten years ago come flooding back. I look into his blue eyes and become lost, ready to drown in their depths. I think of everything we missed, everything we never got to do. It was so long ago but it all came back in a rush, the pain washing over me.

"Please, wait! I didn't want to leave! I was forced out by your father. I didn't take the money, Anna Claire, I promise!"

"You left, dammit! You have no idea how badly I wanted you to fight for me; how badly I wanted to go after you and couldn't. I've spent my whole life doing what my father wanted. He was too powerful, and I knew he would find a way to get you out of my life. I just hoped that you could resist. He told me he paid you and you left. I had no idea you didn't take the money."

"And you believed him?" he asks. I see something else in his expression besides the hurt. Anger maybe? "Of course I didn't take the money! I wanted to leave you a note but I couldn't. What was there to say? Your dad threatened me. He said he would fire my dad at the factory and take you far away, where I would never find you, if I didn't leave you alone. I would have searched for you to the ends of the earth, but my dad couldn't lose his job. My mom was sick with breast cancer and the treatments alone were killing us. I wanted to explain it to you, but I knew you would never forgive me. I couldn't take that, so I left without a word. I was a coward. I know that now. But I don't regret it, Anna Claire, because it made me the man I am today. I wanted to become a fireman and help people that couldn't help themselves. All because I couldn't help my father! And I couldn't save you," he finishes, his voice breaking a bit.

He slowly moves his hand up to cup my face, effectively catching a tear falling from my eye. "I'm so sorry I left without a word. I couldn't save you then, but the world has come full circle because I could save you now."

Tears begin to free flow from my eyes. I'm incapable of saying anything because I just can't catch a thought. I want to say that I believe him, that I forgive him, but I can't. Too much has happened since he left me there alone.

"You may have changed, but so have I. I'm not the impressionable young girl you left behind a decade ago."

"That's for sure," teases Ethan. "You're more beautiful today than ever. And you're exactly like I've remembered you every night in my dreams for the last ten years."

The keys fall from my hand and clamor to the concrete making a high-pitched sound and pierces the quiet, dark night that surrounds us. The wind picks up, and I can feel my dress flap around my weak knees. Ethan moves closer, taking me into his arms ever so slowly. I know he's going to kiss me and I shouldn't let him, but right now, it doesn't matter. All that exists for us is each other. The minute his lips touch mine, the armor I've built around my heart melts instantaneously. I stand up on my tippy toes and put my arms around his neck pulling him closer. Wave after wave of memory fills my head. He feels exactly like he did all those years ago. Actually, he feels better. I hold him close, afraid that if I let him move one inch from me all would be lost again. I let the pain I've kept close to my heart for all these years loose; I kiss him like there is no tomorrow. And in my life, I have to face that there may not be. Because no matter what I ever want, my father will always be stronger than I am. No matter how strong I get, I'm still doomed to the life he chose for me.

Doubled over with doubt and guilt, I break the kiss. Startled, Ethan looks at me. His face is flushed and confusion dominates his expression. I can't tell him about Steve or my weakness. I can't look at the disappointment in his eyes; I get enough of that from my dad.

"I'm so sorry, Ethan, but I can't," I say as tears begin to fall down my face. I bend over to quickly pick up my keys and grab the handle to get into my car. I open it up and try to climb inside, but he stops me once again by his words.

"I've waited for you, Anna Claire, for what seems like a lifetime. You may have someone else but that really doesn't matter. He will never be able to give you everything you need. I'm the only one that can love you the way you deserve to be loved. You can leave here tonight, thinking this is a mistake, but it isn't. It never was. I always knew I would lose if I fought for you so I chose the only path left to me. I waited for you." He takes my hand and places it on his chest.

"In here. You never left. I always had you here inside my heart. Now, it's time for you to come out and be real. It's time for you to live, my love."

I want to say something but the catch in my throat won't let me. I can taste the salt of my tears as they fall upon my lips. I can see the yearning in his eyes, but I'm too emotional to deal with it right now. I take one last look at his beautiful face and hop into the car and drive off into the night, leaving Ethan alone in the darkness.

Chapter Six

~ Scorching Burns ~

The roar of the engine keeps me sane as I drive down the dark road back to my apartment. I turn on the music to try and drown out Ethan's voice in my head. It's no use, the tears just keep coming. The hurt I buried long ago comes bubbling back up to the surface with a vengeance. I thought I was over his abandonment, but his appearance back into my life has made me realize that I only suppressed it. Deep inside, I think I always knew he didn't take the money. Actually hearing him confirm it makes me feel that much more of a coward. As I drive down the dark road through blurry vision, I remember that night like it was yesterday.

~ * ~

The storm raged all around the mansion in an ominous tone. I had my bag packed and ready to leave with Ethan as soon as he arrived sometime around eleven o'clock. We chose this Thursday night in April because my dad had his monthly board meeting. It usually ran very late so he would sleep at the office and not come home until the next day. I chose to wait in the den, snuggled on my favorite couch, watching the minutes tick by on the old grandfather clock in the corner. As the minutes continued to tick by, I kept checking my phone for a text but nothing ever came. I must have sent twenty different texts asking him where he was or updating me on how much longer until he arrived but he never responded. Three times, I got fed up and tried to call him but his phone was off. I told myself it was simply a precaution so that no one could follow him or find out what he was up to.

We had been planning this little escape for months, and talked about it endlessly as we cuddled on a towel by the river or hung out in our favorite tree in the back of my property. The world held such possibilities and we

72

knew that we would be together forever. Yet, forever didn't turn out to be as long as I had predicted.

Eleven o'clock had come and gone with no word from Ethan. I went through every emotion in the book from mad to crying and then hysteria but it changed nothing; Ethan wasn't coming. All sorts of scenarios ran through my head as midnight approached. I wondered if he had died in a car accident while driving to get me; I-85 in Atlanta can be a death trap at night. By one a.m., I was just numb, cold and dead on the inside—sure that tomorrow, and each day after that, would bring nothing but despair. My love had deserted me. What greater pain is there than that?

From behind me, I heard footsteps approach. They sounded like hammers against the wooden floor as they came nearer to the self-made tomb I occupied. I didn't even bother to look up; I would have known those footsteps anywhere. They are made of pure power and unadulterated thirst to succeed at all costs.

"Are you going to stay in here crying and depressed forever Anna Claire?" my father asked with no hint of emotion in his voice.

Though I could have thought of a few distinctly colorful words to say at that moment, I refrained from releasing them. I had lived only a short eighteen years under the rule of my father's thumb but that had been enough to teach me not to spar words with the devil.

"You should have known he would abandon you, Anna Claire. He's trash and brings you down into the bowels with him. You should have known better than to get involved with a no-name guy from south Atlanta. He only wanted you for your money, and he proved that tonight when he took the five thousand I offered him to stay away from you. He couldn't get out of Atlanta fast enough."

My father paused for dramatic effect or perhaps a reaction, but when he got none he just continued. "He's beneath you and always will be. So, get up and start acting like a Hopkins. Or I'll make damn sure that you regret ever letting him into your life."

With those stinging words, my adoring father walked off. The responsibilities of keeping his daughter in check according to his standards of living, all but taken care of in his mind.

Luckily, there wasn't anything else he could do to hurt me. My heart was already broken.

~ * ~

Back home, I lie in bed on my side, facing the window of my penthouse apartment. It's in Midtown, with a beautiful view that overlooks Piedmont Park. From the teak floored terrace, I can usually see the breathtaking skyline of both Midtown and Buckhead. On a clear night like this one, the lights of the city shine like a beacon of prosperity and hope. But tonight, all the darkness holds for me is numbness. I feel as lost as I did the night Ethan left, though with considerably less pain. Despite the fact that time did heal some of my wounds, seeing Ethan tonight brought the pain of desertion from a decade ago all back to the surface. I stare off into the star filled sky, wondering why fate didn't just leave well enough alone.

I wasn't exactly happy, per say, but I was content with the life I am building away from the watchful and tyrannous eye of my father. I worked hard, studied harder and planned extensively for the life I have. A life that I hope matters and gives something good back to the world. Sadly, I've seen so little good in the world my father built for us. It's an existence I never wanted to be a part of, a path that only leads to destruction. At night, I dream of the countless victims my father has left in his wake. Victims I had a part in because I'm too much of a coward to stand against him. I'm a product of my circumstances, yes, but I'm also a prisoner in my own life. I'm the daughter of a man driven by success and money. All he knows how to do is take. And that one fault almost took my life.

I worked long and hard to build a life that's my own and now, my world is turned upside down by a man I thought was long gone. I have no idea what tomorrow will bring. One thing is certain: lying here staring off into space, unsure of my next move, won't get me anywhere. I decide to go to bed and come morning, let the sane part of my brain form a plan. But what plagues me most, as I turn out the light and crawl under my covers, is the fear that the path I choose will be the one that takes me closer to the only man that ever truly touched my heart.

Chapter Seven

~ Raging Fire ~

I walk into the office at my architect firm in downtown Dunwoody, feeling sluggish and out of sorts. The sleep that eluded me most of the night comes down hard on me as I move like a Zombie towards my desk at eight a.m.

"Rough night?" asks Julia with a smirk on her face.

"Not a word," I state firmly, "until I've had my coffee."

Julie just smiles and ignores my grumpiness. In fact, looking closer at her, I now see that she's chirpier than usual this morning.

"What has you all happy this early?" I ask, despite the fact that talking is generally prohibited before my second cup of coffee.

"I had a very nice conversation this morning with a particularly handsome man."

"Oh?" I ask unenthusiastically, wishing she would just get to the point.

Julia smiles in anticipation, clearly happy about something. I about spit out my coffee the minute her next words leave her mouth. "And he left you flowers."

"Flowers?" I ask dumbfounded. "I didn't think they made deliveries this early." My cloudy mind befuddles around, trying to figure out who would send me get well flowers this late.

"They do, if you bring them in yourself. And even though you didn't ask, he brought you pink roses."

I stop stirring the sugar into my coffee the second I hear the flowers are pink. It can't be a coincidence. I throw a strange look at Julia before heading off to my office, two doors down from the coffee maker. I try my best not to look overly eager by running into my office. I skid to a stop the minute I enter the door and see two dozen beautiful, blooming pink roses.

"What did he look like?" I ask as I search for a card.

"Oh you know, tall, muscular, and handsome. He had the most beautiful eyes I've ever seen. Not that I was looking into them for very long."

I roll my eyes and huff at her. "You go through men faster than a Corvette, Julia. Every man you meet has the most beautiful eyes you've ever seen," I tease.

Julia just shrugs her shoulders and laughs. What is there to say? It's the truth, and she doesn't ever apologize for the way she lives. Who am I to judge? If I was that beautiful and didn't have a tyrant for a father, I'd like to think that I'd have tons of boyfriends, too.

"For the record, I love Corvettes, too," she teases back.

I smile back at her, grateful to have her as a friend. We are both silent as I look inside the flowers for a card. Finding none, I begin to look on the desk and floor, hoping that maybe it fell. I'm dying to know if the flowers are from Ethan. I get down on all fours, a feat considering I'm wearing a short red skirt with black pantyhose and heels, and look under my desk. From behind me, I hear Julia laugh out loud.

"Are you looking for this?" she asks, holding up a small white piece of paper in her hand.

I get up and grab the small paper from her, more than a bit perturbed. "You know I was looking for that! Why didn't you just tell me?"

"I would have, honestly, but it was too much fun watching you in a panic. I've never seen you like this before, Anna Claire. Why are you so rattled?"

I shoot her a dirty look and don't bother responding to her question. I don't quite know how to tell her that it's not my fiancé that has my heart racing.

I open up the sealed envelope and read the simple sentence hand written on the paper. It's short, to the point and probably the most romantic thing anyone has ever said to me.

Beauty comes from within, but first you must bloom. Live beautifully, my love, and flourish.

More than anything,
Ethan

I drop the card onto my desk and sink into the closest chair. My heart beats so fast in my chest that I'm afraid it might crash through my ribcage, but I can't stop it. I have ceased to think; now I can only feel. And what I feel is wonderful. For so long, I froze my heart, unable to really let anyone in for fear someone would demolish it again. The one responsible for breaking my heart has come back into my life to heal it. Life really does come back full circle sometimes. It throws some hellish curveballs you would never expect.

"Who's Ethan?" Julia asks from her perch by my office door. I forgot she was there.

"And old friend," I say, not wanting to reveal too much. I sometimes forget how perceptive Julia is.

"A friend doesn't call you '*my love*'. I've never gotten a note like that from any of my boyfriends, so this person is more than just a friend. You can tell me anything Anna Claire, I hope you know that."

I smile at her, grateful to have a shoulder to lean on but not quite ready to accept the offer. "I'm not sure who he is to me yet, so there's nothing to tell. But I promise you will be the first one I call."

"Deal," agrees Julia. Before she can say much else, my cell phone rings. I fish it out of my purse and look at the screen. The name immediately squashes the elation I feel. Guilt consumes me as I slide the screen to 'answer' and put the phone to my ear.

"Hey, Steve. What can I do for you sweetie?" I ask in a sickly sweet tone, hoping he doesn't sense anything different about my voice. Maybe I'm overdoing it? I turn away from the flowers and try to focus on my fiancé But it's so very hard.

Ever the businessman, Steve gets right to the point. "I've decided to invite the Bradleys to the engagement party, so you will need to inform the caterer as well as rearrange the seating a bit. They don't like the Elliots."

I turn to the notepad on my desk and write as he dictates to me. I don't respond because I know I don't need to. Steve doesn't need affirmation; he simply needs me to follow his directions. Which I'm sad to say, I do very well thanks to my OCD. I say "uh huh" and "of course" as he changes a few more things about the party. When he's done, there's silence on the phone. That's something new.

"Is there anything else you need, sweetie?"

"You didn't call last night like usual. I'm wondering why."

I'm sure that the truth—that I was contemplating life with a man I loved long ago—isn't the correct answer, so I go with the most obvious. "I was tired. I fell asleep early after a glass of wine and didn't wake up until morning. Sorry that I worried you."

Placated, he mumbles something similar to a clipped "fine" before hanging up the phone. I whisper bye into the dead line before putting the phone down on my desk and smelling my flowers once more. I inhale the aroma and let it fill me, and guide me, on what I should do from here. Not surprisingly, the roses keep their secrets and I'm just as confused as ever. I'm so engrossed in my own thoughts, I don't realize that Julia is still standing in the doorway of my office.

"Wow, you have it bad, don't you, Anna Claire?"

Shifting my confused look to her, I ask, "What do you mean?"

"This man has you so rattled, I could kiss him. He's woken you up, my friend. And I have a feeling you're in for one hell of a ride."

I look at Julia and smile. I always did enjoy rollercoasters.

Chapter Eight

~ Inferno ~

I work through my indecision most of the day as the hours drone on and on. I rework the designs for the next building my company has contracted to reinvent. It's mind numbing work, but I love the creativity of it and the freedom I get when my mind is working angles and spatial anomalies on how I can best fit a certain number of rooms into one building. Today is no different, save my eyes roaming from my computer to the huge arrangement of pink roses now on the corner of my mahogany desk. As much as my guilt plagues me, my heart keeps coming back to Ethan. Should I meet him again? Do I care if my father finds out? If we do work out, where would we live considering we would have no peace in a city practically owned by my father? I think about how I will break it to Steve and if he'll cry. Then I laugh and realize how stupid that is; Steve never cries.

The day drones on and on like that with my mind oscillating from one extreme to another. Emotionally exhausted, I have little strength left to fight it off. By lunch, I'm exhausted and have designed the same room five times in the last hour. The lack of focus is driving me mad so I take a break and check my email. I have one from Ethan, time stamped five minutes after I arrived at work this morning. I open it up and the only content is a cell phone number. Presumptuous for sure, but I'm still intrigued so I take out my phone and send him a text.

Thank you for the flowers. I put down my phone, expecting to have to wait for a few minutes until he responds but it barely touches the desk before it chimes.

Did you know why I chose pink?

I smile to myself. It seems that I've been doing a lot of that lately. *It was the color of the sunset the first time we kissed.*

Again, the text response is almost instantaneous. *I was afraid you had forgotten.*

It's funny the things you remember, long after you have forgotten them. Time and memory are such fickle beasts. As humans, we are cursed to remember the things we want to forget and forget almost everything we truly want to remember. The paradox isn't lost on me. I want to write something whimsical back, but I honestly don't know what to say. Despite the fact that I'm happier in the past few days than I have been in years, it doesn't change the fact that I'm engaged. The only difference now is that I know in my heart it's to the wrong man. Realization hits me like a Mack truck. Genuine, lasting love indeed does exist. One that can stand the test of time. Even though I haven't seen or spoken to Ethan for ten years, the spark never died. Whatever connection we once had is just as strong today as it was a decade ago. The stories really didn't lie–true love never really dies. It may change over time, but it never, ever diminishes.

Ethan has come back to me after years of fate conspiring to keep us apart. More than that, he's willing to fight for me this time, a miracle within itself. Another chime from my phone brings my attention back to the here and now.

Do you like them? I can hear his vulnerability even through the text.

How could I not? They are perfect. And so was the card. I never thought of you as a poet.

He sends a smiley text before responding. *Robert Thoreau ain't got nothin' on me babe.*

I literally laugh out loud, as I imagine Ethan saying that. I wonder when I became this witless teenager again and shake myself mentally. I really need to get back to work. Just as that thought crosses my mind, another text chimed in from Ethan.

Can you ditch work for the rest of the day? There's something I need to show you.

I hesitate, wondering if it's a good idea to go down this road. Then I realize my heart is already at the end of the road, waiting for me to catch up. Apparently, my mind is very slow and more stubborn than my heart.

Yes. I type and take a deep breath before sending. There's no going back now. I realize, rather ecstatically, that I don't want to go back. I want to move on with the life stolen from me all those years ago.

The second I respond yes, another text pops up on my phone. The only content is an address. My face practically glows as I grab my coat and purse and head out the door. I'm going back to where this all began.

Chapter Nine

~ Eternal Flame ~

I open the door and walk into the half burned remains of the downtown building I almost died in a few short weeks ago. The burnt odor stings my nostrils, but it isn't so overwhelming that I can't breathe. The front walls are as black with soot and debris litters the floor except for one circular area in the middle of the front great hall. Inside the circle is a vase full of pink flowers surrounded by pink petals. As I walk closer, I notice the petals aren't simply thrown down randomly, but rather they spell out a message: *follow the trail.* I look up and see that the petals do indeed form a trail toward the back of the building.

I step around the vase to follow the petals on the floor. My heels echo with each step due to the high ceilings of this old building. Despite the light of the day, the interior is dark. I take out my phone and push the light button to guide my way. I walk down the main hall that leads away from the front lobby, excitement from the adventure making my heart skip beats. I round two corners of the maze-like corridors before the petals stop at a white door. I look up and see a scribbled message: *For Anna Claire—the only woman who will forever hold my heart.* My hands shake as I reach for the doorknob. I take a deep breath as I grasp it; my mind whirls in wonder to see what waits behind door number one.

The moment I open the door, the hall is flooded with light. There are candles everywhere, casting a soft yellow glow on all the light touches. In the middle of the large banquet room sits a round table covered with a soft white tablecloth and two chairs. Candles of all different sizes surround another large arrangement of pink roses smack dab in the middle. As I approach the table, I smell succulent aromas of some sort of chicken dish, sitting on top of the cart just off to the right.

"Hello?" I ask, expecting to hear Ethan's voice but all I get back is my own reverberating off the walls. "Hello, Ethan?" I ask again, feeling confused. "I know you're here so why don't you just show yourself?"

Suddenly, a small fire erupts on the floor from the other side of the table. I gasp and grab my chest, the fear threatening to take over as I take a few large steps back. I soon realize that the small fire is set in a specific pattern. I watch the small spark gather speed as it spreads on the floor, mesmerized by the movements of the yellow flame. It's quite beautiful actually—as long as it isn't chasing you. The flame, which at first had moved up in an arc, now is moving back down in sloping pattern. It reaches a point by my feet and begins to move back up toward the place where it began. I step back two more feet and instantly recognize the shape the flame is making.

My heart flutters rapidly in my chest and I almost literally swoon. I thought that only happened in romance novels, but as light-headed as I feel right now, it must be real. The flame reaches its starting point, completing the heart. I look up and see Ethan come out of the darkness and walk to the middle of the flaming heart and face me. He's dressed in khaki's and a blue polo shirt that matches his eyes. In his hand is a single pink rose. I'm not sure when I begin to cry and I'm certain that I don't care.

"This is supposed to make you happy, not sad, Anna Claire."

I look up into Ethan's confused eyes and smile. I'm as far from sad that I could ever be. "They're happy tears, Ethan. In fact, I think I'm feeling just about every elated emotion conceivable right now. That's probably why I'm crying."

Ethan smiles; it lights up the room even more than the soft fire still flaming around us. "Then I guess this will make you cry even more," he predicts as he takes a small, square black velvet box out of his pocket. He gets down on one knee and opens the box. Staring back at me is a two-carat, sparkling diamond in the shape of a heart. Ethan was correct; the tears begin to free flow and I don't know how to stop them.

"Oh, Ethan," I say after a sniff, "it's absolutely beautiful." Damn, I'm sure I look like Rudolf right now.

"I know it's not as big as you're accustomed to, but it seemed perfect for you so..."

"Stop that right now," I chide as I close the short distance between us and put my finger over his lips. "It's perfect."

Ethan's smile brightens even more as he asks the question I've unknowingly waited over a decade to be asked.

"Anna Claire Hopkins. Will you do me the extraordinary honor of becoming my wife?"

The tears stop instantly as I think of spending the rest of my life in the strong arms of this amazing man, my personal savior. I realize then that I never had a chance. The answer was always the same. "Yes, my love. Absolutely yes," I whisper happily.

Ethan stands quickly, moves forward to take me into his arms and kisses me hungrily. It's a kiss to seal a love that began many years ago and waited patiently until we were both ready to take on my father, leave my current fiancé and fight for a love that was always meant to be. And finally, after a decade of a life void of happiness and romance, I finally feel like I'm home.

THE END

About the Author

Ellyse Roberts' first book was a romance novel set in the London ton. It only took that one book for a romance junkie to be born. Hundreds of novels later, Ellyse decided to take her love for creative writing and create a sweet story where romance isn't dead and true love lasts a lifetime. The Spark is her debut short story.

PROPOSAL UNEXPECTED

By

Elena Kane

Chapter One

Adele sniffed loudly, wiping her reddened nose with yet another tissue for the millionth time. Grabbing the remote, she proceeded to flip through the channels. The same old Christmas shows, which made their grand appearance every year, would not take her mind off the unfairness of being sick during the holidays. As she thought of her husband's company Christmas party starting in a few minutes, she threw the remote down with disgust.

"Of all the stupid times to get a cold," she muttered miserably to Callie. Her calico cat blinked once before turning her head, no more sympathetic than her husband had been. "Humph." Adele blew her nose again; the tender flesh burned painfully with each touch of the lotion-infused material.

Adele leaned her head back onto the soft cushions of the couch, her mouth open wide in a weak attempt to breathe normally. Her whole body ached; her head felt stuffed with cotton, and she couldn't get warm enough. Despite all of that, her true discomfort lay in the fact she hadn't been able to go out in her new cocktail dress, on the arm of her handsome husband. Every year, she looked forward to Rob's company parties—or more importantly—how Rob reacted to her when she came down the stairs all dolled up. Not that he normally thought she looked bad, but he was so rarely home. She appreciated the extra attention. He would tell her how he couldn't wait for all his coworkers to see his hottie wife.

His company always rented out an impressive hotel for the whole night: drinks, entertainment and rooms for the employees included. This year promised to be one of the best parties yet with impressive performances, grand giveaway prizes and rooms twice the size of all the previous years. Adele had been looking forward to the event since hearing the details back in late summer.

"And two days before the big night, a preschooler has to sneeze on me," Adele muttered. She loved her students and enjoyed the new experiences they provided her every day. Dealing with being sneezed and coughed on was definitely not her favorite part. After the first few years of teaching, she'd acquired immunities and it didn't faze her. However, this had been a special virus, destined to make her feel as if she were dying and rendered incapable of attending a party.

"Stupid cold or flu or whatever the hell it is," Adele muttered bitterly. She was seriously beginning to wonder if it wasn't the Bubonic Plague making a comeback. Groaning loudly, she swung her legs off the couch and mentally prepared herself for the vertigo that would attack the minute she got up from her deathbed. She had been talking herself out of getting some orange juice for the past hour, but her taste buds won out. The promise of a wet, soothed throat spurred her on.

"He could have at least stayed home and taken care of me," Adele grumbled as she heaved herself off the couch. She shuffled her feet down the carpeted hallway, stopping at the kitchen counter to rest for a moment, before finishing the rest of her journey to the fridge. "Why does it have to be so far away," she whined to Callie, who had followed her slow progress in the hopes of being fed too. "If you think I'm getting you anything when I just used the last of my reserves to get a glass of juice, you're wrong. You should have helped me convince Rob to stay if you wanted to be fed sometime in the next hour."

Callie gave her another slow blink, turning her head once more in feline disgust. She gave a low meow of indignation before making her way back to the couch Adele had vacated.

"Don't make yourself too comfortable," she called to the independent cat. "I plan on sitting there again." She took a swig of the juice, accidently slamming the glass a little too hard on the counter. Her hands shook badly with such little effort. "If I don't pass out first," she muttered, knowing the cat wasn't listening one way or the other.

She started back toward the couch, pausing every few steps to attempt to breathe and rest before continuing. The room waved uncomfortably before her eyes, making her already nauseous stomach burn with sickness. "See, this is why he should have stayed. I could very well be dying."

She'd tried all afternoon to convince Rob to stay with her, pleading that she felt like death warmed over; he wouldn't be swayed.

"The room has already been paid for and it would be a waste if I didn't go," he argued.

Adele shook her head at the memory, feeling just as insulted now as she did when he'd first made the comment. "What kind of bullshit answer is that," she muttered, slumping to the floor in complete exhaustion. She laid her head down on the soft carpet, fighting the waves of heat crashing around in her stomach.

The phone ringing startled her awake. Fighting pain and nausea, she crawled the remaining distance to where she'd placed it on the arm of the couch, hoping it was Rob. She would tell him he'd better officially say goodbye because she wasn't long for this world.

She looked at the number on the screen, her mind drawing a blank and slid the button across to answer the call. "Hello," she said, painfully aware of how awful she sounded.

"Adele," an unfamiliar voice stammered back.

"This is she." Adele leaned her head against the couch and fought to stay awake for just a few more minutes, though her eyes screamed for relief.

"You don't know me, but I have some important information about your husband."

Adele's heart skipped a beat then fell to the pit of her stomach where it joined the burning sensation. "Is he okay?" she asked, voicing the dreaded question.

"Oh, I would say he is more than okay," the voice dripped sarcasm and anger. "He's currently screwing his secretary in that fancy hotel room the company rented for him."

Adele forgot how to breathe. A blackness, which had nothing to do with her sickness, crashed all around her. Time stood still and words failed her. "Who is this?" she whispered, every other thought scattering in her mind.

"My name isn't important," the voice answered angrily.

"How do you know this?" Adele asked, her own anger showing its ugly head.

"Because he's cheating on me now and I'm the one pregnant with his child."

~ * ~

Adele looked around, temporarily confused by her surroundings. She lay on the floor once more with her face turned toward the couch and her phone still in her hand. *Cheating bastard … another woman … two other women … a baby on the way.* His betrayal bombarded her mind and she retched, unable to hold back the sickness that had threatened her all evening.

The tears flowed hot and fast down her face, causing her nose to run even harder, and she gagged again. She crawled toward the bathroom, leaving a trail of snot and tears in her wake.

"How could he do this to *me*?" she screamed, the shrillness of her voice making her head throb painfully. Her whole life and everything she loved about it, about him, flashed through her mind. It was all a lie. She meant nothing to him. No wonder he wouldn't stay. It was the perfect excuse for him to have the whole night to himself with his mistress of choice.

Adele screamed out again as thoughts of his secretary, Becka, entered her mind. She had trusted, even liked her, and this is how she repaid her? It was all too much. Adele laid her feverish head on the cold tile of the bathroom floor. She sobbed until the tears dried up, and she fell asleep once more.

~ * ~

"Adele. Honey, can you hear me?"

Adele shifted slightly, registering the low voice that made her heart race; it just raced for a completely different reason now. Weakly, she opened her lids just a fraction. The light from the hallway caused her eyes to water painfully.

"Get. The. Hell. Out." She enunciated each word with as much force as she could muster.

"What?" Rob asked, clearly at a loss to what was going on. "Come on, honey. I shouldn't have left you last night. I guess I just didn't realize how sick you were," he said, reaching toward her in an attempt to help her.

"DON'T TOUCH ME!" she screeched. The thought of this man's hands anywhere near her person made her feel sick all over again.

Rob sat back, a look of anger and confusion on his face from being yelled at. "What the hell is wrong with you?" he asked.

Adele sat up slowly. She placed her hands on the lid of the toilet and began the tedious task of getting up from the cold floor. Twice more Rob attempted to help, but Adele screeched at him again. He backed up to the wall where he watched her slow progress. She sat down heavily on the toilet, gasped for air that refused to go into her sick body and glared at Rob.

"Would you mind explaining what this is all about?" he asked, his voice indicating true annoyance.

"Your girlfriend called. She's pissed about your fling with Becka," she spat. She enjoyed watching the color drain from her husband's face, found satisfaction in the way his mouth opened and closed like a fish out of water. "She also told me that you're having a baby. I guess congratulations are in order," she hissed.

"Michelle called you?" he whispered, not bothering to deny it.

"Her name is Michelle? Like as in one of the partners, Michelle?" Adele asked, her voice rising again in anger. "You screwed one of the partners, and then you were dumb enough to cheat on her with a secretary?" If Adele hadn't been so upset that he'd cheated on her first, she would have laughed at his stupidity. "I guess I know who my lawyer is gonna be," Adele said vindictively.

At this, the remaining color in Rob's face drained away, leaving him pale and sweaty.

"Didn't think that one through, did you?"

Chapter Two

Adele sat in the large, comfy leather chair and stared out the window at the sprawling city of Columbus below. High rising buildings could be seen far into the distance, and the sound of cars honking and accelerating penetrated through the closed glass even at that early hour. Her heart broke all over again as memories of life with Rob flooded through her. It had been months since the call that changed her life, and still she mourned for all she had lost.

"Don't do this to yourself," Margo said, looking over her half glasses at her.

Adele wiped the tears from her face and did her best to look as if she was all right, as everyone expected her to be. She kept her face turned toward the window, determined to keep her swollen eyes away from the look of pity she was sure to find.

"Here are the final papers. Everything is signed, filed and now you are officially divorced," Margo said, a broad grin on her face. It couldn't be more obvious that she saw this as a very good thing.

Adele, on the other hand, wanted to curl up into a ball and weep the day away. True, it was over, but that didn't mean it hurt any less. After she'd confronted Rob, she'd approached Michelle, intent on hurting him as badly as he had her. But Michelle reasoned it would have been a conflict of interest for her to represent Adele. Instead, she recommended Margo, assuring Adele that this lawyer was more than capable of ripping Rob's throat out. Satisfied, Adele had called Margo immediately. Now, as she sat in the prestigious lawyer's office, she wondered if she'd done the right thing.

Margo seemed aware of the melancholy mood and placed the neat stack of papers on the edge of her desk. She regarded Adele with a raised eyebrow. "Adele, he cheated on you with at least two different women. One of them just had his daughter. Don't question yourself. Trust me. You were extremely easy on him, too easy if you ask me. He'll get over this and will be screwing more women before the week is out. I guarantee it. Scum like that doesn't change," the lawyer stated firmly.

Adele knew all this, but it didn't stay the permanent ache that resided in her heart. What did this say about her? She couldn't even keep the eye of the one person who was supposed to love her through everything. How could she ever move on knowing that crucial fact about herself?

~ * ~

Sobbing for the fifth night that week, Adele grabbed her phone determined to find someone to talk to, determined not to cry herself to sleep yet again. Her friend Rachel would always listen, like she did many times at work, but Adele felt she'd already reached her quota of complaints given to the poor girl. There had to be some limit for any one person to endure. She looked at her contact list and realization crashed on her like an ocean wave. Most of her friends had moved on after Rob. She had married in her senior year, so her priorities had changed. She went from the crazy and carefree college student to a married woman. Her world suddenly revolved around the incredibly sexy man she felt privileged to call her husband. Without her realizing it, her friends had drifted off, leading their own happy lives. Rob's friends became her friends; or so she'd thought.

"Don't see any of them calling me now," she muttered humorlessly to herself. She wiped her nose on the tissue balled up in her hand; her gaze never left the blank screen of her phone. As much as she willed it, it remained resolutely unmoving. She tossed the useless device onto her couch and buried her face in her hands. Worse, over the past several months she managed to push away almost everyone else in her life, even coworkers she'd gotten on relatively well with despite her overbearing husband. She barely had the energy to wake up and teach every day. Forcing herself to be more than civil to people her own age, only pushed her past her limit of what she could accomplish in a day.

Her gaze shifted past her indifferent cat to pick out different things Rob had bought her over the years. Unpleasant thoughts took hold as she realized they were all bribes meant to placate her into thinking she'd been happy. The complete and utter control she'd let Rob have over her. All the time he'd spent in the 'office.' The fancy presents and clothes he'd bought her instead of actually being a decent husband. She looked at the different trinkets and love tokens surrounding her and saw them in a new light. She clenched her fist and gritted her teeth until her jaws ached.

She strolled across the room, spotting the first unlucky piece of furniture. Grabbing the side of it, she pushed over the large bookcase Rob had given her for her birthday one year. The satisfying crash it made, splintering against the floor, egged her on. Ten minutes later, her entire living room lay in total disrepair. It resembled tornado alley more than a living space.

Still livid with hot angry tears running down her face, she marched into her bedroom and straight toward the closet. Destruction lay heavy on her mind.

"Thought he could dress me up and make me look like a real fool in front of his friends, did he?" Reaching in, she snatched several outfits he had treasured for their sex appeal, but she'd never felt comfortable in. She yanked open her drawer and located the scissors. Within a few short minutes, a fabulous pile of shredded garments littered her floor. She looked back at her closet, her hate and anger dying away as quickly as it had begun.

"Now, what am I gonna wear," she lamented. Realizing she'd demolished over three fourths of her wardrobe in a little under twenty minutes, she hung her head in defeat. She didn't have the money or desire to go shopping for clothes. The weariness of depression, and having used more energy than she'd had in months slapped her rudely. She collapsed to the floor, sobs wracking her body and her mind. The marriage she'd held onto so tightly had left her a worthless and entirely too dependent woman. He had wanted her like that, so he could carry on with the single life behind her back.

"You stupid ass!" Adele screamed at the walls around her. Callie walked in and surveyed the destruction with her haughty eyes, making Adele want to choke her too. She was Rob's cat, but he claimed he wouldn't have time for her and insisted Adele take her. Not wanting to see anything happen to the companion she'd spent more time with than her own husband, she'd agreed. Now, the independent creature seemed more like Rob than she'd ever realized. She wished she'd swallowed those emotions and left the cat behind.

Preparing herself to stand or kick the cat, she was thrown off when

Callie strolled over nonchalantly and rubbed her head against Adele's leg. Adele stared in shock. The cat had never before offered any kind of attention to Adele. Most days, she barely tolerated her—only using her owner for food and water. Other than that, she remained completely aloof to Adele's desire for affection.

Crying for a completely different reason now, Adele reached out, grabbed the fluffy hairball and brought her to her chest. Callie graciously allowed it, even deigning to purr for Adele's benefit.

"You do love me," Adele wailed into Callie's soft fur. "Somebody still loves me."

Chapter Three

Adele waited in line at the deli. An older woman stood in front of her, but she was in no hurry. She had nothing to look forward to but more old movies, Callie, and her tiny apartment. *Woohoo,* Adele thought sarcastically. *Can't wait to get started on that.* Every night, for the past several months, had been a repeat since that horrible night.

"Stupid jerkface," Adele said angrily, a little louder than she intended. The older lady in front of her turned around, giving Adele a very hostile look. "I'm sorry, I was thinking of someone else," she stammered, her face a violent shade of red.

The older lady threw her nose up in the air, turned back to the deli lady and promptly ordered several pounds of cheese and more meat. Adele suspected the woman clearly didn't believe that she might be telling the truth.

With a sigh, she understood the older woman's perspective but felt wronged just the same. She really needed to get a better grip on her inner monologue. This wasn't the first time she'd offended someone by randomly shouting out insults. She shook her head, taking in the variety of meats and other produce available while she waited her turn. *Maybe I should just go home. I can always come back later,* she thought dully. It would give her an excellent excuse to get out of the house if the newest movie didn't live up to her expectations. And lately, nothing had.

Making a decision, she turned around and promptly ran into the person waiting patiently behind her during her mental battle. She backed up quickly and found herself looking into a face she hadn't seen since high school. It had been sixteen years, but she'd thought of him several times since.

"Jack?" she asked, not wanting to assume it was him. He could have had a double that she'd never known about.

"Adele," he responded, the same familiar smile peeking out from his face.

She looked him up and down and made mental notes of what was familiar and what had definitely changed. He was no longer the boy she had dated off and on from middle school through high school graduation. He had filled out in all the right places but with the same warm, brown eyes that lit up when he smiled. And what a smile. It still made her heart skip a beat after all these years. It was what had convinced her to date him. His short, brown hair gave him more sex appeal than the longer, curly style he used to wear.

She didn't say something witty about how nice it was to run into him, quite literally, or tell him how often she'd thought of him since graduating years before. Instead, she found herself bluntly asking, "What the hell ..."

Jack grinned broadly, clearly nonplussed by the question. "I just moved back," he replied, chuckling slightly.

For the second time in less than ten minutes, Adele turned a brilliant shade of red. "Sorry, that didn't come out how I intended," Adele muttered. "How long have you been back?" she asked with a bit more elegance. *Hopefully, he won't write me off as a complete imbecile.*

"A couple of months," he answered, rubbing a hand carelessly across his short hair.

The simple gesture distracted her, and she wanted more than anything to run her own fingers through his silky hair. She remembered how soft it had been the last time she'd felt the strands against her skin. She shook her head to bring her mind back to the conversation and his explanation for returning to their hometown.

"So, I came back here," he finished, looking at her expectantly for some kind of response.

Damn, she thought angrily. *Why on earth did I have to fantasize right when he was talking,* she scolded herself. *Now, I look like an uninterested idiot again.* Instead of asking him to repeat himself, she settled for the chicken way out. "Well, that's great." Mentally, she slapped herself on the forehead. Outwardly, she attempted to look composed and interested. Something she hadn't felt for several months.

Jack looked down at her with a sly grin. "Do you have any plans tonight?" he asked quietly, almost as if he were afraid of her answer.

"Why?" she asked rather rudely again. *What the hell is wrong with you today,* she nearly shouted aloud. "I mean, if you don't consider staying in again to watch movies with your cat as plans, then no, I don't."

Once again, Jack let out a low chuckle, the sound doing something funny to Adele's middle. "I just noticed no ring on the left hand, so I thought I'd ask."

Adele looked down at her left hand. The pain of what she lost hit again, but without the normal gusto she normally felt when looking at her naked ring finger. Five minutes of making a fool of herself with Jack, and the pain faded. *Nice,* she thought with a glimmer of hope starting to take root in her mind.

"Want to go get something to eat? You can choose the place then we can get caught up on all the time we've missed," he went on in a single breath.

Now, it was Adele's turn to smile. She couldn't help it. Something about going out to eat with this incredibly handsome man sounded very appealing. "That sounds great. So, I'm guessing this means that you don't consider movie nights with a pet as plans?" She threw in with a smile.

Jack laughed aloud. "If I did, then you wouldn't be available for dinner tonight, now would you?" he asked, giving her the sexiest smile she'd ever seen.

Her heart gave a little skip, warming her whole body down to her toes. She returned the smile, sure that hers was not half as inviting as his.

"Where would you like to meet?" he asked, his own eyes on the floor.

"They opened a great little restaurant a couple months ago, roughly the same time you came back, and I've been wanting to try it for some time," Adele replied, her confidence and manners returning.

"Sounds great," Jack replied, looking her squarely in the eye.

~ * ~

Adele threw another shirt on the pile of discarded clothes. She stared in disgust at the clutter of clothes on her bed. That one fit a little tight to be appropriate for a 'catch up' date. She wanted him to be interested in her without looking like a hooker. Grabbing a dark gray shirt with quarter length sleeves from her closet, Adele slipped it over her head and looked at herself in the mirror. The shirt still clung a little tightly to her top but then flowed out, so it wasn't super tight around her midsection and brought out the gray in her eyes. It wasn't exactly what she wanted but paired with her 'sexy' jeans, it would have to do. She still needed to fix her hair and make-up.

"Why don't I have anything decent to wear?" she shouted at her reflection as she ran a comb through her hair. *Because you decided to go on a mad destroy-everything-in-the-house-spree,* she scolded herself. "Maybe I should have made him wait until tomorrow night. It would have given me time to buy a new outfit." Shaking her head in resignation, she continued the process of making herself look respectable yet appealing.

Her thoughts trailed back to Jack—again. She'd often thought of him, even scrolling over his Facebook page occasionally. He'd always seemed so content, so happy with life. Adele never dreamed of reaching out to him. She often wondered how different her life would have been if she had married Jack instead of Rob. But their choice of colleges had separated them by too many states and too many miles. Adele sighed.

Thirty minutes later, she didn't resemble the put together hottie she once considered herself, but at least she looked better than the stay-at-home-with-her-cat lady. With a sigh, she took one last look in the mirror, grabbed her purse and headed out to her car with nerves on high alert.

She got in her car and gripped the wheel with shaking hands. How would she make it the four blocks to the restaurant without crashing? Should she be doing this? *You don't have much of a life so getting hurt shouldn't be a consideration. What if he doesn't feel the same about me?*

"Oh boy," she said quietly, hoping the crazy-and-ready-to-party part of her mind would shut up the lock-yourself-up-in-the-apartment part of her mind. If she didn't relax soon, those fabulous armpit and back sweat stains would show everyone the depth of her nerves. "What a great first impression that would be," she muttered. *This isn't your first time with him, you dummy. Remember, you dated him off and on all through middle school and high school.* She shook her head slightly at her logic. That settled it, she needed to get out of the house more.

Pulling into a free spot at the restaurant, she looked around and realized she had no idea what type of vehicle he drove. Pulling her shoulders back, she got out of the car, went in and did a quick head scan to see if he'd beat her there. No Jack.

"How many?" asked a young girl of no older than sixteen.

"Two," Adele answered nervously, wiping her sweaty palms on the thigh of her pants.

The hostess took her to a small table, just on the edge of the main area, with a clear view of the front door. Adele wasn't sure if this was a good thing or not. She didn't want to constantly watch the door while she waited for Jack to arrive. So, she opted for the chair with the back facing the entrance. Now, she just had to fight the urge to turn around every second as if she had Tourette's.

"I can do this," she mumbled.

"I'm sorry?" the hostess asked, clearly thinking that Adele had been addressing her.

"Nothing, sorry. This is good," she said, taking her seat, already beginning the battle to see if Jack had arrived yet. Adele pulled her phone out, determined to look casual and cool when he did finally make his grand appearance. *Plus, it'll keep my mind busy*, Adele reasoned with herself. She started playing a game on her phone that required very little concentration on her part.

"What are you playing?" a low voice whispered near her ear, causing her to jerk violently and drop her phone.

"Geez," she said, clutching her chest to still her racing heart.

"Sorry." Jack looked down sheepishly at her as he walked to the other side of the table and sat down.

Adele saw that handsome smile, still so familiar after all this time, and a broad grin spread across her own face. This was going to be a wonderful night.

The next three hours seemed to fly by. So much had happened to both of them during those sixteen years after high school. Jack had been through an even more difficult divorce than her own. They talked of their careers, homes, fond memories and people from high school; they left no subject untouched. Those quiet nights crying herself to sleep were forgotten with this familiar stranger. Their evening together was more than she could have imagined.

When their waitress asked them for the umpteenth time if they needed anything else, Adele turned to Jack and asked, "My place is just down the road. Do you want to come over? We could watch some movies or play a board game or two."

"I'd love to," Jack replied, the grin on his face showing her just how much he thought of the idea.

~ * ~

Adele pulled into her designated parking spot, wondering where the hell her resolution had gone. She could've sworn she'd made a pact with herself not to invite Jack over after their 'catch up' dinner. She'd decided beforehand that if they had a pleasant evening, they could always schedule another date. She wasn't sure if she was ready to move on, even with someone she'd thought of so often. Inviting him over seemed like the wrong impression to give him. He was *not* supposed to be pulling up in the spot next to her. *Dang it. I'm so weak.* She slammed her forehead into the palm of her hand in frustration. Looking over at him, the voice in her head told her sternly, *no matter what, no kissing. And I mean it, Adele.* She nodded her head in understanding, realizing Jack probably thought she was having an argument with herself just by watching her crazy body language.

She reached for the door handle at the same moment it swung open; Jack stood to one side and held a hand out for her. "Oh," she said, feeling slightly disoriented. She hadn't seen him approach her car and grabbed for the frame in order to keep from falling out.

"Whoop," Jack said, reaching out to steady her and keep her from falling flat on the blacktop. "Sorry, didn't mean to do that." He grinned broadly at her, trying to suppress the laughter that made his shoulders shake.

Adele couldn't help it. She grinned back. He was so easy to be with. "I should have been paying more attention. I was having a bit of an argument."

"Did you win?" he asked, his face adopting an expression of complete seriousness.

"For the moment." Adele swung a leg out, suddenly feeling very self-conscious about showing Jack her tiny apartment. During their many topics covered over dinner, she discovered he had done well for himself. He'd just had a big, beautiful house built with the intention of having a family somewhere along the line. Adele had to watch her pennies to make things work for her financially, and her apartment would scream low budget. Not to mention the fact that she'd gone on a crazy spree and destroyed several valuable items, making her place seem even more desolate. *It doesn't matter. We're just friends.* He had given no indication he wanted more, so she wouldn't expect more.

She led him up the sidewalk, painfully aware that her neighbors were fighting again with the door wide open. Foul words streamed through the screen, and she blushed from embarrassment. Adele shoulders slumped when she saw Jack's look of disgust. *This was such a bad idea.*

She let him in, turned on the light and looked dismally around her. It looked so much worse now than it did when she'd left. "Well, here we are." *I'll see you later,* picturing him turning around and heading right back out the door.

"Do you want to start with a movie? It could drown out your worthless neighbors," he replied, flopping down on the couch and looking completely at ease in her living room.

Adele wished more than anything to have the power to read minds. During moments like these, it would be so helpful. So, she settled for the next best thing. "I'm sorry my apartment sucks." *Hello Ms. Blunt! Where have you been all evening?*

Jack smirked, making Adele's heart start beating a little too fast for that expression alone. He stood, walked over to her entertainment center and started looking at her movies. "Hey, it's yours and that's all that matters."

Adele hadn't thought of it like that and found she smiled despite herself. "Never looked at it that way," she whispered more to herself than Jack.

"So, what will it be?" Jack turned back to the movies, moving them around so he could see the ones toward the back as well.

They settled on a Christmas comedy while talk turned toward high school days and old classmates. Adele fetched her yearbook. Together, they skimmed the pages, commented on different pictures and filled each other in on the events of people from a lifetime ago. Adele was painfully aware of the distance between their bodies; she wanted to be closer. Under the pretense of turning down the TV so she could hear him better, she reached across to grab the remote and managed to scoot a little closer to him in the process. Jack gave her a knowing smile but didn't move away.

What happened to your newest pact? her mind screamed out at her.

I haven't kissed him yet! She shook her head. She really needed to get more friends. These conversations with herself were getting old. Worse, the heated debates took place more and more frequently in her mind. *Pathetic.*

"Why do you do that?" Jack asked, his head tilted to one side as he watched her.

"Uh, do what?"

"Shake your head and mutter."

Dang, he's been watching me. "I spend a lot of time by myself." Adele picked at the corners of her yearbook and realized she sounded pitiful. Tears pricked at her eyes, reminding her how lonely she had been and no one to really blame but herself.

"Hey, what's this about?" Jack reached over, wiping away the traitorous tears trailing down her cheeks.

Adele flung herself up from the couch, storming down the hall and into the bathroom to get a tissue, her face red from embarrassment. This was *so* not how she saw this evening going. When she returned, she said, "I'm sorry. I'm just realizing how I have shut myself off from the world. Rob destroyed so much more than our marriage. He destroyed my self-confidence too. This is the first time I've gone out since the divorce and now I'm crying," Adele wailed, feeling even sillier if that was possible.

Jack held out an arm, grabbed Adele's tissue free hand and pulled her to him. She flopped down on the couch, practically on his lap, and he wrapped his arms around her. He smelled amazing; his arms felt so warm. She snuggled her face closer to his chest, enjoying the way he felt both physically and emotionally. Something she'd not had for a while. Memories of him holding her as a teenager resurfaced, and she found herself grinning through the tears. He had definitely filled out into a very powerful man, one that she wanted to get to know much better.

"Did I tell you how often I thought of you since high school?" Jack whispered.

Adele felt her heart flutter at the meaning behind the words.

"It wasn't every day, but there were lots of times when I just sat back and wondered what or how you were doing." Jack stroked her cheek softly, wiping away the remaining tears.

She lifted her head up, sniffled slightly and looked into those wonderfully intense and warm brown eyes. She saw the concern and something more... His handsome face moved closer. *You told yourself no kissing.* Yet her body remained completely still, anticipating his touch. *Oh well. It won't be the first promise to myself I've broken today.*

The moment their lips met, Adele inhaled deeply and her eyes closed of their own free will. The delicious smell of Jack encompassed her and made her forget the dreariness of her world. She pressed her body closer, wanting nothing more than to feel every inch of him pressed against her.

She heard his groan of pleasure, causing her to gasp and part her mouth slightly. His hands slipped to her waist, pulling her tightly against him as he ran his tongue along her bottom lip. She grabbed the front of his shirt, her fist balling up with the material there. It was so warm.

Adele had just tilted her head to one side when Jack pulled back. Her eyes flew open in surprise and her breath came in pants. She still clutched his shirt painfully tight in her fists.

"On that note, I think I should be heading home for the night." He kissed her nose gently and stood. Adele released her death grip on his shirt while her body slid onto the couch.

She looked past him to the walls. *Did I do something wrong?* Her mind replayed the kiss as she stood to let him out, but she couldn't think of anything that felt off. If someone would ask her how their first kiss as adults went, she would've told them incredible. Yet, that didn't seem to be the case for Jack.

He slipped past her wordlessly, grabbed her around the waist and pulled her close in the process. Lifting her chin so she was looking at him, he said in husky tone that sent chills down her spine, "Just so you know, that was amazing."

Adele blushed profusely, her relief so profound she couldn't respond. He pulled her chin up again, bent his head down and softly kissed her on the lips before strolling out the door. Adele watched him get into his car with a big goofy smile on her face.

"You totally broke every pact you made with yourself, but it was definitely worth it."

Chapter Four

By the next day, Adele still paced around her living room full of memories from the night before. Granted, it wasn't a lot of steps, but it worked well for releasing her nervous energy. She needed a friend to talk to; someone she could tell all about her night.

"What am I gonna do, Callie?" She looked at her cat who gave her typical blink and turn response. Adele rolled her eyes. She really needed to get out more. Grabbing her phone, she searched through her contacts until she came across Rachel, the first person she should have thought of since she was one of her only friends now. She was also a coworker, which Adele wasn't sure what that said about her social life. Rachel always said that whenever Adele needed to get out, she'd be willing to go with her. In fact, she was constantly telling Adele that they needed have dinner or go see a movie. Like everyday reminders. Adele took a chance and shot her a quick text: *What are you up to?*

Throwing the phone on her desk, she resumed her pacing while her thoughts lingered on Jack's eyes and the intense way he held her gaze. Just the thought of it made her heart beat pick up. That was something that hadn't changed at all from when they were teenagers. She smiled to herself and then nearly had a heart attack when her phone sounded. She'd forgotten about the text.

Grabbing her cell, she looked down and sighed with relief.

Not a whole lot. Bored out of my mind. Wanna do something tonight? Like actually out of your house, in the real world, with real people again?

Adele sent a quick reply, asking Rachel if she wanted to grab a bite to eat then a movie. She hit send without having the slightest idea what was showing in the theaters. That would've required her to pay more attention to the world around her.

Sure. Sounds like a great plan! Where do you want eat and what would you like to see?

"Crap," Adele muttered to herself. Thinking quickly, she came up with a little Mexican restaurant and then suggested that Rachel pick the movie since she chose the place to eat. Rachel agreed and they decided to meet around five.

Putting her phone down once more, Adele couldn't help but feel proud of herself. A date and a night out with a friend—all in the same weekend. There may be hope for her yet. Looking down at her watch, she groaned. Three more hours to kill.

"I should have asked if she wanted to do some shopping, too." She looked at Callie who studiously ignored her. "But then again, I would probably run out of things to say." She decided to read for a while, before getting ready, but ended up pacing her living room again. This was turning out to be the world's longest day.

~ * ~

Adele pulled into the parking lot and spotted Rachel's car right off the bat. *No waiting game for me tonight* Scanning the restaurant, she caught sight of Rachel's flaming red hair and began to make her way across the room. As she weaved around the tables, a hand reached out and grabbed her arm, stopping her progress. Startled, Adele looked down to see who would be so bold. She found herself looking into the familiar blue eyes of her ex-husband.

"Rob," she breathed, too paralyzed from shock to say much more. She'd spent months avoiding the places Rob went—fear of this moment always in the forefront of her mind.

"You look good," he replied in that low seductive voice that made her heart race. His eyes raked over every inch of her body, causing her cheeks to redden in humiliation.

"Let go." She jerked her arm back, desperate to get away from the man that had torn her heart in two, stepping on the pieces with his new baby girl thrown in the mix. She'd pleaded with him for years to have a baby; the answer had always been no. Now, she knew why.

"What are you doing out and about?" he asked casually, completely unaware of the torture he put her through. He reached for a glass, bringing it to his lips and causing a host of old memories to flow through her mind.

"I'm meeting a friend," she managed to choke out.

"There you are, Adele." Rachel stepped up to Adele's side, eyeing Rob with obvious disgust. "Hi, asshole. Imagine meeting you at this lowly place. Trying to pick up cheap broads with no taste?" she asked Rob.

"Have we met?" Rob asked with a look of surprise.

"Nope, I'm not in to giant jackasses. But I see some trampy looking blondes over there." Rachel turned and pointed to a pair of women by the bar, obviously trying to catch his attention. "Maybe you would have better luck with them. It looks like they would be willing to sleep with anything that crawled in their bed."

Adele nearly choked on the laugh that threatened to bubble from her throat. She knew Rachel had seen several pictures of Rob on her desk, not to mention all the times Adele had confided in her through the whole horrible process. Rachel could be a little feisty, but she never imagined this.

"Well, fiery little thing aren't you?" Rob asked, a sneer on his face.

"Yep, don't let any other thoughts cross your mind. I know what a sleaze you are." Rachel grabbed Adele's arm, steering her toward their table. "Why did you even stop?" she whispered into Adele's ear before sitting down. "Once you saw him, you should have kept on walking."

"I was just surprised," Adele muttered, her face still flushed from the recent encounter.

"Whatever you're thinking, stop it right now." Rachel picked up a menu, eyeing Adele sternly over the top of it. "I don't know exactly what's going through your head, but I know enough to realize that you're thinking about that scum and all you've 'lost'. So you can just stop that right now. Rob is the world's biggest prick; just ask the other two women and his daughter."

Adele swallowed the lump in her throat that appeared every time she thought about his daughter. She hated being reminded of the little girl Rob now had with some other woman. Grabbing her own menu, she scanned the food items several times, never truly seeing anything in front of her. Tears pricked at her eyes and she blinked repeatedly, doing her best to appear strong. *Why did I think this would be such a great idea?* A hand reached over, pulling her menu down so she could see the concerned look on Rachel's face.

"Do you want to find someplace else to eat?" she asked soothingly.

Adele shook her head, knowing it wouldn't matter where they went; her appetite was gone. "It doesn't matter." She looked over toward the table Rob had been sitting at only to find he'd gone.

"He left shortly after we sat down." Rachel's voice drifted over the menu she hid behind.

"Figures." Adele wiped her eyes hastily, more angry than hurt. She glanced down at the menu and decided on cheese nachos. It was simple and the first thing she'd been able to make out while looking at the cursed laminated paper. You couldn't go wrong with cheese and chips.

"So, what's up?" Rachel folded her hands in front of her and gave Adele a knowing look.

"What do you mean?" Adele, still frustrated with her response to Rob, had trouble making sense of Rachel's question. Of course she would still run into him, they did still lived in the same town. She should have moved farther away. Like to Alaska or China.

"I mean, you never want to go out. Well, not since … Anyway, back to the question at hand," Rachel explained, cutting across Adele's inner plotting to look into apartments in another state or planet.

Adele fought to bring her thoughts back to the conversation, but Rob's appearance had totally shattered her concentration. She scrunched her eyebrows, focused on the brown eyes staring at her and the tension in her chest began to ease. She sighed, memories from the night before replacing the anger. "I went out last night." She looked up at Rachel and held back a laugh. Rachel's lower jaw hung somewhere around her chest.

"You mean, like an actual date?" Rachel asked, still looking dumbfounded. "And you waited until now to spring that one on me?"

The look on her friend's face made her want to roll on the floor laughing. She settled for a giggle.

"I need details. Who was it? Where did you go? I'm guessing it went well, which is why you wanted to meet with me," Rachel started.

Adele held up a hand to stop Rachel from a further attack. "He was a guy I dated off and on all through middle and high school."

"Serious?"

"Yeah. I ran into him at the grocery store and we—" Adele's phone cut her off with a ding. Startled, she looked down and found that Jack had sent her a text. Unable to conceal the merriment of being texted by him, Adele looked up to see Rachel rolling her eyes at her.

"You're surprised, aren't you?" She shook her head at Adele. "Welcome back to the real world, Adele. We missed you."

Chapter Five

I'm here.

Those simple words, lit up against Adele's black phone screen, made her heart race in anticipation. She arranged to meet Jack the next evening so she could finish her girl's night with Rachel. However, that proved to be an extremely difficult task when her mind continued to wander back to him and their incredible night. She thought of all the time they'd wasted with other people. They should have just married out of high school and saved themselves the grief of having married the wrong person. *Geez, second date and you're already planning your wedding.*

Rachel had taken the whole night in stride, laughing when Adele repeatedly asked, "What?" after almost everything she said or asked. By the time the night ended, Adele had apologized repeatedly for being such a poor companion. Rachel just waved it off and proclaimed that she was just glad to see Adele happy again.

Adele shook her head slightly to bring herself back to the present and took a calming breath. She opened the door wide, watching Jack as he walked up her sidewalk.

"Hey, stranger. Didn't I just see you a couple nights ago?" she teased.

"Naw, I was with a different girl. Super cute. Maybe you know her." Jack's eyes twinkled with mischief.

"Is it serious?" Adele asked, her face a mask of mock concern. She stepped out of the way so Jack could get past her, but instead he grabbed her waist and pulled her close to him. He bent down, kissing her softly, effectively blowing all thoughts out of her mind. She reached up, sliding her hands into his short brown hair and pulled his face closer to her own. She angled her head a little and parted her lips, letting a sigh escape her when his arms tightened around her waist. Her tongue slid along his lips and ventured further into the recess of his mouth. His hands tightened on her hips, lifting her slightly. She started to explore more when he drew back, the twinkle in his eyes replaced by heat.

"Now, that's a greeting." His voice, low and husky, did something funny to Adele's middle—not to mention the tattoo her heart was beating in her chest.

Pulling her hands back to her side, she closed the door behind him and turned to see him plop down on the couch. "So, movies at home then?" she said with a laugh. She stopped then, realizing her laughter was finally returning after the divorce. She'd forgotten how nice it felt.

"Did you have anything else in mind?" he asked, watching her from his spot on the couch.

"Nope, sounds perfect. What would you like to see?"

After several minutes of debate, they decided on a comedy as Adele had spent far too much time crying over real life. Adele lay back on the couch. Her knees curled up next to her body, she looked down at Jack at the other end of the couch. She didn't want to seem too pushy, but he was entirely too far away for her taste.

"What are you thinking about?" Jack asked as he grabbed her foot and stretched her leg out so it was lying across his lap. He reached for the other foot, doing the same to it.

Adele enjoyed the way Jack casually ran his hand up the length of her calf—a feeling she'd missed the last several months. She shook her head and turned her gaze back to the movie but didn't see any of it. Her attention was solely on Jack and his gentle caresses. Making a sudden decision, Adele sat up and swung her legs off his lap. Placing her feet on the floor, she got up and turned to face him. She stuck a knee on either side of his legs and sat down on his lap while staring at his handsome face. She placed her hands on his face and just stared. There was something so beautiful, so calming there in his smile; she just wanted to soak it up.

She found his eyes last. His look held surprise and passion while his hands found their way up to her hips. Running a thumb over his lower lip and across the stubble that covered his face, her fingers found their way into his hair. She held his head and bent down, gently brushing her lips across his own. They barely touched, but it sent shivers down Adele's back. She ran her nose along the length of his, keeping her eyes open so she could see his expression.

"Sorry, the movie wasn't holding my interest," she whispered softly, her mouth just above his own. She couldn't believe she was doing this. She'd never been the aggressor in a relationship before and found the role strangely exciting and empowering.

He gripped her hips tighter, pulling her closer before claiming her lips with his own. Adele sucked in a breath, her heart racing with the simple gesture. She wrapped her arms around his neck, refusing to let go. Kissing him felt too good. He groaned and slid his hands around to her backside. He grabbed her, picked her up slightly and shifted her weight so she could feel more of him. She threw her head back, trying desperately to catch her breath.

Jack wound his fingers into her hair, pulling her head back further and exposing her throat to his soft lips. His lips blazed a trail down her jawline, nibbled her ear slightly and sent goose bumps down her body. She was so warm from his caresses. He continued to the exposed skin at the base of her neck. "You're so beautiful," he whispered over and over between molten kisses.

Wanting more, Adele grabbed the collar of the simple t-shirt he wore and pulled it aside. She ran her tongue along the collarbone before biting down gently, causing him to moan aloud. He smelled so enticing, and Adele wanted more.

Jack ran his hands up her sides and around to her back before bringing them up to her shoulders. He held her there, pressing her even closer to him. Adele gasped. Definitely not the teenager she remembered from their younger days together. Where he had been long and lanky before—more bones than meat—now he was all man.

Adele looked down, Jack's eyes burning into her own. Her heart beat wildly, while her thoughts recollected. Suddenly, she realized that she didn't want *just* sex.

"Jack, wait." Even to her own ears, she didn't sound very convincing. Pushing him slightly, she pulled away to look down at his handsome face again. *Will I ever get tired of looking at him?* "Can we slow down? This is going a little fast."

"Says the woman who climbed onto my lap." Jack chuckled huskily, causing Adele to blush with the truth of it.

"Yeah, didn't think that one through." She scooted back and fought to regain her breath, and the desire to climb back onto his warm and oh-so-inviting lap.

Jack continued to stare up at her; the look on his face told her plainly where his thoughts were.

"It's just, I want this relationship to be more than ..." To be honest, she wasn't sure what she expected, but she didn't want the whole thing based on sex. It felt too much like what Rob would have done.

"You don't want it to be built on sex," Jack finished, with one eyebrow raised in amusement.

Adele shook her head, feeling like she may have jinxed the whole thing by being presumptuous.

Jack stood, pulling her back in his arms and kissed her forehead sweetly. He bent his head lower and kissed her lips, almost making her regret the decision to get off his lap. "We'll take this day by day and see where it leads us."

Chapter Six

Adele snuggled further under her blankets, letting the warmth surround her. She smiled to herself, thoughts of the last couple of weeks drifting lazily over her. True to his word, they'd sat down and watched the remainder of the movie, snatching kisses throughout the entire thing. Afterwards, Jack had left but not before arranging to meet with Adele the following weekend, and promised to talk to her every day in between. He'd made good on those promises and even managed to sneak in time with her during the week. She'd received more texts and spent more time talking with him than she did with Rob for the past year.

Jack continued to surprise her with his thoughtful and sincere compliments, and beliefs in her as a person. He did little things like telling her good night before bed every evening or sending her pictures of his smiling face, making her feel warm all over. He bought her small things like a pack of gum in her favorite flavor and kept her preferred drink stocked at his house. He made sure to ask how her day went and listened to her when she told him. He soon became the first person she thought of when she opened her eyes every morning and the only person she dreamed of at night.

Rolling over, Adele grabbed her phone, shot Jack a quick good morning text then got out of bed and headed for the shower. Flipping on the radio, one of her favorite songs blared out of the speakers. She sang at the top of her lungs, much to Callie's annoyance from by the way she flew from the room. Adele turned on the hot water and let it soak into her skin. Showers were so relaxing and enhanced her good mood.

Adele decided, after the annihilation of her old closet, it was time to update her wardrobe. She wanted something for her future dates with Jack.

Something that would really catch his eye. She smiled, thinking about how different someone could be even after knowing them for so long. It was a wonderful feeling to have that much history with someone, yet still have the chance to discover something new.

Stepping out of the shower, she dressed in a pair of tight jeans and a simple, light blue cotton long-sleeved shirt. She combed her hair before scrunching up the light brown locks, creating a loose curl, and finished with a touch of make-up. Surveying herself in the mirror, she realized the lost and depressed Adele was slowly fading into a more confident and happy woman. She liked the change and internally thanked Jack.

Giving her hair one final pat of satisfaction, she slipped on a pair of shoes, grabbed her purse, flung open the door and nearly collided with Rob.

"What in the hell are you doing here?" she spluttered, not caring how rude she sounded. She didn't have to impress him. The goal now was to refrain from beating him to death with a frying pan.

"When I saw you at the restaurant the other day, you just looked so good. I realized what a complete fool I've been." He looked intently at her, his expression sad.

Adele could see the longing in his eyes. She could even detect the remorse he might have felt, but that didn't stop her from wanting to stomp all over his pretty face. "Your point?" She crossed her arms angrily over her chest, her good mood vanishing.

"I'm sorry for everything. How can I make it up to you?" He reached out to her, attempting to take her face into his hands, but Adele slapped the hands away.

"So, you go screwing around with God knows how many women, and you expect me to take you back because you thought I looked good one day?" she asked. She stared hard at Rob. He was clearly experiencing a mental breakdown to think she'd even remotely consider taking him back

"Adele, please. I really am sorry, and I'm willing to do anything to prove it." He held out his hands again, reaching slowly for her.

"You touch me and I will personally slap the crap out of you," she spat. "Keep your damn hands off me. They're not wanted here." She looked coldly at him, wondering what she ever saw in him to begin with.

"Adele—"

"Don't Adele me. You have a daughter with someone else! After I spent years trying to convince you to have a baby with me!"

"That was an accident!"

"And that makes it better?" Adele threw her head back and laughed. Sure, she sounded like the wicked witch from Oz, but she didn't care. It felt good to tell Rob off. It felt good not to love him any longer. She had Jack to thank for that, too. "What's the real problem, Rob? No one will have you? In between girls?" Adele clasped her hands in front of her, adopting an expression of mock concern.

"No, I just realized what I lost," he shouted, making Adele smile. She'd unnerved him. He only yelled when he thought he was losing.

"Too bad you didn't realize that sooner. I was there in front of your face for eight years, and now you realize what you had. I don't know how you found me, and I really don't care. The fact of the matter is, I've moved on. So if you step foot anywhere near my home again, I'll call the cops and have you thrown out. You're not welcome here. Quit bothering me. We're done." With that, Adele slammed the door on his startled face.

Taking a deep breath, she sank onto the couch as her mind reeled from the encounter. She realized she'd meant every word. She no longer cared about his looks or what he thought. He didn't matter to her. If he couldn't see what he'd lost before, she wouldn't spend any more time trying to show him now. Jack saw her, knew her and still wanted to be with her. He was willing to take the time to learn everything he'd missed over their years apart. That meant more to her than she'd been willing to admit. Moreover, when she was with him, it just felt right, like it was meant to be.

Smiling, she realized there was someone she wanted to see more than anyone else at that moment. Grabbing her purse once more, she headed out the door and to her car.

Fifteen minutes later, Adele pulled into the driveway that was becoming extremely familiar to her after several visits. It screamed bachelor's pad, but Adele didn't mind. It meant she was the first since his divorce. A fact she suddenly took pride in. He wanted to be with her; he'd chosen to start something with her after his own painful split.

Marching straight up to the door, she knocked loudly. The butterflies in her stomach went crazy. *What the heck? Five seconds ago, you were fine.*

The door swung open, revealing Jack in a t-shirt and gray sweatpants. He looked down at her, surprise and pleasure on his face. "Hey," he said, a grin replacing the shocked look. "I didn't think I'd be able to see you until tomorrow."

Adele stared into his eyes, her heart melting all over again. She really did love looking at his face. It had to be the most beautiful and honest thing she'd ever seen. "I didn't want to wait that long. Rob came over and—"

"Rob came to your house?" Jack asked, the smile dropping from his face. "Why?" He held the door open for Adele, wordlessly indicating she should come in.

She slipped past him and then turned on the spot so she faced him again before continuing, "He said he realized what he'd lost and wanted me back. For the first time, I realized I had no feelings at all for him. I could care less what he wants. You matter to me. Even after everything I've been through—college, marriage, divorce—you were always at the back of my mind. I don't think I ever got over you. I'm not sure why we ever broke up, but it had to be either some silly reason or a divine one. Maybe we just needed to grow up a bit, before we could really appreciate each other the way we were always meant to." She took a step closer to him, her heart racing. She knew what she said was true, but that didn't stop her from nearly having a coronary when saying it aloud. Jack could easily reject her, tell her it was too fast or that he didn't feel the same way. It seemed like a lot to ask of him.

With an expression too serious for Adele's comfort, Jack took a step toward her, his hands by his side. "What are you trying to say, Adele?" His voice was low, cautious even. It made Adele swallow thickly.

"I ... I ..." Her heart thudded entirely too loudly in her chest. She had overstepped their boundary and had no way of recovering from it. "I want to be with you. I feel like I've always been meant for you. It just took several years for me to realize it," she whispered. There was no going back, but she wanted it out there just the same.

Jack reached up, cupping her face gently. He pulled her to him and kissed her. He reached around, grabbing her waist tightly so she could feel the heat of his body soaking through her clothes. She wrapped her arms around his neck; her lips parted and met his tongue with her own. Placing a hand on the back of her head, he held her there. The kiss deepened, making Adele's head spin. She could do this forever with him.

They stayed that way for several minutes. Their tongues and hands explored with such a passion, Adele thought she would catch fire from the heat of it. Jack pulled his head back but his arms remained tightly around her waist, holding her close to his body.

"I love you," he whispered, startling her.

She realized she'd just confessed the same thing when she heard the words fall from his lips. He spoke of a commitment she didn't think he was ready to share with her. She looked at him wordlessly, unsure if she should return the statement.

"You're right and I've felt the same way. I have for years. Like you, I've been struggling with the reality of my life and failing miserably. I have thought of you so many times since high school, it's rather embarrassing. When I was offered the opportunity to take a job here, I jumped on it; the first thing crossing my mind was seeing you again. I didn't know if I'd ever have another shot with you, but I couldn't rest until I knew for sure. This may be the craziest thing that I've ever done but …. Marry me?" he whispered. "You're right, we were meant to be together and I don't want to waste another moment."

Adele's heart stopped altogether. "We just started seeing each other again." She was ready to take this relationship to a more serious level, but marriage hadn't even crossed her mind. *Has he been drinking?*

"How long did you date Rob before you were married?" he asked, bending down to kiss her lips gently.

"We dated almost three years before we even got engaged."

"And I dated Emily for nearly five." He ran his nose the length of Adele's neck, making it entirely too hard for her to think straight. "Both of those relationships ended very badly indeed, which brings me back to my original question. Marry me, Adele. We have more history together than anyone else I've ever met, and nothing has felt this right."

She pulled herself back, looking into the most beautiful brown eyes she'd seen. It was a face, she understood with sudden clarity, which she wanted to spend the rest of her life looking at, waking up to, and being with. Her heart swelled with the realization that he was right. They had been reacquainting themselves for the past few weeks, but they had a history together. Besides, she'd followed all the rules with Rob, and look where that had left her? In that instant, she knew exactly where she wanted to be—wherever Jack was. Swallowing the knot of happiness in her throat, she smiled. "Yes, I'll marry you."

THE END

About the Author

Elena Kane lives in a small town in Ohio where she teaches preschool.

She absolutely loves it because she is free to be herself. Elena has three children, two boys and a girl, and they are the light of her busy life.

She loves the Green Bay Packers and swimming, is determined to live on a sunny beach someday, and—most importantly—she loves to read! Reading is her way to relax and forget her worries. She loves getting on her treadmill with a good book!

Other works by the author with Melange Books, LLC

Frozen Dreams (Frozen, A Winter Romance Anthology)

Connect with Elena at:

www.facebook.com/elenakanewriter

ONE PERFECT MOMENT

By

Tara Fox Hall

For every first kiss and last kiss goodbye, and everyone who every hoped to have one perfect moment with the one they loved...and got more than they wished for.

"Do you think we'll see any cheerleaders, Ice?" Allen murmured to his friend, his usually calm blue eyes alight with excitement.

"Even if we do, they'll probably look a lot different than the last time you saw them at one of your games," Dustin "Iceberg" Bergman replied, shifting his feet as he leaned onto the bar. He reached for his glass then took back his hand, resisting the urge to take another sip of his drink. As much as the alcohol might soothe his nerves, the last thing he wanted to do was deaden his senses. "And don't call me Ice, either. It's either Dustin or Dusty now."

"Some of us liked our high school years," Allen said with a mock glower. "We didn't need to rebel against everything and anything, and wear black leather jackets."

"We never wore any black leather jackets," Dustin retorted, cracking an involuntary smile. "So I didn't get into sports like you did, so what? It's not like I was a criminal or anything!"

"I can recall once or twice when you ended up in jail for the night," Allen teased. "Remember that prank you pulled? The homecoming queen's crown—"

"We don't need to get into all that." Dustin motioned to his friend to keep his voice down.

"Uh, that's exactly what reunions are for," Allen said, giving him an odd look. "Why are you so nervous, anyway? It's not like you're unemployed and living with your parents. You've got a thriving carpentry business, and you're in good shape, unlike some." Allen patted the beginning paunch of his own formerly flat stomach. "So what's got you so riled up?" Before Dustin could answer, a football friend of Allen's came over, loudly singing something. Allen turned to him and began talking.

"Nothing," Dustin murmured, relieved to not have to bring up the source of his anxiety. Yet even as he brought his glass to his mouth, one name came unbidden to his mind: Coriander.

What will she look like after ten years? Even if she cut that long blonde hair, those blue-green eyes of hers will still be deep enough for me to drown in all over again. What if she doesn't remember me the way I remember her? What if she sees me and looks right through me? Worse, what if I see that same disillusionment in her eyes the moment she realizes it's me?

~ * ~

"Cori, hi!"

Coriander pasted a smile on her face as a heavyset brunette approached her. She delved into the depths of her memory in search of a name to go with the earnest, smiling face. "Brenda?"

"Yes, of course, Brenda," the woman said, her smile widening. "God, Cori, you look great! You look just like you did in high school! You haven't changed a bit."

Cori nodded, continuing the conversation in all the right places, even as she scanned the crowd for someone to save her. While Brenda had been an acquaintance more than a decade ago, Cori hadn't come tonight to chat about old times.

You know why you came tonight. There's just one person you're hoping to see, even if you're scared to death to face him after how things ended between you.

Cori forced herself to utter an excuse, and then moved away from Brenda, greeting some of her old classmates warmly, nodding to others. With a small graduating class and the blessing of popularity, there was almost no one here Cori hadn't known by the end of her senior year. They had all known her as well: friendly, outspoken, eager to volunteer for activities in the community and never one to ridicule someone unpopular, even when tempted by those around her who did.

It's nice to remember a time when I was innocent. At least until that night I met

Ice.

Cori flushed at the memory and slipped into the nearby bathroom, shutting herself in a stall. She sat for a moment on the toilet seat, trying to come to terms with the sudden memories flooding her mind.

Ice catching her gaze across a crowded room. Leaving her last class a day later to find him in the parking lot with the unspoken invitation, a cigarette dangling from his mouth, holding the car door of his black Torino open. The wild ride that followed down one country road after another, windows down, the intoxicating smell of wildflowers strong and undeniable. The stop at the ice cream stand, where he'd treated her to a small baby cone when she'd refused anything else on the grounds of her strict diet. The walk by the banks of the nearby river, the long pauses in their easy conversation whenever their gazes locked again. Cori desperately hoping the dark boy-man would take her in his arms the way she had fantasized, yet terrified to make a move herself to touch him. The thunderstorm that moved in just as they returned, driving them back into the car and into one another's arms. The long kiss that followed, steaming up the car windows completely.

Cori closed her eyes, drew in a long shuddering breath and hugged herself as she released it with a tremor. *How can a kiss that happened more than ten years ago make my heart race so fast?*

Ice and she had been inseparable after that kiss, even though her friends and his were vocal in their disapproval. Cori and Ice dated all through high school, shunning the major dances and games for long walks and late night talks by the light of fireflies. Cori had never been so happy and thought she had found her soul mate. Entirely without meaning to, she began to plan their future after high school: college, marriage, then children and careers. Maybe not in that order, but those ambitions were a certainty.

On the night of what would have been their prom, Cori wanted to cement that future. Ice had never pushed for more than passionate kisses or some light touching in all their time together, in spite of his so-called bad reputation. He'd also never mentioned getting married, or anything beyond maybe some college, if he could decide on a major. That they wouldn't go to the prom was a given; that they'd spend the whole night together—their first night all alone—was, too. In Cori's opinion, that night was the perfect moment to move things to the next level. She had never thought Ice would be anything but a learned guide on her journey to becoming a woman. And after she had given herself to him, he would ask her to be his forever, and their happily ever after would start then and there, The days would stretch out before them toward some unknown, yet wonderful future.

You never think that a moment you looked forward to that much, planned to a T, could be anything except perfect. God, was I wrong.

Cori had assumed that Ice, a man of the world, had sex before her. That night Cori saw Ice for what he was: just a boy her own age who wanted to impress her and appear much more knowledgeable. Not that she'd acted much better, being a virgin herself. The night had been a complete disaster as soon as it had moved beyond kissing to hesitant, then desperate fumbling. And while the young couple had managed to consummate the act, both of them had been embarrassed and disappointed.

Funny how something I wanted so much to bring us closer together only drove us apart.

After they had sex, Cori had been unable to let go of her fantasy and the inadequacy of the real experience. She'd distanced herself from Ice, even said a few sarcastic comments that made her flush in memory. She'd refused to call him by his nickname, telling Dustin that he didn't deserve it. She wasn't sure why but that had seemed to hurt him the most. When he'd walked away from her that day, he'd walked out of her life. A month later, she'd gone to his home to make amends, but Dustin had already left for college in another state.

Cori bit her lip. *All these years, and you've never heard a word from him. Dustin probably will give you a wide berth, if he doesn't just say something cutting that's long overdue. What do you expect, that he'll just forgive you for being a jerk? Fall down on his knees and tell you to give him another chance?*

"I don't want any of that, in any case," Cori murmured aloud. "I'm already engaged to Stefan."

Stefan Van Kellam II, a name right out of a romance tale. The man himself is cool, collected ... and the best gentleman I've ever known. He's been a perfect boyfriend, a perfect lover, and so far the perfect fiancé. So why am I here thinking about someone else?

Cori blinked, then stood up and left the stall, making her way to the mirror. Though her makeup was still fresh, her face was flushed. Hurriedly, she splashed some cool water on the inside of her wrists and then patted her cheeks. *You have nothing to be embarrassed about. You're getting exactly what you've always wanted. Dustin has nothing to do with your future, only your past. Now get out there and be nice to everyone. Tomorrow you can forget all of this and go back to your perfect future.*

Resolved, Cori put her head up and her shoulders back then marched back out to the party.

~ * ~

Allen came back over to Dustin at the bar and slapped him on the back. "Enjoying yourself yet?"

"Of course," Dustin answered, still scanning the crowd for a glimpse of Cori.

"She just came out of the bathroom," Allen said with a knowledgeable smirk. "Looks like she's kept in shape, too."

Dustin shot a surprised look at Allen, and then his hungry gaze fastened on Cori. She stood talking to a tall man he didn't recognize. He drank in the sight of her: those graceful hand movements she'd always used in conversation, her infectious laugh, and the way her face practically glowed when she was truly happy about something. *I used to make her that happy once. Will she ever give me that chance again?*

"If you're waiting for the perfect moment, this is it," Allen quipped. "I have it on good authority she's not married."

Dustin was already moving, throwing down the last of his drink for courage as he headed toward Cori. He was almost to her when she turned suddenly, their gaze locking on one another. That same electrical charge jolted through Dustin in an instant, sweeping away the years without her. With an irresistible urge to kiss her, he reached out to bring Cori into his arms.

"Hey, Iceberg!" a voice called from behind him. "Ice!"

Cori dropped her gaze instantly, breaking the connection. Dustin took a deep breath, his hands falling again at his side as an old friend grasped his arm, turning him as he launched into conversation. Dustin smiled then quickly excused himself to go to Cori, only to find she had vanished. Feeling a twinge of fear, Dustin raced toward the nearest exit.

~ * ~

Idiot! You almost let him kiss you without even saying a word! So much for your resolve. Cori hurried to her car, fumbling with her keys to try to get them into the lock faster. She had to get away from here before Dustin came after her. She knew that familiar look in his eyes. The one he always used to have when they were coming to the end of the night, and he wanted to kiss her.

The game we played that led up to the kiss. Kind of a repeat of our first date, where we both wanted to kiss but held off until we couldn't stand it anymore. We were never like normal teens, groping at one another the moment we got alone together. We were always telling jokes, and teasing one another, laughing at each other and the weirdness of the world. The more time we spent together, the more pregnant with meaning the pauses between our words became; the heated chemistry between us built ever stronger. We weren't mature enough to know what to say, far too young to quote romantic poetry, even if we could have gotten past our shyness. So, we said nothing. But it was all there in our eyes—that pure longing—a wanting so strong it threatened to eclipse everything else. It only took looking into his eyes again tonight for me to want to give everything I am and take everything he has to offer ...

"Cori! Wait!"

Cori shuddered and turned, keys forgotten in her hand as Dustin jogged up to her. She took in his slim physique, his earnest clean-shaven face, the dark hair curling over his collar. *How many times did I run my hands through his hair as we kissed?* Resisting the sudden urge to touch him, Cori shoved both of her hands into her pockets. She bit back a curse, as the keys tore a small hole in her pocket lining.

Dustin shoved the dark hair out of his eyes with his hand, his hazel eyes staring down into hers. "Hi, Cori."

Say something. "Hi, Dustin."

He shifted his weight nervously. "I didn't want you to leave without saying goodbye."

"We never said hello yet," Cori quipped. A sudden grin appeared unbidden on her face. "Don't you think we should start there?"

Dustin stared down at her for a moment, then burst out laughing. Cori joined in almost immediately. The familiar combined sound comforted them both and evaporated the tension between them like so much smoke.

"Yes, I do," Dustin said, his expression much more relaxed. "Hello, Coriander. It's wonderful to see you again."

"It's wonderful to be seen," Cori said, smiling. "I'm glad you came, Dustin."

"I wanted to see you," he said simply, staring at her.

The tension that had so abruptly left flowed back in a tidal wave, engulfing Cori. She stared up at him like a deer caught frozen in headlights, waiting for him to accuse her, to call her a bitch for her behavior, to tell her that he'd only come to give their teen love an adult ending, to cauterize the still seeping wound. Instead of accusation, Dustin looked at her with hungry eyes, as if he had asked some question and still awaited an answer.

126

"Why?" she managed to squeak.

"I've missed you all these years," he murmured and stepped close, his arms going around her.

Why did you leave then? Cori wanted to scream. Instead, she shut her eyes, leaning into the warmth of his chest.

"Do you have anyone?" Dustin murmured. "I'm single now."

His question snapped Cori back to reality. Unease and self-reproach settled in her chest like a contagion. *Don't do this to him; don't add new insult to old injury.* She took a step back, moving out of Dustin's arms. "I'm engaged, Dustin. I'm sorry, I should have—"

"It's all right," Dustin said quickly and took a step back himself. "It's not like I gave you a lot of time to bring it up, Cori." He forced a smile. "I'm glad you're happy, really. When I thought of you over the years, I always hoped you were happy."

Cori gritted her teeth. Her eyes shifted from the ground to her car, anywhere but at Dustin, unwilling to see his hurt expression. He had never been able to hide his feelings from her. *But then he didn't try, did he? There isn't a duplicitous bone in his body. Unlike you, who practically grew up lying …*

"Do you have some time before you head back to … um, where are you now?" Dustin continued. "Maybe we can do lunch or dinner?"

"I live just over the state line," Cori said, wincing at the unnatural cheerfulness of her tone. She felt relief to have kept her true feelings hidden. "But I'll be here through the weekend for the dinner and dance tomorrow night."

"Great," Dustin replied, appearing to ignore her tone. "We can catch up there."

Cori stared at him a moment and considered telling him it wasn't a good idea. It would be better to just walk away now and leave the old wounds alone. *But was it? Down deep, she still had questions of her own, if not an apology that was long overdue.*

Dustin shifted his weight, tilting his head as he looked at her. "If you want to, that is."

How can he look at me like that and make the rest of the world fall away as if it's nothing? Cori forced a smile, then reached out and clasped his hand in hers. "That would be fun, Dustin," she affirmed. "Of course I can't wait to catch up. I've got close to a decade of embarrassing moments to share with you." Her smile widened, becoming genuine. "You're going to die laughing, probably."

Dustin took her hand in his, and then kissed the back of it. "Believe it or not, I've made more than my share of mistakes," he said huskily. He looked up at her meaningfully. "But I think you already know that, Cori."

Get out of here right now. Right now before something happens! Cori managed a quick smile, turned and opened her door, then slid quickly into the front seat of her rental car. She shut the door and cranked the key in the ignition, not daring to see if Dustin was still there. At that moment, he knocked on the glass. Apprehensive, Cori lowered the window.

"So tomorrow night, then?" Dustin asked. "I'll be there right at five, when it starts."

Just the same: absolutely oblivious to how he affected her. Cori laughed aloud, and then nodded. "I'll see you then. But forgive me if I'm a little late, I've got a lot—"

Dustin bent down in a smooth motion, planting a soft kiss on her forehead before she could react. "Drive safe," he whispered. With a last touch of his fingertips across her cheek, he turned and walked away.

Cori drove to her hotel in a state of shock. She managed to park, stumble up to her room and get inside before sinking down onto the bed. Still entranced ten minutes later, her cell phone rang, jarring her out of her stupor. She fumbled in her purse for her phone. "Hello?"

"And how did it go, my decadent flower?" Stefan murmured in a sexy tone. "Were you the belle of the ball, the way I always imagine you?"

Cori laughed, glad that her fiancé could not witness the flush that suffused her cheeks. "I got a fair number of compliments, but there was no dancing. That's tomorrow night."

"Yes, that's right, you told me," Stefan agreed. "So you enjoyed yourself? I'm glad. My reunion last year wasn't that much fun."

"That's because you were an introvert in high school, and you're still one," Cori teased. "You don't like to socialize unless you're made to."

"True," Stefan replied. "I always have my eye on the next mountain to climb."

"Overachiever to the end," Cori teased. "I hope your day was productive, then?"

"Of course," Stefan teased back. "I always work hard, especially when it's something I want badly." He paused. "Now you're sure you'll be home Sunday night by six? I have an early appointment that day for lunch, but I'll be home by then. I can bring us some Italian or maybe Thai."

"Sounds great," Cori agreed. "And yes, I'll be there by then. I'm meeting my stepmother to try on several wedding dresses, but that's earlier in the day."

"Goodnight then, darling," Stefan said lovingly. "Give me a call if anything changes."

"Goodnight," Cori said, hanging up the phone. Then she turned it off and headed into the shower, deliberately doing her best not to think about anything but Stefan and their wedding plans.

Four hours later, Cori still tossed and turned, trying her best to get Dustin out of her mind. His hazel eyes still haunted her, just like the sadness in his voice when she admitted to being engaged.

~ * ~

Across town at his mother's home, Dustin was also trying to sleep and having no luck. Thoughts of Cori kept him awake: how she had felt in his arms, the way she had looked at him when he'd touched her, that same panicked freeze she used to get right before he kissed her and unleashed their shared passion.

But she didn't let you kiss her tonight, did she? No, she's engaged. Everything you hoped for is dust in the wind. And you're a double jerk for thinking that someone like her wouldn't have a boyfriend. God, she'd probably have fabricated one if she didn't, just so you'd get the picture and back off.

Dustin's eyes snapped open. What if Cori had said she was engaged just to make him back off? *There's one way to know for sure.*

Dustin got up then carefully tiptoed down to the living room to his mother's laptop computer. He logged onto Facebook and searched for Cori, locating her after only a few failed attempts. Pulling up her page, he worried for a moment that she would have the information he sought private. Then the page loaded and all his worst fears were confirmed.

Cori is engaged. Worse, it's to some tall handsome guy who looks like he stepped off the cover of Gentleman's Quarterly. Her profile pic was of her and her fiancé— Stefan somebody with a Roman numeral after his name—with the last posting from a week ago, announcing their formal engagement.

Why the hell didn't I contact her sooner? If I had, it might be us up there on her page instead.

"Doing some late night surfing?" his mother commented knowingly from behind him.

Dustin logged off the computer then closed the lid. "Yeah, but I'm done now."

"You're only done if you give up," his mother said meaningfully, before heading back to her bedroom.

"What?" Dustin asked in confusion, turning his head to look at her.

"I think you know exactly what I mean," his mother replied as she left the room. "If you still love her, don't give her up without a fight."

Dustin got up and went after his mother, following her into her bedroom. "This isn't a Lifetime movie," he said angrily. "You don't just say things like that and walk offstage and everything works itself out."

"No shit," his mother said, her crude words catching Dustin off guard. "It's real life son, and that means it's messy. It means that in a story with a love triangle, someone walks away alone at the end. It means that a lot of times people that love each other don't end up together because life gets in the way. And if you want to buck those odds, you'll have to hold nothing back and go after what you want with everything you've got."

"Which means?" Dustin challenged.

"Tell her exactly how you feel. Give her a reason to give him up and pick you instead, before you lose this last chance to be together. And think hard about what you're willing to give up, because odds are you're going to have to sacrifice something, too."

"I don't understand," Dustin said angrily.

"You're not two teens falling in love out of high school anymore. You've each had lives of your own now for ten years. She's old enough to know what she wants and so do you. Decide if it's each other, and if that's worth more than everything else in your life right now."

Dustin swallowed hard. "And what if it's worth it to me but not to her?"

His mother looked away. "Then she's not worth you changing your life," she said in a much gentler tone. "And you'd be foolish to give up your happiness for someone like that, Dusty, especially if you already have what makes you happy."

"I like my life," Dustin said slowly. "I like never knowing where I'm going to be working next week, and calling the shots myself instead of answering to some boss. "

"You have to be true to yourself," his mother said after a pause. "You only get one life. But my advice is not to ask her for something you aren't willing to give yourself."

Dustin looked at her a moment, then walked silently out of the room. To his surprise, his mother didn't call him back.

~ * ~

Cori primped in front of the mirror, turning this way and that, and wondered for the third time if she should put her shoulder-length hair up.

An elegant bun with a few curls by my ears would really look sophisticated, especially with just jeans and a simple blouse.

You know Dustin likes it better down.

Why do I care if he likes it better? He's just a friend.

He'll never be just a friend, and you know it.

Oh, who cares, I'm late enough as it is!

Cori grabbed her purse and keys from the dresser. Locking the hotel door behind her, she ran down the hall to the lobby, darting out the door to her car. As she slid behind the wheel and started the engine, she realized she'd left her cell phone in the hotel room in its charger.

Telling herself there was no point going back for it, she put the car in drive with a quick glance at the clock. With a muttered curse, she peeled out of the lot.

Making the drive in record time, Cori hurried through the front door of the restaurant, grateful for the reunion sign, which pointed toward the back private room. She grabbed up her card with a quick smile at the greeter whom she recognized but couldn't put a name to. *Gerrie. Thank goodness for nametags.* A DJ played some popular music from her high school days, but no one was dancing. The majority of minimally decorated tables were only partly full, some with couples, and others with small groups of men or women looking at wallet pictures or their phones. She quickly saw Ice—*Dustin, he wants to be called Dustin now*—with his friend, Allen, and several other couples at one of the center tables.

Allen saw Cori, and then nudged Dustin. Dustin looked over at his friend, and then his head turned in Cori's direction. He gave a wide smile. Instead of beckoning her to join them, he excused himself and made a beeline for her. Cori waited nervously, exchanging quick hellos with several people as she waited nervously for Dustin.

"So, where do you want to go?" he asked impishly.

"Um, I thought the point of this was to stay here and be friendly to our classmates," she said mock-slowly.

"We can if you want," Dustin replied, putting his hands in his pockets with a shrug. "But you and I never followed the crowd. So if you wanted to do something else, I'm game."

Cori stared at him, trying to tell if Dustin was kidding or not. He had been famous for his pranks in high school, but she had never been on the receiving end. *He's serious.* "Like what?"

"I thought maybe we could get ice cream," he said, tilting his head and looking up at her through his dark lashes. Those sparkling hazel eyes stirred her thoughts, making her heart race. "And maybe take a walk. It's a nice night."

Cori laughed. "I'm old enough now I don't go without dinner, not that I ever liked to. So you'll have to sweeten the deal with some French fries and a burger or something."

"I can do that," Dustin said. "There's a diner a few blocks up that serves great food. I always stop there when I'm in town to visit Mom."

Cori looked at him, wavering.

"Look, go and see the food for yourself," Dustin said, motioning with his head to the buffet table. "We're better off with burgers. Whoever negotiated for this restaurant to cater tonight must have done it for a personal kickback. There can't be any other reason."

Cori laughed out loud, causing several of her classmates to look over at her. She quieted with effort, still considering. "Fine, but we have to come back for a last song. I never got to dance at my prom, you know."

A cloud passed over Dustin's face, and then he nodded, his smile fading. "I know, Cori."

Cori looked down, appalled at herself. *How could I have said that, now of all times? What's wrong with me?* "I'm sorry I said that, Dustin. I—"

She felt his hand close over hers, as he leaned in to whisper, "I'll have you back for the last song. And you'll get your dance. Fair enough?"

Cori nodded as she let him lead her away, blinking back sudden tears. *None of this is fair. But if this is all we get, then I'm going to enjoy tonight until the last moment.*

Dustin led her out of the restaurant and to his truck, opening the door. After she got in, they drove in silence to a small diner. After parking, Dustin held the door for her again as they entered. The waitress seated them quickly with menus and took their drink orders.

"I don't think they have ice cream," Cori offered as she perused the menu, trying to lighten the mood.

"We can have pie or cake then," Dustin said with a grin. "What matters is that we have time to ourselves." He put the menu near the center outer corner of the table, just as the waitress brought his coffee. "I'll have the chicken sandwich with a large fry."

"No burger?" Cori teased, handing her menu to the waitress as well. "Well, I will have one and some fries, too. Medium rare for the burger, please."

The waitress walked away, leaving them alone. Cori's gaze flitted over the new furnishings, noting with a slight sadness that little of the diner she remembered from her youth remained. *The jukebox, the tables, the counter ... it's all changed. Even the color scheme is different.*

"I was just kidding about the ice cream," Dustin said easily, sipping his coffee. "I just wanted to be alone with you, Cori."

It hadn't been an accident that Dustin had brought her here, the same diner they'd had their weekly date in during most of senior year. Her throat suddenly parched, Cori quickly sipped her water then cleared her throat. "I'm glad, Dustin, because I have something to say to you."

Dustin's gaze rose from the table and locked intently on hers.

"I'm sorry," Cori said quietly. "I was a jerk that night we broke up. I'm sorry things didn't go well—"

"Shh," Dustin said softly, taking her hand in his. "We were both young, and we made a lot of mistakes. You don't have to apologize for something we both had a part in."

"I do," Cori responded resolutely. "I always wanted to. I'm sorry it took so long for me to say it."

"I'm glad you did." Dustin kissed the back of her hand, then put it to his cheek, running her smooth skin against the slight stubble of his jawline. "I'm sorry, too. I should never have let you go."

Cori's breath caught in her chest, the sensation of his touch electrifying.

"It would have gotten better, you know. Practice makes perfect." Dustin shot her a grin.

Cori laughed again aloud, Dustin joining in. Then he released her hand. "So we're alone. Tell me what you've been doing the last decade. Leave nothing out."

There was no odd shyness, no worry that some event of the last ten years would need to be edited out in its retelling. For the next half hour, Cori freely told Dustin of her college days, her first job as a telemarketer, her second as a bank clerk, and the third and last, that of official public liaison for a large chemical company. "It's a lot of paper, mostly," Cori finished. "But its good money, as my stepmother says."

Their food came, and they began to eat hungrily.

"And how is your family?" Dustin continued, after a moment. "I know you didn't used to get along with your stepmother. Are things better now?"

"No, it's your turn," Cori countered firmly, eating a fry. "I've told you all the highpoints you missed for the last ten years. I've showed you mine. Show me yours."

Dustin smirked at her, then launched into his own retelling: his brief stint in college before deciding it wasn't for him, his foibles learning the carpentry business and his recent moderate success. "I'm not sure if it's what I will always want but right now, like you, it's good money and I'm happy with it. I like the freedom of not having to answer to anyone."

Is it only an old boss he's referring to, or is he still smarting from an ex's past demands? Cori kept the thought to herself as she ate her last fry, then pushed back her plate. Dustin had already finished a few moments ago. "I'm very glad that you're doing so well," she said with a smile. "I noticed that your F-150 truck looks like it's brand new."

Their waitress appeared. "Dessert?"

Cori began to make excuses, but Dustin was already ordering. "A piece of chocolate cake to go please."

"That had better be for you," Cori said as the waitress left to get the cake.

"It's for you, for later tonight," Dustin said. He stood and put down some money to cover the bill. "You always craved something sweet as soon as it got dark."

Maybe, but cake's not what I'm craving tonight, Cori thought to herself hungrily, reluctantly dragging her gaze from Dustin to dig in her purse for tip money. She put a few dollars onto the bill then tossed several of Dustin's back to him, even as he protested. "That's fair," she said, interrupting him. "I've already let you buy dinner. Now do you want your walk? We're not that far from the river, and the night is going fast."

Dustin nodded then followed her out. Cori turned to hold the door, catching Dustin admiring her shapely derriere encased in her tight jeans. "Enjoying the view?"

"Yes, ma'am," he said in a fake drawl, making them both erupt into laughter.

They walked along the street, laughing and joking, until they reached the former site of the ice cream parlor they had visited years ago.

"I'm surprised it closed," Cori said sadly, looking at the boarded-up, weathered structure as they walked past it to the river. "It's really a great location."

"Another bigger chain opened down the block nearer the mall," Dustin explained with a shrug. "Everything changes."

Not everything, Cori thought with a stolen glance at Dustin as they walked. *I still want to be in your arms as much as I did then. I'm still waiting to see if you'll kiss me at the end of the night, and hoping like hell that you will.*

They walked down the short dirt path to the river, treading carefully on the heavily shadowed path. "Kids must not come down here much anymore," Cori said, picking her way after Dustin.

He held back a briar bush's long trailing stems, so she could step past. "I think kids today are less interested in getting dirty." He shot her a grin. "Not like we were, Cor."

Cori stumbled on a hidden rock as she went past Dustin. He grabbed her quickly before she lost her balance. Cori fell hard against him, her right hand pressing against his chest. She looked up into his eyes like a frightened deer, and then managed a squeaky laugh. "Sorry."

"Not a problem," he murmured, taking her small right hand in his callused palm. "I'll lead you."

Cori trembled slightly as she followed Dustin out of the deep shadows to the brightly lit water's edge. The night was clear but chilly, a promise of the coming autumn. A full moon hung high above, bathing them both in silvery light.

"It looks the same," Cori said in relief, gazing out over the moonlit water. *Our first night together in ten years. Do I really want it to be the last?*

"It's not," Dustin murmured, a trace of sadness in his tone. He turned to her. "We should go back to the party."

The remorse in his words galvanized Cori into action. Her hands reached up for Dustin, her fingers threaded into his hair and gripped fast, bringing his lips down to meet hers in an ardent kiss. Dustin reacted at once. His arms pulled her close into his embrace even as he deepened the kiss, his mouth opening on hers. Cori sighed into him, wanting nothing more than to devour him, to meld their bodies into one thought, one being. Dustin's hold on her strengthened at her soft whimper, his arms molding her body to his. The kiss lasted until they were both breathing hard, their hearts racing, as they finally broke apart.

"Everything doesn't change," Cori whispered, closing her eyes and touching her head to Dustin's.

He kissed her forehead gently. "Untrue. This is the first time I can ever remember you kissing me. What happened to patience?"

Cori laughed, hugging him. "I was afraid you might never get around to it."

"I might not have," he said gently, kissing her cheek. "You're engaged, Cori."

His gentle words were like ice water flowing over her naked skin. "I know," Cori said. She flushed and stepped back out of his embrace. "I—"

"You don't have to explain," Dustin said, grabbing her arm before she got out of reach. "But we should go back now, or you won't get your dance."

With her thoughts churning between desire and her chagrin, Cori followed Dustin back to his car in silence.

~ * ~

They entered the dance at a quarter to ten. About half of the people had already left, but a few tables were still occupied. Several couples were slow dancing to Lionel Richie's *Say You, Say Me*. Dustin led Cori to the dance floor, put his hands on her waist and began to sway to the music.

Cori hung her arms around Dustin's neck, adopting his swaying motion so they moved together to the slow beat. *I'd forgotten, after learning how to dance for real with Stefan, that this was how we danced as kids.* Pushing the thought from her mind with a sliver of guilt, Cori closed her eyes, luxuriating in the feel of Dustin's touch.

Why couldn't that night have ended differently years ago? We could have had this and so much more.

Thoughts of that long ago night flooded Cori's mind. Dustin got the tent from his brother and pitched it near the river. They prepared over a matter of weeks slowly, so that no one would be wise to the fact that they weren't going to the after prom parties. Even enlisting some of Dustin's friends, like Allen to help cover for them. Cori packed an overnight bag, along with some snacks and a bottle of champagne. Her giddy excitement as she dressed in her strapless baby blue prom gown and applied her makeup. Then the anxious wait while her dad and stepmother snapped pictures, and she worried something would occur to stop their magic night from finally happening.

Cori sighed. *If only.*

The prom itself had been fine for the short time they had been there. After saying hello to all their friends and posing for some pictures, Cori and Dustin had separated, changed their clothes in the bathroom and snuck out separately. Meeting back in the parking lot, they had walked to their tent, triumphant and exultant over what was to come. And then …

Cori hugged Dustin tighter but couldn't stop the relentless march of her memory.

We'd forgotten glasses for the champagne, and neither of us liked the taste anyway. He was dressed for a night of camping; I'd dressed in lace lingerie under my clothes … and the temperature was unseasonably warm, close to eighty degrees. We were both way too hot but afraid to open the tent flap and let any more mosquitos in. My hair fell flat and my makeup ran. And then …

Cori let out an involuntary sigh. *In the stories, the hero and heroine always come together, even the first time. Yet, all I felt was pain for a while. Dustin didn't want to hurt me, but he wanted me so badly that it frustrated him terribly to have to wait. And we touched and kissed, trying to make it work, trying to give me time to catch up to him. But when he finally loved me, he came quickly, leaving me with only faint stirrings of pleasure. The second time was the same, only worse: by then, I was dying for want of him, desperate to be filled and fulfilled. Instead, he came again, without me.*

Cori burrowed into Dustin's shoulder, not wanting him to see how upset she was. *I remember lying there afterwards, Dustin still breathing hard beside me, and resenting the hell out of him. My own bitter determination took hold of me. I straddled him and ground away for all I was worth. The sheer relief when I finally came made me cry out. But my disappointment rose up almost before that pleasure faded. I didn't come with him. He hadn't waited for me.*

Hell hath no fury like a disillusioned teen. And I gave him all my wrath the next morning, one cutting remark after the other, until he finally gave up trying to find out what was wrong and walked home alone, leaving me there with the tent.

"I'm sorry again," Cori whispered. "For everything."

"Don't be sorry," Dustin replied tenderly. "This is your dance, and by the looks of it, the DJ's packing up. Enjoy it while it lasts, with no recriminations."

Cori nestled her head on his shoulder and didn't reply.

~ * ~

Dustin forced himself to breathe, his mind coming up with scenario after scenario of how to stop the night from ending. The love of his life was in his arms, just like she'd never left. And that kiss they'd shared had been hot as lava. *But she's wrong that everything's the same between us. She's got a fiancé. And even though we talked for more than an hour, I never brought up my own romantic troubles … or the fact I'm freshly divorced. How can I move us forward and out of the past, so she believes we could have a future together?*

Dustin hugged Cori tightly as the last strains of the song ended. There was so much he wanted to tell her, but would any of it be welcome? If he let her go tonight without saying what was in his heart, would he ever be able to live with himself?

Cori separated from him then looked up at him. "Thank you for the dance."

"You're welcome," he managed.

A classmate of Cori's came up, wishing her a goodnight. Dustin felt hands pulling at him, too. Allen and several of the other guys asked where he'd been all night, the former giving pointed looks at Cori and a nod of congratulations. Dustin fended them all off as fast as he could without being rude then turned to Cori, only to see her slip out the door. Cursing, he ran after her.

He caught up to her at her car, just as she was about to open the door. "Wait!"

Cori turned then dropped her keys. She cursed once herself, then picked them up, casting a musing glance his way. "Didn't we just do this?"

Dustin raked his hand through his hair, trying to find the right words, knowing that whatever he said would fall short of how he was feeling.

I love you. Don't leave. We can make it work somehow, if you only give me a chance.

Before Dustin could speak, his phone rang. He stared at Cori for a moment as it continued to ring.

"Shouldn't you answer that?" she asked finally. "I can wait."

Reluctantly, Dustin answered the phone. "Hello."

"Hi, son."

At the first tones of the gravelly voice of his father, Dustin inwardly groaned. *He never calls me, and he chooses this moment of all moments to start ...* Dustin drew a shuddering breath, knowing instantly that something had happened, and it wasn't good. "What's wrong?"

"Your mom's had a heart attack. She went to the emergency room at General Hospital. She's stable, but I thought you should come. I've already called your brother and sister—"

"I'll be right there," Dustin answered hollowly, then hung up. He turned to Cori, only to see she was already in her car, the window rolled down. "Get in," she said. "I'll drive you."

Dustin didn't stop to wonder how Cori knew something was wrong, or why she wanted to drive him. He just eased shakily into the front seat and sat back, worried thoughts flooding his mind. "My mom's in the hospital. General, on the south side of town. Head to the emergency ward."

~ * ~

At the hospital, Cori let Dustin off in front of the emergency entrance. He jumped out of her car and hurried into the hospital, straight to the receiving desk. He was still waiting in line when Cori joined him a few moments later.

"How is she?" Cori asked him breathlessly.

"She's still in the emergency room," the desk clerk said to Dustin. "She's going to be staying tonight. They're getting her room ready now." The woman handed him a printed out map. "Just follow the path marked in red arrows."

Dustin thanked the woman then headed to the emergency wing with Cori in tow. After a bunch of twists and turns, they found Dustin's mother in one of the emergency bays, protesting to the staff doctor who told her she had to stay the night.

"I'm fine—"

"Mrs. Bergman, I'm advising you to stay the night for observation. You've had a mild heart attack—"

"She'll stay," Dustin interrupted, going to his mom's side. "Do what he says, Mom. You can't risk your life."

139

Dustin's mother looked about to reply but noticed Cori, who offered her a tentative smile. "You look well, Cori. It's good to see you, in spite of the circumstances."

"Your son is right," Cori said persuasively. "You should stay the night. You don't want ... um, you want to stick around."

Dustin shifted his weight. *Just what Cori needed tonight on top of everything else, to be reminded how she lost her own mother when she was eleven to a heart attack.*

Mrs. Bergman opened her mouth as if to reply then closed it and nodded. "I guess I can stay one night."

Orderlies arrived with a bed and collected Dustin's mother. As they were leaving, Dustin's brother and sister arrived with their spouses and some of his mom's things, taking Dustin's attention. They all walked his mother up to her new room to get her settled in. It was close to midnight when he finally exited his mother's room and noticed Cori, dozing in a chair just down the hall. He crouched down in front of her then touched her arm lightly, giving her a start as she opened her eyes.

"Sorry," he said tenderly, taking her hand. "You didn't have to stay."

"I thought you might need a ride home," Cori said with a yawn.

"Actually, I do," Dustin said apologetically. "My siblings all came in the same compact car, and there were no extra seats. Not that I need to hurry, as they've commandeered my mom's spare bedroom and couch too." He forced a smile. "But I'm so tired the floor looks good to me."

"Stay with me," Cori said, the words falling unbidden from her lips. She colored at once but didn't take the offer back.

Dustin looked at her searchingly. "You don't mind? You've got room?"

"My room comes with a sleeper couch in the sitting area," Cori explained quickly. "It's separate from the bedroom. You can use that."

Dustin nodded. "I'd be grateful."

Exhausted, Cori drove Dustin back to pick up his car in case of emergency, and then had him follow her to the hotel. She led him inside the room, kicked off her shoes and sank down on the couch with a sigh.

You're in my bed, technically. Jerk, don't say that, she'll think you just accepted her offer to sleep here, hoping to get laid. "Thanks for saying what you did, Cori. I wouldn't have put it past mom to check herself out and try to go home."

Cori's smile faltered. "I was glad to do it. Losing my own mom wasn't something I'd wish on anyone else, least of all you."

Dustin sat down beside her, being careful to keep his distance, lest she think his motives were more than just comfort. "You never answered me before. How's your family?"

Cori grimaced slightly. "Everyone's the same. My father is still self-absorbed, and my stepmom is still trying to climb the social ladder and getting nowhere. The most I've seen them is lately, when we've been planning the wedding." Before Dustin could reply, Cori hurried on. "But I'm glad you're getting along with your mom. I always liked her."

"She always liked you," Dustin assured.

"And your dad?" Cori added quickly.

"About the same as yours: into his own thing, like he's been his entire life," Dustin said with a shrug. He took her hand in his. "Do you really want to talk about this?"

Cori's pulse rate shot up as Dustin's touch. "Did you have something else to say?"

Yeah. Don't marry him. Marry me. Dustin closed his mouth firmly, until he was sure the words wouldn't escape. "Don't you think we should talk?" he murmured finally, squeezing her hand in his.

Cori swallowed hard then gathered her courage. "Yes." She paused again, making herself force out the words. "Why did you leave without saying anything to me?"

Dustin loosened his grip on her hand, though he didn't release it. "You basically told me that I didn't deserve you. I knew I'd let you down, even though I never meant to. What else was there to say?"

"I'm sorry," Cori said, bringing Dustin's hand to her chest and holding it with both hands. "I never meant to hurt you."

Dustin's lips parted even as he moved forward to kiss Cori's parted, inviting lips. But as he bent down, the large diamond on her ring finger flashed as if in warning, and broke the spell.

It doesn't matter what might have been, only what is. "It's okay," Dustin said lightly. Releasing her hand, he moved back to the other end of the sofa. "Do you want the shower first?"

"Please," Cori said gratefully, getting to her feet. She walked into the bathroom and shut the door.

As the shower began to run, Dustin went into the bedroom and grabbed the extra blankets and a pillow from the bed. When he removed the pillow, the vibrator that had been resting beneath it, rolled out onto the bedspread.

Why did she bring this with her? Some fiancé. He must not be taking care of business. Carefully, Dustin put the vibrator back where it had been, put the pillow back on top of it and grabbed the other pillow off the bed. He made up the couch then took off his shirt, leaving on his jeans. Stretching back, he rested his arms above his head, listening to the water run.

She's in there naked.

Dustin shifted, images of Cori's luscious body swarming through his mind. His body responded automatically; an erection formed that was painful in its intensity. He tried to ignore it. The longer the water ran, the harder it was to keep his thoughts off his old flame.

What if she uses the vibrator tonight and I hear her? Will I be able to stay out here, listening to her soft orgasmic cries and not go in there to answer them? Imaginative scenarios burst over Dustin's eyes, flooding his senses with pictures of the two of them coming together, their naked bodies entwined, joined, moving in tandem until the sweet rush of climax engulfed them both.

Dustin drew a long shuddering sigh. *No way you're going to get through saying goodnight, much less the few hours until morning, unless you handle this now.* Saying a prayer that Cori would stay in there another few moments, Dustin undid his pants.

~ * ~

Cori finished washing her hair, then went to soap up her face one last time. The well-used bar broke into several pieces in her hand. Muttering that the hotel bar was so decorously thin to begin with, Cori stepped out of the shower and walked dripping across the tile to the extra bars near the sink. She snatched one up and unwrapped it, then moved to the garbage can near the door. As she tossed the wrapper, a low groan made her pause.

Another groan came, this one more insistent than the last. Riveted, Cori pressed her ear to the door and listened. As the moans intensified and quickened, Cori drew a long, shuddering breath.

He's out there masturbating.

Cori's first impulse was to open the door because she desperately wanted to watch, though she knew it was wrong. Instead, she stayed motionless on her side, trying not to breath.

"Cori. Cori."

For a second, Cori thought somehow Dustin knew she was there

142

listening. Then Dustin gave a loud groan then several more, the last trailing off into a satisfied sigh. Then came the sounds of a muttered curse and tissues pulled from a box.

He came, thinking about me. Cori swayed, her one desire to open the door and go out to Dustin in her wet skin, showing him with her touch that she was all too willing to sate his every desire. Instead, she retreated to the shower and got back under the warm water. Shaking, she touched herself at once, rubbing the swollen nub between her thighs, an involuntary gasp of pleasure lost in the pounding spray of the water. The climax built almost at once, all the longing and lust for Dustin raging through her like a flood, her back arched as she came, her soft cries lost in the pounding of the water.

Slowly Cori sank down onto her haunches, hugging herself. When her breathing slowed, she turned off the water and got out, toweling herself dry.

There was no noise from the other room.

He hadn't meant to be overheard. It was just a stressful day, and he needed some release. You were a convenient fantasy. Tonight just brought up all the old feelings, nothing more.

Cori sighed, then wiped off the fogged up mirror with the edge of the towel. *That's all bullshit and you know it, except for the being overheard part. His feelings—and yours—are as real as they ever were. The only real question is what are you going to do about how you feel?*

Cori opened the door slowly, unsure what to say to Dustin yet determined not to hide her feelings. But she needn't have worried. He was fast asleep, wrapped in a blanket with a peaceful expression on his face, his dark hair mussed.

Cori looked down at him, then reached out and touched his cheek gently with her fingertips. When Dustin stirred then moved on his side away from her, the blanket covering him slipped off his shoulders to reveal his muscular back.

Cori stood transfixed, watching the rise and fall of his deep even breathing. She reached out a hand toward him again then took it back. To wake him would ensure an inevitable outcome that they had both done their respective best to avoid. Stifling a sob of sheer need, she fled into her bedroom and closed the door.

~ * ~

Dustin woke with a groan, his back stiff and sore. Blinking his eyes, he swung his legs over the edge of the bed and sat up. Last night's events came back in a rush when he realized the bed was instead a couch. *Kissing Cori. Mom in the hospital. Staying here for the night. Fantasizing about Cori, then falling asleep after.* He looked toward Cori's door, but it was shut, with only silence on the other side.

Dustin rubbed his eyes then yawned, wrinkling his nose. Everything else could wait until he had a shower.

Several minutes later, he emerged clean under yesterday's clothes and looked toward Cori's door. Still shut. Not wanting to wake her, especially if she regretted last night's conversations, he penned a quick note on hotel stationary and left it on the table.

Cori,
I'm going to head to the hospital this morning, but I want to see you again. Please give me a call.
Dustin

Dustin listed his cell phone and home phone then paused, wondering if he should leave it at that. Deciding that note alone was too reticent, he threw caution to the wind and added on a few sentences.

I love you. I know you still love me. Don't let this second chance slip away. What we have is worth fighting for, no matter what.

Hoping that would be enough to sway her to give him a chance, Dustin grabbed his things then left the room.

A few moments later, Cori emerged hesitantly from her room. The moment she saw Dustin missing, she ran to the window, just in time to see him climbing into his truck.

Cori watched Dustin drive away, tears coming to her eyes that she quickly brushed away. She closed the curtains and slowly walked to the table to read his note, dejection settling about her shoulders.

He still loves me. He still wants me. Cori put down the note with shaking fingers, and rubbed at her eyes.

How can it have happened so fast, falling back in love with him? My carefully crafted, perfect future awaits me. Yet, I don't give a damn for any of it because he's not a part of it. The foundations of my life are crumbling, and I don't care because all I want is to be with him.

Cori took a deep breath then collected herself, just as someone knocked at the door. Pasting on a smile, she went and opened it, relieved to see her stepmom until Cori saw the expression on her face.

"Who was that I just saw leaving here?" her stepmother asked sharply. "That man?"

God, I don't need this now. "Dustin, and nothing happened," Cori replied, heading into the bedroom to pack. "He and I met at the reunion party last night, and we reconnected."

"We will discuss this now," her stepmother said harshly as she followed Cori and shut the open suitcase with a snap. "You're upset, Cor. So something happened. Did he spend the night?"

Cori faced her stepmother, her own fears and emotions causing her normal self-control to snap. "Yes, he did. And nothing happened, all right? I was the little lady you raised me to be! All I wanted was to spend the night in his arms, and I kept my distance instead! I did what you expected of me, just like I've done my whole fucking life!"

"Don't you use that language with me," Cori's stepmother retorted harshly. "Though I'm glad to hear you didn't let your emotions get out of control—"

"Now that you have heard it, get out," Cori interrupted, striding to the door and flinging it open. "We're not going to lunch or anything else today. I can pick out my own damned dress just fine."

Her stepmother's expression softened slightly as she gave a small sigh. "I know you care about him, it's clear," she said gently. "But you're crazy to consider this man when you have Stefan. He loves you very much, you know."

A fresh wave of guilt hit Cori. "I know," she whispered.

"Don't you love him?"

"I do," Cori said, swallowing hard. "It's just—"

"Then stop leading on Dustin," her stepmother finished. "You're just going to hurt him. Tell him you can't see him anymore and cut it clean, Cor."

Cori rubbed at her eyes. *Good advice, if it didn't make me feel like I was dying inside.*

"Dustin must know you're engaged," her stepmother went on. "And for all you know he's engaged himself, or already married—"

"He's not," Cori grated out, her eyes spitting sparks. "He would have

145

told me. He's not like that. Now please leave."

She walked out without a backward look, and Cori slammed the door behind her.

Incensed, and wanting to prove Dustin's virtue, she checked under the name he had given her on Facebook and located the correct page with a few keystrokes. And got the shock of her life

Cori looked down at the computer screen, and the warm feeling died inside her as she read the words on Dustin's page. *Married. He's married.*

I should never have opened myself up to him again. God, I've been such a fool.

Cori's cell phone rang, still in its charger. She went to it and picked up, forcing a smile. "Good morning, Stefan."

"And how are you?" Stefan asked curiously. "I called and left you a message last night, but you didn't return it."

"I'm sorry," Cori said. "I was at the hospital with a friend whose mother had a heart attack." She went on to explain what had happened, leaving out her own feelings for Dustin, as well as his note from this morning.

"That was kind of you," Stefan said. "But will it cause a delay, or will you still be here by six? I know there was a brunch you planned to attend to wrap up the weekend."

"I'll be there by six," Cori assured him, leaving out that she wouldn't attend the brunch. "I'll leave within the hour."

"I can't wait to see you."

"Me either," Cori said, biting her lip. "Thanks for being so understanding." She hung up the phone then began packing.

~ * ~

After visiting his mother in the hospital that morning, Dustin had lunch with his siblings then drove home, arriving in the early evening. He unlocked his front door and rifled through the sheaf of mail on the table, glad he had his neighbor pick it up for him. After unpacking, he dusted off the top of his old laptop with a cough then logged on. It took him three tries, as he'd forgotten where the caps were in his standard password, before his Facebook page opened up before him. As the pages loaded in increments, his eager expression changed to one of confusion, then horror.

Oh no. I left my status married.

Swearing, Dustin typed commands on the keyboard and updated his

146

status to single as fast as possible. Then he checked his messages, giving a groan of relief to see there was nothing from Cori demanding an explanation. *She hasn't been on my page yet, thank God.*

After liking a few picture tags that his high school chums had posted of him on their pages, Dustin went to Cori's page. Hers was oddly blank of recent posts, save the older engagement announcement, as if she hadn't posted anything since before their reunion.

With a smile, Dustin typed her a quick message to call him when she'd had a minute to herself, and that he looked forward to hearing her voice.

It was in her eyes, and in the way she kissed me, that she still loves me. I let her know how I feel; now the ball's in her court. And I've got a hell of a wait before me, because knowing her, it could go either way.

~ * ~

Cori took the long way home, enjoying the late summer weather even as she tried to sort out her feelings. Stefan didn't expect her until six. She had a lot to think about, most importantly, what she wanted now.

Dustin's who I want but he's no good for me, even if he and I still do have feelings for one another. And Stefan is good for me, but can I really go ahead and marry him now, knowing that he only gets me by default? Can I really be happy with him now? I thought we were marrying for all the right reasons, but something is missing. I just didn't see it until now.

With a sigh, Cori got out of her car and went up to Stefan's front door. Using her key, she let herself in, calling out that she was home. The faint sound of the shower in the guest bathroom was just audible over the sound of the dishwasher in the kitchen.

Curious, Cori went to the guest bathroom and opened the door. Her eyes opened wide as she beheld Stefan and another man with wet hair, both of them dressed only in towels. Both turned to her in pure shock. The unknown man gave her a forced smile, grabbed his clothes from the counter and left. Stefan simply dropped his towel and began dressing.

This can't be what it looks like. But what else can this be, really? "Stefan, is that man your lover?"

"Yes, sometimes," Stefan answered reluctantly. "I'm bisexual, Cori. I'd hoped to introduce you to Armand gradually, to have you get to know him before I told you. But this is probably better, really." He turned to face her, taking her hand. "I never wanted to hide this from you, love. But I felt as if you needed me to be the perfect man for you, and I didn't want to let you down. I wanted to be your white knight, your hero."

It would be easy to call him a few foul names and use this as an excuse to break things off. But what's the point? I'm not upset really, because I don't love Stefan as more than a friend. And if he needs this to be happy, then he does need someone like Armand who can love him the way he needs to be loved, instead of someone who loved the idea of him and not the reality.

Cori squeezed his hand in hers. "You aren't letting me down by telling me that this is who you really are, Stefan." She let go of his hand then moved to the door. "Come talk to me when you're dressed."

Stefan buttoned his shirt. "Are you breaking off our engagement?" he said simply. "Now that you know the truth?"

"I don't fault you for who you are," Cori said honestly. "I'm not going to marry you, no. But that's not only because of Armand and you. It's because of me, too." She took a deep breath. "I still have feelings for someone else. Even if I hadn't discovered your secret, I'd still break off our engagement. I'm sorry, Stefan."

"We could still make it work," Stefan offered, his expression crestfallen. "We could have a great life, Coriander."

"Yes, we could," Cori said softly. "But that life isn't the one that I truly want." She went to the bedroom and began to pack.

Where to go? My wedding is off, the two men in my life are otherwise occupied, and what little I have left of my family isn't supportive. Why the hell didn't I ever get a dog?

'Cori, where are you going?" Stefan said as he followed her into his bedroom, upset. "I don't want you driving in your state."

"You don't really have anything to say about it anymore, do you?" Cori snapped at him, throwing the last of her clothes into a duffle bag. She took off the engagement ring from her finger and set it carefully on the dresser. "This belongs to you—"

Stefan grabbed hold of her, even as she struggled. "Don't think I didn't love you or didn't want to spend the rest of my life with you," he whispered sadly. "I meant everything I said. I'm sorry that I couldn't be more perfect for you. " Abruptly, he released her.

Cori took a deep breath, trying to control her emotions. "I'm not angry with you, Stefan. I'm relieved, actually." She forced a smile. "I beat myself up sometimes because you were so good that you made me feel like I couldn't measure up to your level of perfection. Finding this out about you doesn't make you a bad person to me. It just makes you human." She gave him a quick kiss on the cheek then walked out the front door, even as he called after her to stop.

~ * ~

Several hours later, Dustin arrived at Cori's house. In spite of his resolve to wait for her to make a move, there was too much at stake for him. He needed to know where he stood, especially with her upcoming nuptials. Dustin took a deep breath, and rang the doorbell. No one answered.

Stymied, he debated climbing the back privacy fence and peering in the windows when his cell phone rang. He answered at once, hopeful at the unfamiliar number. "Cori?"

"Sorry, it's just your mother. I'm calling from your brother's new Smartphone."

"I'm glad you're feeling better, Mom——"

"Save it. Did you go after Cori like I said you should?"

"I went to her house. She's not here."

"She's likely at her fiancé's house. Go there."

"Mom, I can't stalk her."

"You aren't stalking her. You're letting her know that you care. Now get moving. The address per the Internet is 187 Bradfern Lane. It's across town."

Shaking his head, Dustin returned to the car and drove to Cori's fiancé's house. He felt foolish as knocked on the door. Stefan answered, freshly showered and fully dressed, his dark hair glistening. "Yes?"

"Is Cori here?"

Stefan looked him up and down. "Who are you?"

"A friend from her reunion. My name's Dustin."

"She never mentioned a Dustin," Stefan said, his tone curious rather than unkind. "In any case, she's not here. And it's unlikely she will return, I'm afraid."

"Why?" Dustin asked anxiously. "Is she okay?"

"I was told it wasn't any of my business anymore," Stefan said with a sigh. "She broke off our engagement this morning and left with all her personal effects."

Rapture flooded Dustin. *This had to be because of her feelings for him!* "Do you know where she is?"

"I assumed she went home," Stefan said with a shrug. "She was in one of her moods and not inclined to say much."

"She's not there," Dustin said worriedly. "I just came from there."

Stefan opened the door. "Please come in."

Dustin followed him down the hall to the kitchen, where another man was making a gourmet meal in the kitchen. "I'll just be a moment, Armand." Stefan headed into the bedroom, pulled out his wallet and thumbed through the contents until he came to a credit card. Pulling it out, he called the number on the back as Dustin paced nervously.

"Yes, I'd like to check if my card was used recently." Stefan recited a number and all the relevant information then listened for a moment. "No, don't terminate the card. The charges are fine." He hung up the phone, and then scribbled down an address on a pad of paper. Ripping the top sheet off, he handed it to Dustin. "This is where she is."

Dustin gaped at him.

"I gave Cori a credit card to use for wedding expenses when she told me she didn't have any of her own," Stefan explained. A bitter smile formed on his lips.

"Why are you helping me?" Dustin said, pocketing the information. "Not that I'm ungrateful, but I expected you to want to deck me, worst case scenario."

"I'm seldom dramatic," Stefan said dryly, heading back to the front door. "But Cori is, and to have her leave so calmly the way she did makes me worried for her." He looked Dustin up and down again. "Even if you have anything to do with her leaving." He opened the door. "Go to her. Maybe you can make her happy."

"I'm sorry," Dustin said awkwardly.

Stefan looked at him for a moment, eyes narrowed, then punched Dustin squarely in the left cheekbone. Dustin went down on one knee with a grunt, head ringing.

"But I did owe you that for taking whatever chance we might have had away from me," Stefan said angrily, looking down his nose at Dustin. Then he slammed the door.

Dustin got to his feet then made his way carefully to his car, wincing in pain. *God, Cori, the things I go through for you.*

~ * ~

The sound of a car door slammed in the silent night air followed by abrupt cursing.

Oh no. No, he can't have found me! Not unless he's spent the last three hours driving here ...

Cori ran to the hotel room door, threw back the deadbolt and rushed outside. Yes, it was Dustin, his black hair wild, his clothes wrinkled from the long drive. He stood before her, stretching slightly.

"Why did you come here?" she screeched at him.

"Because I love you," he said simply. "I always have. I always will. And I'm not married, like my Facebook page said. I just got divorced a few weeks ago, after a long separation." He paused. "I know that you broke it off today with Stefan because of us."

Cori stared at him, her heart racing, and rapidly blinked back tears. "There isn't any us."

"Stop denying how you feel," Dustin pleaded. "If it was going to fade, don't you think it would have all those years we were apart?" He took a step closer. "No one else makes me feel the way you make me feel. No one else ever could." He took her in his arms. "And even if they could, I wouldn't want to feel this with anyone else but you."

Cori let out a desperate cry, pulling back her hand and slapping Dustin. He stood staunchly, staring down at her. Then with a wordless moan, Cori grabbed hold of Dustin's face with her hands and guided his mouth to meet hers.

The first meeting of their lips was pure bliss. The intense emotion fueled an almost punishing kiss as each of them fought to devour the other. Cori moaned softly, then opened her mouth, licking at Dustin's lips. With a groan he opened to her, tasting her sweetness, his hands tangled in her hair. Dustin's momentum pushed Cori backwards, until she was splayed against the hotel wall. He kissed her with abandon over and over, down her throat and back to her lips. Finally, he drew back, his eyes almost black with lust. "Stay there," he ordered.

Cori shivered at the desire in his words and leaned against the wall, her chest heaving.

Dustin ran to the car, and then ran back with a duffel bag in one hand and a small cooler. He looked at Cori, leaning against the outside wall, and then grinned. "I didn't mean literally," he said. "Just didn't want to break the moment."

There was a boom of thunder from above.

"Seems like nature is already doing that," Cori said with a laugh. "Let's get inside before we get wet."

"I picked up some snacks and more cake," Dustin stated as he put the cooler contents into the mini-fridge then took off his shoes. "Sorry, they're covered in mud."

"I don't care about that," Cori said, coming close to him. She took his hand and pulled him into the sitting room. "I love you." She kissed him for all she was worth, her arms going around his neck.

Dustin groaned and kissed her back, his hands moving to unbutton her shirt. His hands caressed her breasts then slid under the cotton material to cup the soft mounds. She let out another urgent moan. Her nipples tightened at his touch as he tweaked and rubbed. Then she let out a sharp gasp as his mouth engulfed the sensitive reddened skin, sucking and teasing. Without pause, Dustin moved his attentions to the other breast, eliciting cry after cry from Cori as she trembled in his embrace.

Possessively, Dustin's hand slid into the top of her jeans, reaching down to cup her womanhood, the soft, swelling folds already moist with her excitement. He slid a finger inside then gently rubbed. Cori groaned, then pulled away, going for Dustin's shirt, pulling it over his head. Then she unbuttoned his jeans, sliding them down so he could step out of them.

Dustin picked her up in his arms, and then carried her to the bed. He lay her down, his hands roaming her flushed, warm skin, his mouth sucking and teasing until she couldn't stand it any longer.

"I want you," she whispered, freeing him from his confining underwear. "Please take me."

Dustin needed no further encouragement. He slid on a condom procured from his jeans, spread Cori's legs and slipped inside. Entering easily to stroke her body with his own, Cori and Dustin began moving in rhythm. Unhurried, their movements were slow, wanting to enjoy each other instead of rushing their lovemaking to its inevitable conclusion. As much as the couple both wanted to come, they had both waited too long for this moment to hurry it one moment faster.

~ * ~

Cori gave a groan, and then turned in Dustin's arms to face him, her naked thighs brushing his. He opened his eyes and looked down at her sleepily, a huge grin on his face. "Marry me?" he asked, drawing her small body tight against him.

Cori laughed with a nod and gave him a kiss. As they separated, she murmured, "I'm glad you didn't wait any longer for the perfect moment to ask me, or I was going to have to ask you instead."

"This is the perfect moment," Dustin said huskily, looking into her eyes. "You're in my arms. We're together, like we always should have been. And you love me like I love you." He brushed his lips gently across her cheek. "It doesn't get any more perfect than this."

"I'm glad we want the same things," Cori said softly, hugging him. "I wasn't sure we'd ever be on the same page."

"We're in the same book, in the same chapter, reading the same page," Dustin said lovingly. "Trust me, I wasn't going to miss this chance."

"I'm glad we finally got it right," Cori said dreamily as she caressed his cheek, running her fingers through his hair. "But I want more than one, if it's okay with you." She giggled, seeing his expression. "Moment, that is. Not that I'd be opposed to more of the other shared joys later today."

"This is just the first of many," Dustin assured her. "I promise you that, my sweet Cori." Then he pulled her close for a passionate kiss.

THE END

About the Author

Tara Fox Hall's writing credits include nonfiction, horror, suspense, action-adventure, erotica, and contemporary and historical paranormal romance. She is the author of the paranormal action-adventure *Lash* series and the vampire romantic suspense *Promise Me* series. Tara divides her free time unequally between writing novels and short stories, chainsawing firewood, caring for stray animals, sewing cat and dog beds for donation to animal shelters, and target practice.

Connect with Tara at:
Website: www.tarafoxhall.com

Other works by the author with Melange Books, LLC
Return To Me
Surrender to Me
The Origin of Fear in Spellbound 2011 Anthology
Night Music in Midnight Thirsts II Anthology
Partners in Midnight Thirsts II Anthology
Kink in Wicked Christmas Wishes Anthology
The Oath in Wicked Christmas Wishes Anthology
Bedtime Shadows Anthology
Make Me Behave Anthology
Latham's Landing, An Anthology
The Oath
Her Frozen Heart, in Frozen Anthology
Night Music, a Novella

The Promise Me Series
Promise Me, Book 1
Broken Promise, Book 2
Taken in the Night, Book 3
Taken for his Own, Book 4
Promise Me Anthology, Book 4.5
Immortal Confessions, Book 5
Her Secret, Book 6
Point of No Return, Book 7
Lost Paradise, Book 8
Dark Solace, Book 9
Eye of the Storm, Book 10
Tempest of Vengeance, Book 11
Sundown-Serena, Book 12

Coming Soon
Hope's Return—Promise Me Series, Book 13

RUNNING LATE

By

Caroline Andrus

For my mom.
She introduced me to books and I've never looked back.

~ Present Time ~

The time on the clock sitting on the nightstand flashed 3:43 PM, taunting Paige and reminding her of her relentless lack of punctuality.

"Shoot!" she cried as she pulled her sweater over her head and grabbed her cell phone from her bed. She was supposed to meet her boyfriend at the coffee shop in exactly two minutes.

For the past few weeks, Will had been acting strange and Paige was starting to worry. She would ask him what was up and he'd just say, "Nothing" and change the subject. They used to spend nearly every free moment together, but lately he was making excuses to get away from her. It felt like he was hiding something.

Logically, she knew she was probably being crazy, but she couldn't help but wonder if there was someone else. It had been seven years since they'd first met and their relationship had reached a plateau; things had to change one way or another, and she was terrified that he was bringing their love story to an end. She had convinced herself that he wanted to meet her in public so that he could break up with her quietly, somewhere she wouldn't make a big scene.

~ * ~

~ Seven Years Ago ~

"How much?" Paige asked the barista. A stray lock of hair escaped the messy bun she had pulled her long, ash brown locks into earlier, and was now dangling in her face. With a frustrated sigh, she pushed the offending stray hair behind her ear, and struggled to pull her wallet from the book bag she carried, which weighed in at roughly one hundred and twenty pounds of college textbooks.

"No charge," the barista replied.

Paige looked up from her struggle in surprise, her wallet temporarily forgotten.

"Huh?" she asked, pushing that pesky stray hair out of her face once more.

"You're covered."

Paige blinked in surprise. "Is this one of those 'pay it forward' things?"

The barista shrugged. She looked around conspiratorially before leaning in to inform her, in a hushed voice, "See the guy wearing the blue hoodie, sitting at the table in the back corner?" When Paige went to turn around, the barista whispered, "Don't look at him now. He's watching us. When you walked in I was at his table, refilling his coffee, when he asked me to charge your drink to his card."

The barista left and Paige casually looked over her shoulder and spotted him instantly. He was watching her. When her eyes locked with his, he glanced down, appearing to be trying to hide his smile.

Paige quickly turned back to the counter and frowned. Did she know him? He didn't look familiar. Paige was pretty sure she'd remember those haunting brown eyes. Of course, Paige was usually running late and didn't pay much attention to her surroundings. She sure paid attention now, though. He was super cute, with short brown hair and a tan complexion. Though his hoodie and jeans covered his body, he appeared to be physically fit as well.

She made her way to the other end of the counter and waited another minute for her drink, her eyes continuously making their way back to the handsome young man.

When her drink order was up, she carefully grabbed the paper cup and held it in both hands, appreciating the warmth after coming in from the chilly, fall weather. She summoned all the courage she could muster, spun around, squared her shoulders and made her way to his table.

"Thanks," she said, stopping beside him. His focus was on a textbook resting on the table in front of him. Despite his intense focus on the book, she noticed his eyes weren't moving across the page.

He looked up and gave her a shy smile. "You're welcome." There was an awkward pause before he said, "Would you like to sit down?"

She felt her face flush and nodded, taking the seat across from him. She was completely self-conscious of her appearance. She'd been running late for her morning class and had made it just in the nick of time, but only at the expense of looking like an absolute slob. Clearly, he must have felt sorry for the girl sitting in front of him who looked like she lived on the streets.

"Thanks," she said, her eyes locked on the coffee cup in her hand, her fingers tracing the letters printed on the paper. She removed the lid and blew on the piping hot liquid; steam rose and fogged her glasses. She had been in such a rush she hadn't even had time to put in her contacts.

"I've seen you around," he said.

Was that hesitation she detected in his voice? "You have?" she said in surprise.

"Yeah. You always come in here around this time."

"Oh." She couldn't deny she was a creature of habit.

"I'm Will."

"Paige. Do you go to the U of M?" she asked. They were near the college she attended, which was why this was her coffee shop of choice, close to both her dorm and her classes.

He nodded. "Yeah, I'm a junior. Majoring in Business Management."

"I'm a freshman. Undecided."

Is he too old for me? she wondered. She was eighteen and fresh out of high school, that meant if he was a junior, he was at least twenty-one. She'd only had one boyfriend in high school and he'd been the same age; she'd never had the confidence to really date.

"Still don't know what you want to be when you grow up?" he asked her playfully.

She laughed. "Nope. Not a clue. What made you decide on Business Management?"

They spent the next hour talking about school and family and life. Paige was completely smitten and she was pretty sure he was, too. Especially when he asked for her number, then programmed his own into her phone. They parted ways when Paige realized she had only ten minutes to get to her next class and it was a fifteen-minute walk.

Will offered to walk with her, but she respectfully declined, needing some time to process her coffee date. Was it a date?

She spent most of that class—and the next class—daydreaming about Will instead of concentrating on the lectures. She hoped nothing covered that day would end up on the finals.

~ * ~

~ *Present Time* ~

Paige grabbed her purse from her dresser, knocking a framed photo to the floor.

"Shoot!" she cried, hurriedly reaching down and grabbing the frame. Thankfully, it was not broken. She paused a moment to smile at the image before her, a photo of her and Will on their first date. She returned it lovingly to the dresser, and slung the purse over her shoulder, after throwing her phone inside.

~ * ~

~ *Seven Years Ago* ~

"What if he doesn't call?" Paige worried, staring at her phone.

"He's going to call."

Classes were over for the day and she was lying on her stomach on her bed, staring at her phone. She'd shared all the juicy details about her meeting Will with her roommate, Lauren, who was playing the part of reassuring friend.

"What if he doesn't?"

"Shut up!" Lauren exclaimed with a laugh. "He's going to call. If everything you told me about this morning is true, he's as into you as you are into him."

Paige rolled onto her back, her phone still clutched in her hand, and shut her eyes.

"You're probably right. He did really seem to be into me."

"Of course I am."

Before either girl could say one more word, Paige's phone began ringing. She stared at it. "WILL" was displayed in big, bold letters.

"Omigosh! It's him." Paige stared at the device, which continued to ring and vibrate in her hand.

"Answer it already!" Lauren insisted.

"Oh, right." Paige hit the talk button and said, "Hello?"

"Hey stranger," came Will's voice from the other end of the line.

Her heart fluttered up into her throat and she smiled.

"What's up?" she asked, trying to keep her cool.

"Just finished classes for the day. I was wondering if you had dinner plans."

Lauren had come to sit beside her on the bed and had her ear pressed to the other side of the phone, trying to make out Will's side of the conversation. She gave Paige a thumbs up.

"Um...not really, I had planned on just eating down in the mess hall."

"Well, if you could bring yourself to break those plans, I was hoping I could take you out."

"I suppose the mess hall would understand if I cancelled," she tried to joke.

"Do you like Italian?"

"Who doesn't?"

"Good answer. Can I pick you up at 5:45?"

"Sure."

She gave him her dorm info and made plans for him to meet her in front of the building.

"Oh. My. Gosh," she breathed as she hung up, clutching the phone to her chest.

"Told you he'd call," Lauren said with a smug smile. Paige watched as she stood up from the bed and walked to Paige's closet.

"What are you doing?"

"You're not wearing *that* on your first date, are you?"

She glanced down at her U of M hoodie, old faded jeans, and worn sneakers.

"No. It's a wonder he even asked me out after seeing me like this." She felt her face heat up in embarrassment as she pushed the stray hair out of her face once more.

"I'll help tame that beast, too." Lauren gestured to Paige's hair.

"What would I do without you?"

"Let's hope you never have to find out."

Will had called at about four thirty, so the girls had plenty of time to make Paige presentable.

After a shower and a wardrobe change, followed by hair and makeup,

Paige was ready.

"There," Lauren said as she bobby pinned the last stray hair out of Paige's face. "He'll wonder if you're even the same girl!"

"Hopefully that won't scare him off," Paige said with a laugh. "He did buy coffee for the me with the untamed hair and grunge clothes."

"He probably thought you were homeless," Lauren joked.

Paige glared and punched her friend playfully in the arm. She couldn't be too offended since she'd had the exact same thought after all. "I don't do mornings."

"Believe me, I know."

At 5:40, the girls headed down to the front entrance of the dorm. Lauren insisted on escorting Paige, under the pretense of being a witness, just in case Will was actually a serial killer. Paige knew the real reason; her friend wanted to get a good look at Will, to see if he lived up to Paige's description.

It was exactly 5:45 when a green SUV pulled to a stop in front of them. Paige waited with baited breath until she saw Will step around the front of the vehicle and smile at her. He looked delicious in a nice pair of blue jeans and a crisp button down dress shirt. Until that moment, she hadn't been aware that college guys even owned dress shirts. She hadn't been quite sure what to wear herself, but Lauren had insisted that you can never be overdressed. She had said, "It's best to look better than everyone else, versus looking like a slob in comparison." Therefore, Lauren had helped her pick out an earth tone print dress from Paige's closet, paired with Lauren's brown cowboy boots and brown leather jacket.

"You look amazing," Will said as he stopped directly in front of her. They stood awkwardly for a moment, neither quite sure of the appropriate greeting. A hug? A handshake? Surely it was too soon for a kiss.

Lauren broke the tension. "Hi, I'm Lauren, Paige's roommate."

"Will," he introduced himself, offering Lauren his hand.

"Now, I want you two to have a good time, but I expect her home by 9:30," Lauren deadpanned.

Will looked confused for a brief moment before Paige cut in. "She's kidding." She forced a laugh, then glared at her friend.

Lauren grinned innocently. "But seriously, before you go, stand next to each other and smile!"

Will put one arm around Paige's shoulder. Even through her jacket, she could feel the warmth of his hand on her skin, sending tingles of pleasure straight down her arm. She looked up at him, a smile on her face. Lauren quickly snapped a couple photos on her phone and said her farewells.

"Shall we?" Will gestured to the SUV.

"Let's shall."

Will opened her door and helped her in, then returned to the driver's side.

"Where are we eating?" she asked to fill the silence.

"Have you ever been to Donatelli's?" he asked.

She shook her head.

"It's a family restaurant in a suburb northeast of here. They've been around for years and years. My parents took me and my sisters there a lot as kids."

"Sounds good," Paige replied. "How many sisters do you have?"

"Two. I'm in the middle. Rachel is twenty-five and Sarah is seventeen."

"Do you get along with them?"

"For the most part. I think there's a big enough age gap between each of us that we don't have as much sibling rivalry as we would have if we were closer in age."

Paige nodded.

"What about you?" Will asked.

"What *about* me?"

He chuckled. "Do you have any brothers or sisters?"

"Nope. It's just me."

"Do you like being an only child?"

She shrugged. "I don't have anything to compare it to." She paused in thought for a moment. "I always picture myself having at least three kids though, in the future."

Was it bad dating etiquette to talk about how many kids you want on a first date? She blushed, afraid she'd made a faux pas. Too late now.

"Only three?" Will asked. She looked up at him in surprise his face was dead serious. "I want at least seven. Maybe more."

Her mouth fell open. "Seriously?"

He broke into a grin, then laughed. "No. I don't think I could handle that many. I want at least two—that much I know."

Paige tried not to smile. She failed miserably and broke into a fit of giggles as well.

Despite her first date nerves, Paige found it easy to keep up a conversation with Will. By the time they arrived at the restaurant twenty minutes later, it felt as if they were old friends. Almost. She was still a little nervous, but she was feeling more and more comfortable with Will as the night wore on. They talked about their hometowns, their school careers, their childhood friends. They discovered that both of their families spent a week or two each summer driving up to Northern Minnesota and renting a cabin on one of the many lakes. For all they knew, it was possible they had spent time at the same resort at one point during their childhood. Not likely, but it was fun to imagine.

When Will returned her to the dorms later that night, their bellies full and leftovers in a box, Paige was both sad the night was over, and relieved to be able to relax in her dorm and tell Lauren all about the date.

"So, this is me," Paige said, looking out the passenger side window at the dorm looming before them.

"This is you," he echoed.

Paige turned to face Will.

"I had a—" they each started at the same time. They both stopped and laughed.

Will gestured for Paige to go first.

"I had a really good time."

"Me, too."

Paige stared into his eyes and melted. She seriously felt like her insides were turning to goo. Her heart sped up as she stared at the smile playing on his lips.

Will leaned forward and Paige froze. Was he going in for a kiss?

He continued to lean closer and finally she snapped to it and leaned forward to meet him. Their lips met and Paige savored the warmth of his mouth on hers. The kiss was short, but intense. Paige felt like she was soaring. She felt like she could run a marathon. She had no idea how she would possibly sleep tonight after experiencing this kiss.

They slowly parted, eyes opening and staring at each other. Paige felt a smile tugging at the corners of her mouth. It matched the one she saw on Will. They took their time, just staring at each other.

A horn honked somewhere outside their world, breaking the moment.

Will quickly opened the driver's door and climbed out, walking around to open her door.

He offered his hand and helped her out.

"I had a great time," she said.

"You already said that." He grinned at her.

She blushed and looked down at her boots.

"Will I see you tomorrow?" he asked her. "At the coffee shop?"

She nodded. "You can bet on it."

He walked her to the door, and as she made her way down the hall, she could feel his eyes still on her. She looked back before she turned the corner and waved. He waved back, then returned to his SUV and drove off.

Paige rounded the corner and let her body sink back against the wall. Wow.

~ * ~

~ *Present Day* ~

Paige's purse buzzed, bringing her back to the present.

"Crap!" She set it on the bed and began digging, pulling out eyeliner pencils, her wallet, old receipts and finally her phone.

New Text, the display read.

She quickly unlocked the screen, expecting the text to be from Will, asking where she was.

Hey, what's up? she read. It was not from Will, but rather his sister, Sara.

Running late to meet Will! she quickly texted back.

She threw the purse over her shoulder once more and decided her phone was best left in her hand.

3:46 the time on her phone warned her.

She rushed to the front door. She was now officially late.

~ * ~

~ *Seven Years Ago* ~

"You okay?" Will asked.

"Hmm?" Will's voice jarred her back to reality. She had been staring out the passenger door window of Will's SUV, lost in thought. Her attention turned to Will at his question.

He glanced over from the driver's seat and laughed. "You look worried."

"Me? Worried?" She gave a fake laugh. "Why would I be worried?"

"You shouldn't be. They don't bite and they're all excited to meet you."

"Great," she replied in a flat tone.

Will laughed again. "They're going to love you."

She returned her gaze to the world outside. Will reached out and gently squeezed her leg.

"You think so?" she asked softly.

"How could they not?"

She looked back at him once more. They were at a stoplight and he was looking at her seriously.

"I love you, and so will they."

She smiled at him and placed her hand on top of his.

It had been three months since their first date and she was as smitten with him as ever. Every morning they met for coffee. He always beat her, and therefore always paid. She would walk in, see him at the back corner table, and find her coffee sitting in front of him, ready to be consumed. When neither of them had too much homework or studying to do, they went to the movies, out to dinner, or spent time with one another's friends. Lauren had even been on a date or two with Will's roommate, Ben. They didn't click like Paige and Will did, but seemed okay to hang out together despite the failed attempt at romance. Will had even convinced Paige to attend one of the college football games. She wasn't a fan of sports, but being with Will made it an enjoyable experience. He had played Football in high school and patiently explained to her what was happening. None of it stuck, but she appreciated the gesture.

And now it was time to meet the parents. Paige knew she was being neurotic, but she couldn't help being nervous. She really, really liked Will. She was pretty sure she loved him. You only get one chance at first impressions and she didn't want to blow it. Not only was she meeting the parents, but she was also meeting both of Will's sisters.

She went over what she knew about the sisters in her head once more. Sara was a senior in high school and played Volleyball on her high school team. Rachel was older than Will and had just started a job at a big technology company based in the cities.

"We're here," Will announced.

The car pulled to a stop and Paige looked out at a modest two-story house in a nice suburb of the city. She took a deep breath and opened her door. Will rushed around to help her out. Despite the three months of dating, he was still ever the gentleman.

He held her hand, led her up the front steps and pushed open the front door.

"We're here!" he announced, stomping the snow from his boots on the mat inside the entryway. Paige followed suit and held her breath, wondering which of Will's family members would greet them first. Or would they all come running at once?

"Will!" A blonde blur rushed by and jumped on Will.

He laughed and took a step back, wrapping his arms around what could only be his younger sister.

"Whoa, Sara. Are you trying to kill me?"

She hopped down and took a step back, smiled at him, then turned her attention to Paige.

"Hi, I'm Sara," she said with a grin. She had her long hair pulled back in a high ponytail and was dressed in leggings and an orange school hoodie.

"Paige." She gave Sara a small smile.

"Shut the door, Will! You're letting in all the cold air." A man who could only be their father poked his head through the doorframe of the next room and scolded him.

"I'm trying to, but your daughter is assaulting me!"

Will turned around and closed the door behind them. He hung his coat on the hook in the foyer and took Paige's jacket, hanging it beside his.

"Ready?" he whispered close to her ear, planting a kiss on her cheek.

She just nodded and forced a smile. She was *so* not ready.

They slipped off their winter boots and Will led her into the kitchen where his mother was busy moving from counter to stove to microwave, back to counter, getting a big family meal ready. Will's dad was standing by, waiting for his wife to direct him to grab this, or chop that, or "move out of the way."

"Hi, Mom," Will greeted her, his hand still lightly grasping Paige's. She stood a step behind him, as if he could shield her from his well-meaning family.

"Will!" she cried, setting a pan on the stove and rushing over. Paige felt his hand let go of hers as his mom wrapped him in a hug. She sucked in a deep breath, her safety net gone.

Will's mom released him and looked to Paige, a genuine smile on her face. "And you must be Paige."

"Hi," she said softly. She cleared her throat. "Yes, I am. It's nice to meet you."

"We've heard so much about you. It's about time Will brought you around," she said, winking at Paige before turning back to the stove. "Dinner should be ready in about ten minutes. Rachel should be here any moment as well. Go make yourselves at home in the living room."

"You sure you don't need any help, Mom?"

"Your father and I can handle it. Besides, Sara has been dying to see you."

They left the kitchen and entered the living room. Will took a seat on the couch and pulled Paige down beside him, putting his arm around her shoulder and drawing her into him. Sara took that moment to make her way into the living room as well and plopped down on the other side of Will.

"Will, are you still coming to my Volleyball tournament next weekend?" she asked. "You promised, remember?"

"I will be there," he confirmed.

"Good." She looked to Paige. "You can come, too. If you want."

Paige looked to Will, who said, "What do you say? I know you're not a big fan of sports..."

Paige smiled at Sara. "I'd love to. I hear you're really good."

"Aw, Will, have you been talking about me?" Sara joked. "Only good things, right?"

Paige nodded. "All good. How long have you been playing volleyball?"

"I started in sixth grade. I tried soccer and basketball, but I was no good. Volleyball comes easy to me though, and my coach is really awesome."

"I hated playing volleyball in gym class, it always hurt my wrists."

"You were probably hitting it wrong. At the game, you'll have to watch my hand placement. It's fun."

"I'm here," a female voice came pouring into the room from the front entrance.

"Rachel!" Sara cried, jumping up from the couch and running to the front door.

"Breathe," Will whispered, patting her leg.

Paige sucked in a deep breath. "I am."

Sara returned to the room, a tall young woman with hair the same shade of brown as Will's on her heels.

"Hi, I'm Rachel," she introduced herself to Paige, sticking her hand out.

Paige returned the handshake and said, "Paige."

"Will, you didn't tell us she was so pretty," Rachel stage whispered to her little brother.

Paige blushed and caught Sara rolling her eyes.

"Soups on!" their dad called from the dining room.

Rachel flashed a dazzling smile at Paige and followed the sound of her father's voice, Sara quickly followed, leaving Paige and Will alone once more, if only for a moment.

"She seems nice."

Will jabbed her in the ribs. "They like you."

Paige knew there was still plenty of time left to screw things up.

He led her to the dining room where they each took their seats, passed around dishes of food, and proceeded to dig in. Coming from a family of three, Paige was a bit shocked at how loud and rowdy dinnertime could be when you threw in two more family members and a guest. Will's parents and sisters threw questions at her left and right; what was her major, what city did she grow up in, and so on and so forth. By the end of the meal, she felt like an honorary member of the family. She wasn't one hundred percent comfortable with them yet, but when Will's mom hugged her goodbye, she knew she could grow to really love his family.

"Told you," Will said as he slid into the driver's seat next to Paige.

She rolled her eyes in reply.

He laughed, knowing that she knew he'd been right.

~ * ~

~ *Present Day* ~

Paige rushed down the hall from her bedroom, knowing she was already late to meet Will. Considering she was pretty sure this was the end of them as a couple, she paused a moment to think about their relationship.

~ * ~

~ *Six Years Ago* ~

"How have you never been here?" Will demanded, completely flabbergasted by the bombshell Paige had dropped.

It was nearing the end of their first summer together and the pair was walking around the Minnesota State Fair, enjoying the last of summer before classes began once more.

Paige shrugged and grinned. "My parents were too busy working to take me. We usually made it to the Renaissance Festival or Valleyfair, though."

Will shook his head, still in disbelief.

"This is The Great Minnesota Get Together," he informed her. "We are starting a new tradition for you right here and now."

She shrugged. "Whatever you say."

"This place is amazing," he informed her. "I mean, where else can you eat ostrich on a stick?"

Paige wrinkled her nose. "I'm not sure I'd want to."

"Okay, what about mocha on a stick?"

Her ears perked up. "Did someone say coffee?"

Will laughed, knowing he had her there.

"Go on, tell me more," she said. "Give me more reasons to love this place, besides coffee on a stick, and the fact that you love it."

He sighed. "Where to start..." he trailed off, lost in thought. "There's Sweet Martha's, the best chocolate chip cookies around; concerts at the Grandstand—"

"Will?"

Will and Paige both turned to find the owner of the voice calling his name.

"Abby," Will said, acknowledging the leggy blonde who stood before them. "How are you?" he asked cordially.

"Great," Abby replied. "I'm just starting the medical program up in Duluth."

"Good for you."

"What about you?" she asked.

"I'm starting my last year in the business program at the Twin Cities campus."

"That's great," she responded, a dazzling smile on her pink lips.

Paige just stood there like an idiot. She hated social situations where she was the third wheel.

"This is Paige," Will said, putting his arm around her. "My girlfriend."

"Nice to meet you," Abby replied genuinely.

"You too," Paige responded, forcing a smile in return. "How do you guys know each other?"

"Oh, just high school," Will said nonchalantly.

Abby laughed. "Just high school?" She raised her eyebrow at him, then turned back to Paige. "Will and I dated from, what was it, Will? Sophomore year of high school through freshman year of college?"

"Something like that," Will replied.

Paige's jaw dropped. "Wow. That's a really long time."

"Everyone thought we were going to be together forever," Abby stated in a dreamy tone of voice.

"But clearly they were wrong." Will was starting to sound annoyed.

"Anyway," Abby continued. "I can't believe I ran into you. What a small world."

"Very," Will said.

"I've got to catch up with my friends, good seeing you."

"You, too."

"Bye," Paige called. "So..." she said to Will once Abby was lost in the crowd.

Will didn't respond, just kept his arm around her shoulder as they continued walking.

"Bad breakup?"

"Something like that," Will said.

"Care to elaborate?"

He squeezed her shoulder. "We just had different goals in life."

They walked in silence for another moment.

"Did you love her?" Paige asked tentatively.

"I thought I did then," he answered. "But now? I think it wasn't so much love, but that we were used to each other. We were too young to know what love is."

"So you were my age when you broke up?"

"Just about."

"Who broke up with who?" Paige was curious. Abby was beautiful, there was no way Will would have broken up with her. Would he?

"Do we have to talk about this?"

"Sorry..." she trailed off. She'd clearly hit a nerve.

He sighed. "Sorry," he apologized for being short with her. "She broke my heart. Let's leave it at that, okay?"

169

"Okay," Paige answered. She wrapped her arm around him and leaned against his side. In the almost year they had been dating, she had fallen head over heels in love with Will. She was determined not to break his heart as well.

~ * ~

~ *Present Day* ~

Paige had her hand on the doorknob, ready to rush to the coffee shop when she felt a furry critter brush against her legs. She looked down to find her cat, Gemma, rubbing against her ankles and meowing.

"Did I forget to feed you?"

She pulled her hand from the doorknob and walked into the kitchen to find Gemma's food dish empty. She quickly poured some dry food in the dish and gave the cat a loving stroke, feeling the vibration from the cats purring in her hand.

"Good kitty."

~ * ~

~ *Five Years Ago* ~

By her junior year of college, Paige had finally settled on a major in education; she wanted to teach elementary age kids. By her junior year she also had an off campus apartment with Lauren and a part time job at a daycare center, and she and Will were still going strong.

"Happy anniversary," Will said as she walked into the coffee shop and met him at their usual table for their morning coffee. He had graduated the previous spring and had landed a job in the city, so he was still able to attend their morning coffee date.

He stood up when she reached the table and gave her a kiss on the lips, his right arm wrapped lightly around her. She still tingled all over when they kissed, and though this kiss was brief, it left her frozen for a moment with a smile on her face.

"Happy anniversary," was her breathy reply as he released her from his embrace.

"I've got big plans for tonight," he informed her as they each took their seat, a suspicious grin crossing his face.

"Should I be worried?" she questioned.

He laughed. "No hints," was his playful response.

She wrinkled her nose and glared at him. "At least tell me how to dress."

"Casual."

"Casual? Our second anniversary is casual?"

He laughed again. "Trust me. And no more hints. Just dress casually and I'll be by your apartment as soon as I'm off work at five-thirty to pick you up."

"Okay..." she said skeptically, wondering what he possibly had planned for their big day.

She reached for her coffee and realized there was also a large blueberry muffin with delicious crumbly top sitting in front of her as well.

She gave Will a questioning look.

He grinned and shrugged. "Some people have cake to celebrate. I figure we can have a muffin."

She shook her head and smiled before cutting the muffin in half and giving one piece to Will, keeping the other for herself.

~ * ~

Classes seemed to drag on forever that day. All Paige could think about was the big surprise date Will had planned. She literally had no idea what he could possibly have in mind.

When she returned to her apartment after classes Lauren was already there.

"So," Lauren began, "big plans tonight?"

Paige narrowed her eyes at her. "I'm not sure."

Lauren giggled and turned her back on Paige, unsuccessfully trying to hide her grin.

"Oh my, God. You know!" Paige cried.

"I'm sure I have no idea what you could possibly be talking about."

"Uh huh, look me in the eye and say that."

"Fine. I know, but I can't tell you!"

"Who do you like more, Will or me?" Paige tried to guilt her friend.

"I love you both. I won't choose sides. I'm Switzerland and you'll find out soon enough."

Paige glared at her friend as Lauren wandered off to her room.

"What are you up to tonight?" Paige called out to Lauren's retreating back.

"Oh, nothing special. Just meeting a study group for my Chem class."

Paige wrinkled her nose. Lauren was super smart and was a biology major. Just the thought of science gave Paige a headache, but being roommates with Lauren was very convenient when Paige had taken her required math and science courses. She was pretty sure she never would have passed the classes without Lauren around to dumb it down for her. Not that Paige was dumb; she was just more into reading and writing than calculations and hypotheses.

"I'll probably be gone late," Lauren added. She'd exited her room with her book bag over her shoulder. Paige was surprised Lauren's bag wasn't bursting at the seams, and did not envy Lauren's evening of studying the periodic table or whatever it was they were doing in that study group.

"Okay, well...try to have fun I guess."

Lauren grinned. "You, too."

"Stop tormenting me!"

"Bye!" Lauren waggled her fingers playfully as she pulled open the door to their apartment and stepped out.

Paige checked the time on her phone. It was only five. She had at least half an hour until Will picked her up. She didn't need to change, since apparently they were being casual tonight. Not knowing the plan was nearly killing her though.

She grabbed a book and read until her phone chirped. She checked her text messages and found a new one from Will: *Just leaving work. Be there in ten. Can't wait to see you.*

She smiled and set down her book, double-checking her hair and makeup in the bathroom mirror.

Right on time, Will knocked on the apartment door before pulling it open. Paige had given him a copy of the key so he could let himself in and out as he pleased. She was grateful that Lauren didn't care.

"Hey beautiful, you ready?" he asked.

He was dressed in jeans and a t-shirt, his leather jacket protecting him from the brisk fall weather waiting for them outside.

She grinned and grabbed her coat from where she'd tossed it on the back of the couch when she came home from classes. "Absolutely." She gave him a quick peck on the lips, but was pulled into a deeper kiss when he circled his arms around her, holding her in place. He pulled his face back, looking into her eyes.

"Why the rush?" he whispered.

"Are you seriously going to make me wait any longer?" she asked. "You know I hate surprises. I haven't been able to think of anything else all day."

He quickly leaned in and kissed the tip of her nose. "You know I love you, right?"

Butterflies filled her stomach. "I love you, too," she softly replied.

"Okay. Let's go."

They locked up the apartment, took the stairs out the front door and got into Will's car. He wouldn't say anything about their destination and Paige spent the car ride guessing.

"Are we going to the fairgrounds?" she asked, as they passed a sign indicating the state fair grounds were off the next exit.

"Nope."

She frowned. "The zoo?" was her next guess, knowing that was also in the direction in which they were heading.

"Getting closer," he hedged.

She frowned. "I give up. Just tell me!"

"We're almost there."

Will refused to say another word, no matter how much she whined and pleaded, until they pulled up to a little hole in the wall building.

Paige frowned. "Where are we?"

Will grinned and quickly got out of the car. She waited while he walked around to open her door. She knew better than to try to get out of the car on her own. Will enjoyed the simple gesture of his affection and Paige was okay with that.

He escorted her to the building, opened the door and to her surprise, discovered they were at the animal shelter.

"What are we doing here?" she asked.

"Happy anniversary, I know you miss having a pet, so...pick one."

"What?" Paige was completely taken aback.

"Seriously. You can choose any one you want."

"What about Lauren? I don't even know if she's okay with a pet being in the apartment."

"Don't worry. I asked her. She has no problem, so long as you or I pay the pet fee at the apartment. And clean up after it."

Paige broke into a grin and threw her arms around Will, pulling his head down to give him a kiss.

"Thank you," she whispered.

"You're welcome," he whispered back. "Now let's go find us a pet."

She removed her arms and they explored the shelter. With her schedule busy with college and her job at the daycare, and Will's busy work schedule, a dog was out.

But a cat was perfect. They admired the tiny kittens, but ultimately Paige fell in love with a three-year-old cat named Gemma. She was a gray tabby and walked right up to Paige, rubbing her body against Paige's legs.

"Gemma is a real sweetheart," the girl working at the shelter told them. "She was surrendered by a couple who moved overseas for work and weren't able to bring her with. She's great with other pets and kids, too. If I didn't have so many pets already I'd have loved to bring her home myself."

"What do you think?" Paige asked Will.

He smiled at her. "What do *you* think?"

"I think she's perfect."

"We'll take her," Will announced as Paige continued to stroke Gemma's silky fur.

They filled out the adoption paperwork, Will paid the fees and Gemma came home in a cardboard box—along with a bag of cat essentials.

Upon arriving back at Paige's place, Gemma cautiously exited her box and began exploring the apartment. Paige and Will snuggled on the couch and watched her.

"Thanks, Will," Paige said, turning her face up to look at him. "She's perfect."

"I'm glad," he replied, lowering his face to gently kiss her lips.

They were interrupted by a loud grumbling coming from her stomach. Paige laughed. "Sorry. I didn't eat. I assumed we were getting dinner."

"I texted in an order. It should be here any minute. Surprise."

"You really are full of surprises tonight."

His lips met hers once more and stayed in place until dinner arrived some time later.

~ * ~

~ *Present Day* ~

With Gemma fed, Paige was out of reasons to delay. It was now 3:49. Will was probably planning on breaking up with her due to her inability to arrive *anywhere* on time. She rushed out the door, locking it behind her.

The time was 3:50 when she got into the car and started the engine. The radio greeted her with a song she hadn't heard since the first really big fight she and Will had experienced. She quickly switched the station and continued on her way.

~ * ~

~ *Three Years Ago* ~

Paige rested her head on Will's chest as he held her lightly in his arms, swaying to the music on the dance floor. She breathed a sigh, enjoying the moment. The air around them hummed with romance.

The song ended and they gently broke apart as a fast dance track began playing. Will led her back to their table for a break.

Paige watched the wedding guests around them, some dancing, others chatting; all having a great time.

"Are we having fun?"

Paige turned to find Rachel behind them, one hand on each of their shoulders. It was her wedding day and she looked absolutely glowing in her white gown and veil.

Paige nodded and Will yelled above the music, "Absolutely! How about you?"

She beamed. "Best day ever!" she cried. "When are you two going to finally get hitched?"

Will laughed. Paige froze.

Was she serious? Sure she and Will had been together for four years, but she was *not* ready for marriage. Was he ready for that? Oh God, what if Rachel knew something she didn't. Was Will planning on proposing? They didn't even live together yet. Did she *want* to live with him?

"You should be focusing on your big day, Rach, instead of ours," Will said with a laugh.

She stuck her tongue out at her brother. "I have to go mingle!"

Paige watched her retreating back.

Will placed his arm around her shoulder and pulled her close. She felt stiff as a board.

"You okay?" he asked, leaning down to speak into her ear. His breath tickled her in a good way, sending goose bumps down her arms.

She nodded.

"Good," he said before planting a kiss on the side of her head. "Love you."

She nodded again.

She felt awkward the rest of the night, but tried her best to hide it. Why was she such a spaz? Rachel was the one bringing up marriage, not Will. She shouldn't freak out until Will actually proposed. *If* he proposed. Did she want him to propose? Maybe. In the future. But not now.

When the reception was winding down, they said goodbye to the family and headed out to Will's car. He opened the door and helped her in before returning to the driver's seat.

Instead of starting the car, he turned to her.

"I've been thinking," he said.

Oh, God. Here it comes.

She closed her eyes in anticipation.

"With Lauren moving away for grad school, I was thinking maybe we could get a place together."

Huh? That wasn't a wedding proposal. But living together? That was almost as big of a step. She wasn't ready for that. No way.

"No," Paige whispered.

"No?" he asked.

Paige nodded.

"Why?" he asked, sounding a little hurt.

"I don't think I'm ready for that."

"Why not?" Will asked.

"Because I'm only twenty-two," she answered.

"So what?" he demanded, his hands clenching the steering wheel of the car in frustration.

"I'm not ready!" she all but yelled, the emotions she had been bottling up since Rachel's comment finally bursting forth.

"Paige. We've been together four years now. How long is long enough?"

"I don't know." Paige stared out the window in a sorry attempt to avoid the matter at hand. "Just drive."

Will turned the key in the ignition and pulled out of the lot. They drove in silence for a few minutes before he started up again.

"It makes logical sense. You're graduating in a couple of months. Lauren is moving away for grad school. I don't understand why you won't move in with me."

"I'm just not ready," she whispered.

"Do you want to break up?" he demanded.

"What?" she cried, turning back to face him. "No! Why would I want to break up?"

"I don't know! It just makes sense for a couple that has been dating as long as we have to move in together, and you won't even entertain the idea. It makes me think you don't want to be with me anymore."

She and Will had the dream relationship. Nearly every morning they shared their coffee dates, most evenings they spent together either alone or with friends. Sometimes she slept at his apartment, other times he slept at hers. But when his sister Rachel brought up the topic of Will and Paige getting married, her brain went into overdrive and she sort of freaked out. Her head was spinning. She was too young to start thinking about marriage. She started questioning dating the same guy for so long, starting at such a young age. She didn't want to break up, but the thought of progressing the relationship? She wasn't sure she was ready for that. She wanted things to stay exactly as they were.

"I'm just not ready."

"I don't know what that means!" he yelled.

"Watch out!" Paige screamed.

Too late.

In his anger and frustration, distracted by the argument, Will failed to notice the brake lights on the car in front of theirs. Paige squeezed her eyes shut and threw her hands up to shield herself from the impact.

The next thing she knew, her seatbelt was jerking her back and the car came to a shuttering halt. Her eyes flew open and she looked over to see Will with his head against the steering wheel.

"Will!" she yelled, reaching over and shaking his arm. "Will!"

"Paige?" he groaned, lifting his head up and turning to her. "You okay?" He sounded groggy.

"Oh, God. You're bleeding!" She was frantic. He had a nasty gash on his forehead from the impact. She looked around the cab of the car, searching for *what* she didn't know. She was in panic mode. "9-1-1. We need to call 9-1-1!"

There was an urgent knock on Will's window and Paige's eyes searched for the source.

Will slowly reached forward and pressed the button to roll down the window.

"Are you okay, man?"

"I think so..." Will trailed off. "I didn't see...too late..."

"Call 9-1-1," Paige urged the man at the window.

"Cops are on the way."

"Were you in the other car?" Paige asked. It suddenly dawned on her that they were not the only ones impacted by the accident.

"No, but they're fine. Just a bent bumper. You guys took the worst of it."

"I need to…" Will started to say, but didn't finish. He reached for his door handle.

"Stay there. Cops are on the way with an ambulance."

"Don't need an ambulance." He looked to Paige again. "Right?"

"Will, you need the ambulance. I think you hit your head harder than you realize."

"I'm fine," Will insisted.

"No. You're not. You can't even complete a sentence. Stay put until the cops and ambulance get here."

The man continued to block the driver's door so Will had no choice but to stay put, for which Paige was grateful.

Finally, the cops and ambulance arrived. They loaded Will into the back while Paige talked to the officer and explained what happened from her perspective. They let her into the ambulance with Will, leaving the car to be towed to a local repair shop.

Once at the hospital, Will was diagnosed with a concussion and was to be kept overnight for observation. Paige insisted she was fine but they examined her as well and she was given the all clear. "Will," she whispered, lying next to him on his hospital bed.

"Mmm?" he replied. He was lying back with his eyes shut, but she knew he was awake.

"I'm sorry," she whispered.

"No, I'm sorry," he whispered in return.

"You really scared me."

"It wasn't intentional."

"I know." There was a long pause. "Will?"

"Mmm?"

"I was wrong."

"What?" He turned his face to her and opened his eyes.

"I was scared to move forward with *us*. For a while there, between the crash and the hospital, I didn't know if you were really going to be okay."

"Of course I'm going to be okay. It was a minor traffic accident."

"You hit your head pretty hard."

"I'm fine." He turned his head back, his eyes falling closed again as his head rested on the pillow.

"Will?"

"Mmm?"

"I'll do it," she stated.

"What?"

"I'll move in with you."

He smiled. "My plan worked," he joked.

Paige punched him lightly in the arm, then snuggled up next to him again. From the moment of the impact, she couldn't imagine her life without him in it. She knew now that she was ready to take this next step. She was going to move in with Will.

She stayed with him as long as the hospital would allow, before calling Lauren to come pick her up. Will's family had been called by the hospital upon him being admitted. They had spoken with Paige, who had assured them that Will was going to be okay. They were on their way, as well.

~ * ~

~ *Present Day* ~

Now Paige sat behind the wheel of her car, staring at the coffee shop. It was well past the time she'd agreed to meet Will, but she couldn't bring herself to move just yet. She wasn't ready to face the inevitable.

Maybe he's not breaking up with me, she thought in an effort to convince herself to get out of the car.

~ * ~

~ *One Month Ago* ~

"Oh, look, Ben is getting married," Paige said. She was lying across the couch in the apartment she shared with Will, opening the day's mail, her feet resting in his lap.

"Good for him," came Will's nonchalant reply, his gaze never straying

179

from the game on TV.

Paige frowned at the shimmery white paper in her hands. Ben had been Will's college roommate and unless she was mistaken, he had only been dating his fiancée about eighteen months.

Eighteen months. Not even two years. She'd been with Will for going on seven years. Sure she'd freaked out a bit about the idea of moving in together, but that had been three years ago. Shortly after the car accident, she and Lauren had given up the lease on their apartment and she had moved into his. Sure, they had their share of arguments over dirty laundry left on the bathroom floor and someone leaving only a few drops of milk left in the carton in the fridge, but they were happy.

"Eighteen months, right?" Paige asked.

"Hmm?" he replied, his eyes still glued to the screen.

Paige sighed and sat up, moving to the center of the couch and leaning against him.

"Ben and his fiancée," she clarified. "They've been together about eighteen months, right?"

"Huh? I dunno. Something like that."

Paige foraged on. "That seems like such a short time to be getting married already."

"I guess."

"I mean, how long do you think a couple should date before they get married?"

Will glanced at his phone. "Sorry, babe, I'm late."

"Late for what?"

"Just a guys thing. I must have forgotten to tell you. I'll be back later." He gave her a peck on the cheek and bolted out the front door.

Paige's heart sank.

What is going on with him? she wondered. He'd been a little short on conversation the last couple of weeks, but never had he walked out in the middle of a conversation with her. *This conversation* was *pretty one sided*, she reflected.

Was Will's heart just not in it anymore? Was he delaying the inevitable? A break up?

~ * ~

~ *Present Day* ~

Taking a deep breath, she opened the door and stepped out of her car. The scent of the coffee beans hit her senses and she couldn't help but smile. The scent of coffee always reminded her of Will.

She shut her car door, braced herself, and marched forward to the front door.

Swinging the door open her eyes automatically fell on Will, seated at their usual table in the back with two mugs of coffee before him. He stood upon seeing her and met her halfway to the table.

"You made it," he said, kissing her softly on the lips before guiding her back to their table.

"Of course I did," she said as lightly as she could. "Why wouldn't I?"

"Well, you were running even later than usual," he teased.

She rolled her eyes. All throughout their seven-year relationship, Will had teased her about her inability to arrive anywhere on time. When she told him she'd decided she wanted to be a teacher he had laughed, then apologized. When she asked what was so funny he had simply put on his most charming smile and asked, "Can teachers get detention for being tardy?"

"I had to feed the cat," she stated. That was part of the reason. He didn't need to know she was dragging her feet.

"Ah," he replied, relaxing back in his seat. "Gemma wouldn't let you out the door."

"You know how she is. Sweet as can be, but won't let you out the door if her dish isn't full."

"Well, thanks for not letting our girl starve."

"I wouldn't dream of it."

There was an awkward silence.

"Will—" Paige began, just as Will began to speak.

They laughed.

"You go," Paige said, bracing herself for the inevitable.

"Okay." Will took a deep breath. "Paige."

"Yes?" she said meekly.

"I was hoping we could talk about us."

Here it was. She sucked in a breath, preparing for the blow, and nodded.

"Seven years is a long time to be with one person. I mean, I feel like I've known you my entire life. You're basically my best friend."

Here it comes. He just wants to be friends.

"Paige," he continued. He raised his right hand and looked somewhere behind her. Paige glanced around and saw a barista coming to the table with a plate. She set the plate in front of Will, who blocked whatever it was with his hand. That was odd.

"Paige, I don't want to be your boyfriend anymore," Will said in a rush.

Her heart stopped. She knew this was coming, but she had desperately hoped she was wrong, that he wasn't breaking up with her. But here it was. He didn't want to be her boyfriend anymore.

"What I mean is," he continued, "Paige..." He pushed the plate toward her. She looked down to see a large blueberry muffin. Stuffed in the middle, sparkling under the dim lighting, was a diamond ring. When she looked back at Will, she found he was down on one knee beside her. "Will you let me be your husband?"

Paige was stunned. Her day had certainly done a one eighty from what she had expected. From thinking he was going to break up with her, to receiving a marriage proposal. Her mouth opened but nothing came out. She blinked rapidly. Her eyes were starting to burn.

"Breathe," he whispered.

Paige sucked in a deep breath and looked from the muffin to Will and back again.

"This is the part where you say yes," he said softly.

Paige stared at the slight curvature of his lips as he smiled at her. Yes? Of course she would marry him.

"Paige?" The smile faltered. "Say something?"

Oops. She hadn't said it out loud yet.

"I thought you were breaking up with me!" she blurted. Okay, that hadn't been what she meant to say.

"What?" Will asked, leaning back in surprise, confusion plastered all over his face.

She laughed. "Yes," she whispered. "Of course, yes." The burning in her eyes subsided as she felt a tiny droplet of water leak from each eye. She laughed as Will broke into a grin. He reached over and pulled the ring from the muffin. Wiping the crumbs from the band, he gently took her hand. She watched as he slid it onto her left ring finger. It was a little sticky from the blueberry, but she didn't mind.

"For a second there I thought you were going to say no," he said, the relief evident in his voice.

"I thought so, too," came a voice from behind her. She spun around to see Will's sister Sara wearing a huge grin, flanked by an equally gleeful Lauren and Rachel.

She turned back to Will who was still kneeling before her, his hand still clasped around hers. He shrugged and said, "I was pretty sure you'd say yes. I didn't want to wait to share the good news."

Paige leaned forward and kissed her future husband on the lips.

THE END

About the Author

Caroline Andrus was born and raised in the St. Paul suburbs where she now lives with her husband, two daughters, and Henry McCoy—her cat, who is actually a wild cougar trapped in a housecat's body.

She divides her time between writing, Facebook, designing, and managing her household. In her spare time, she enjoys reading, rocking out to the radio, and gardening (but only in the hot summer months.)

She is passionate about both reading and writing teen fiction, and is pretty sure she will forever be eighteen at heart.

Connect with Caroline at:
Website: www.CarolineAndrus.com
Facebook: www.facebook.com/CarolineAndrusDesigns
My twitter is @FaerieTears

CAPPUCCINO DREAMING

By

Louise Redmann

"For my husband, who never stopped believing in me."

I walked up the narrow wooden stairwell of the coffee house, hoping the coffee would kickstart a new life. My old had died in spectacular fashion ten minutes ago. The precariously full cappuccino on the tray threatened to slosh over the side, and I strove to control my trembling hands. Today was an excellent contender for worst day of my life, definitely above being picked on in school for wearing thick glasses with huge rims or knocking an open bottle of organic cleaner into my boss's lap.

My boyfriend had booked a table in the Peacock for Saturday night. *The Peacock.* When he told me, I was so excited. This restaurant was top of my list for romantic dates. Not any more. Lying, faithless...a hundred epithets crowded my mind, but I decided he wasn't worth the headspace.

A man in a suit rushed down the stairs, as though late for an important meeting. The bag containing my new, expensive black shift swung from my left wrist and unbalanced the tray. I attempted to right it, but instead I stepped on the hem of my skirt and fell up the stairs. The cup clattered to the floor and hot coffee gushed down, drenching my skirt and everyone behind me. Shrieks and curses erupted, depending on whether the drenchee was male or female. I froze in my awkward position on the steps, debating whether to run up and hide in the corner, or down the stairs and out the door.

Laughter burst out from somewhere above my head. Not the unkind laughter that had erupted farther down, but more of a sympathetic amusement, if there is such a thing.

His eyes, brown as the sprinkles on my cappuccino, seemed lit by a soul who had known only joy and laughter. In contrast, my own freshly wounded soul lay exposed, its bleakness mirroring the grey drabness of the wall beside me. I fumbled to put the empty coffee cup back on the tray, grateful when my chestnut hair screened my heated face.

My life with Calum flashed as an ugly truth before me. I had been used and discarded. He would not propose on Saturday night; he was going to break up with me. I blinked hard. How cruel, to be confronted with such a truth while prone on the floor. The muttering on the stairs grew louder.

"Here, grab my hand."

He was still there, that man who had sliced me open with one smile. I glimpsed another self—one vibrant and exuberant—something I had never been with Calum. I had been more anxious to please than concerned about my own identity. My life with him appeared dull, colorless now, like a watercolour compared to a vivid oil canvas. Who was I?

My heart pounded slowly; its every beat magnified in my ear as it told me what would happen if I touched him. Somehow, I knew my soul, my hitherto dormant soul, would awaken. I didn't want to feel that power, that connection; yet I craved it, needed it.

I reached out. His hand enclosed mine and heat flowed into me. At his audacious grin, I felt something break up inside me. The crack was loud, like ice in a thaw. I thought he must have heard, since he turned on the stair and surveyed me thoughtfully for what seemed like a minute but must have only been three or four seconds.

He guided me to a seat near the window. "I'll be back in a minute."

I dropped my bags on the floor and sank into the faux-leather armchair, studying those around me to see if anyone was pointing and staring, hiding sniggers behind their hands. Now, camouflaged amongst coffee-drinkers self-absorbed in their own groupings, I relaxed. And felt the wetness against my thighs.

Ugh, how delightful. By the time he returned, I would smell of stale milk and coffee. I glanced at the bag containing my new dress. Should I race to the restroom and switch clothes? I would have done that in a heartbeat for Calum, but something made me hesitate. For once, I wanted to be accepted for who I was, rather than what I looked or smelled like. I dug in my purse for the small bottle of perfume I carried around to spritz whenever I met Calum after work. Empty. I shook it and squirted. Nothing. Oh, well. Maybe I could persuade him I was trying out a new perfume.

Using a tissue, I dabbed at my skirt. Fortunately, it was black, so any stains wouldn't show. I had unknowingly spilled coffee on tight white trousers once, and then conducted a presentation of our latest organic cleaning product with a mocha stain on my right inner thigh. Throughout the demonstration, I thought everyone was staring at my crotch. I kept my body turned sideways as much as possible, either craning my neck around in an awkward, ungainly manner, or looking like I was desperate for the toilet. Better a stain than a hole, though.

With a sigh, I scrunched the tissue, left it on an empty, adjacent table and turned toward the window. It had mucky fingerprints until about half way up the pane. Doubtless, some young child had eaten his marshmallow in slow bites, the foamy sweet reduced in hot hands to a sticky mess painted onto the glass.

The sidewalks were slowly emptying. Shops would close in the next half hour. The gold statue standing on a box looked to be staying the night. A little girl put money in the tin, and then squealed when the statue bent and offered his hand in a show of gratitude. Shadows lengthened to span the road. Still sunny. Odd, I could have sworn a massive, thunderous cloud had engulfed the sky when I entered the coffee house.

The cream stone of the eleventh century cathedral gleamed like marble in the early March sunshine. I had often fantasized about being married to Calum in that splendid church. The lump in my throat increased.

"I got you another coffee to replace the one you lost." He set the cappuccinos on the table, together with a collection of pastel-coloured sugar packets and several napkins.

Something inside me clenched. Feeling cared for was not something I had often experienced with Calum. It was usually the other way around. After the two years spent catering to his every need and making myself indispensable, I had been convinced the posh restaurant meant he'd realized how much he needed me. Ha. How foolish I'd been. I drew the coffee nearer and forced my lips into a half smile. "That's very kind of you."

"Kindness, pshaw. Call it curiosity." He removed his caramel leather jacket and slung it over the back of the chair.

I dragged my gaze from his jeans-clad backside and feigned interest in the coffee. The leaf emblem was exquisitely sifted in cocoa. It seemed a shame to stick my spoon in. I did, though. I scooped up a mountain of froth, sprinkled some sugar on it and stuck it in my mouth.

My face heated at his raised eyebrow. To cover my embarrassment, I waved the bundle of napkins. "Are you worried I might spill coffee on you, too?"

He took a swallow of his cappuccino and wiped a foam moustache from his upper lip. "Spilling one coffee in a day is misfortunate. Spilling two...well, suffice to say, I would run very far, very fast. If you're clumsy with coffee, what will you do with my heart?" He placed his hand over his chest and grimaced as though in pain.

"I think your heart is safe. It's on the other side of your chest."

"You know," he said, cocking his head, "I am not at all sure my heart is safe from you."

Confused and a little flustered, I emptied the sachet of sugar into my coffee. Some spilled over the side, and I rolled my eyes at his stifled chuckle. His humour and openness appealed to me after two years of being told I was clumsy. He was a bit older than me, I estimated around thirty-five. Mahogany hair cut short, beginnings of a shadow along his chin. Perhaps—

"Well, I can see why you tripped," he said, wagging a finger. "Distraction."

I slurped the coffee, instead of sipping it delicately as I had intended. "I beg your pardon?" Although I understood full well what he referred to, I wanted him to explain, to talk more. His full-bodied voice slid past my ears like melted chocolate down my throat. Part of me wanted to slouch in the chair, close my eyes and just listen—like I did with a Jeremy Irons movie. Or Donald Sutherland. Mmm.

"You are a daydreamer," he pronounced. "You were fantasising about meeting a fabulously good-looking man with short brown hair and blue jeans. Admit it."

I stirred more sugar into the coffee and licked the cocoa-infused froth from the spoon. "I was thinking about Donald Sutherland, actually."

His eyes widened slightly, and I ducked my head to conceal my smile.

"Sure you don't mean Keifer?"

"Oh, I'm sure. I saw Keifer on Top Gear the other day. The voice is definitely reminiscent of the great man but …" I threw the spoon at the tray. It landed half on and half off. "Nope. Didn't do it for me."

He poked the spoon back on to the tray, face gloomy. "And instead of meeting Donald here, you met me."

His gaze dipped to my lips, and a thrill travelled through my body. It had been a long time since Calum had looked at me in that way. Had he ever looked at me like that? I rubbed the bare skin on the underside of my ring finger. "I was not looking for Donald, but I am glad to have met you."

I liked this guy. He made me laugh, something Calum rarely did; he made a good sparring partner, something Calum rarely did.

"You're lonely."

"Will you stop it?" He had called me lonely and distracted. A lonely daydreamer. Was I anything more? I fiddled with the wet patch on my skirt, uncomfortable at how accurately he had read me when, until moments ago, I had not known myself.

He raised his hands. "I apologise. Some people I read more easily than others. Being a doctor, you learn to tell who is disguising the pain and who is exaggerating. When I saw you on the stairs, you looked lonely to me. Easily spooked. I knew you weren't meeting anybody."

I pressed my lips together. "I'm not lonely. I like coming here by myself, listening to conversations. It's a moment of peace in an otherwise talky day."

"Eavesdropper." His eyes glinted. "I bet you hate the phone."

I despised the phone. "I like to look at someone when I'm talking to them. If we're on the phone, how can I tell if they're pretending to stick two fingers down their throat or making faces?"

He tried to look shocked and grin at the same time. It produced an odd, contorted expression on his face. "I cannot imagine you knowing anybody like that."

I knew too many. How strange that I had never seen it until now. "Sometimes I long for deeper conversations, you know? With some people, it's so hard to connect, and forcing a conversation is like wading through treacle. It's like trying to orgasm but not able to get to the peak. Repeatedly. Over and over." I glanced at him. His eyebrows were so far up his forehead they looked like they might pop off. "I guess a guy like you wouldn't know that kind of frustration."

Rather shocked that such words had come from my mouth, and that I had been talking about Calum, I lifted the cup and sipped. Today was a day of revelations, each one more astonishing than the last. The aroma of coffee filled my nose, stimulating my laggard memory. I had known and fantasised about Calum for years, always at a distance. I never felt worthy enough to join his group of adoring females. One of our first dates had been walking along the beach in the evening. I had felt rich, beautiful; Calum had chosen me. And then he had refused to buy me an ice cream because he feared it might ruin my figure. I had always erred towards the plumper side, and to hear him say he loved my figure boosted my self-esteem. Except, he had not been saying he loved it; he had been telling me to lose weight. I clacked the cup back down. Part of me wanted to go back outside and find the pompous, rude—

"A girl like you shouldn't know that frustration either."

Frustration? What was he talking about? Oh yes. I squirmed in the chair. "What do you know about girls like me?"

He rubbed his chin slowly with a forefinger. "Clearly not enough. I assumed you to be lonely, and now I realise I may have got it wrong."

But he hadn't. Now I realised how lonely I was, how starved for harmonious company I had become. Pride forbade me to acknowledge this to him. "You do not seem to be the lonely type," I said. "You claim I must be, yet if you have never been lonely, how can you perceive it or understand it in others?"

He tipped his cup to me. "Brava. But now you are making assumptions about me. What makes you think I have never been lonely?"

"You are very free with your opinions, whether you laugh them, speak them or look them." He did not react. I searched his eyes for a clue. Nothing, so I continued, "I would think such freedom leads inevitably to loneliness or popularity. Since you are very confident in expressing your opinions to a total stranger, I assume that you must be popular, not lonely."

"Have you never heard how you can be lonely in a crowd?" He pressed his finger into his cheek. The skin indented and an urge to kiss the dimple flooded me. I wrenched my gaze away, afraid he would see and know. When I had gained control of my emotions, I chanced another look. He was scooping up the remains of the foam in his cup, so either he had noticed my discomfort and was being gentlemanly in not showing it, or he was oblivious. I hoped the latter. There was silence between us for some moments and to prolong the conversation, I asked, "So, are you?"

"What, popular?" He gestured around. "Do you see me with a large company of people? Do you see me with even one other person?"

"No," I said, "but they may have left before you."

He heaved a sigh. "Very well. A friend of mine had just left, much to my relief. She wanted me to go on a blind date with an old school friend of hers. Badger, badger, badger. So I agreed just to keep the peace."

Something caught in my throat. I would have loved to go on a blind date with this guy. Maybe I should join an online dating website. "A blind date sounds like fun. What are you grinning at?"

"You. Your face is so expressive. First, you frowned, then you shrugged, then you stuck your lower lip out in a pout. I don't need to ask what you were thinking."

"Why don't you tell me if you're so clever, and I will tell you if you were right."

"Ha, I'm not going to fall for that one. No matter what I say, or how bang on I might be, you will tell me how way out I am, how erroneously wrong I was, how I've misjudged you."

I sucked my lips in between my teeth and then released them again. "Let's agree you cannot possibly know what I was thinking. So, are you going on the date?"

"Of course. Why not?" He ran a hand over his close-cropped hair. "It should be an interesting evening." That naughty grin again. "If you give me your phone number, I will let you know how I got on."

I gave him a steely look. "Earlier, you informed me that I didn't like the phone."

"I thought you might like to answer my calls." He dismissed the comment with a wave of his hand. "If not, then I will text you. Come on, write the number on a napkin." He rummaged around for a clean one and handed it to me.

I screwed it up and flicked it towards him. The paper ball skidded over the edge of the table. He caught it and unfolded it, making a great show of surprise. "You didn't write your number. I must conclude either you do not possess a phone, something I find incomprehensible in today's age, or you find me repulsive. Since the thought that I might be repulsive to you scares me to death, I must think you have no phone. Oh, I have it." He clapped a hand to his forehead. "You, yourself, do not possess a phone. You have a company phone!" He flopped in his chair with relief and threw the napkin at me again. It landed in my coffee with a gentle splosh. "Looks like I have to buy you yet another coffee."

The gleam in his eyes dared me to refuse. Another coffee. I had always loved the smell far more than the taste, and actually preferred tea. It was the sociality of coffee I enjoyed, the feeling of belonging, of taking part in a familiar ritual with strangers who were not so strange, after all. Gleefully, I said, "I don't like coffee."

Laughter erupted again. "Of course you don't. Well, fortunately for you and me, they don't just serve coffee here."

Our gazes met and held. Something sparked in the air between us. Warmth diffused through my entire body. I tingled in places I hadn't tingled for a long time. For a moment, my soul brushed his. Panicked at the connection, floored by how alive I had felt for that split second, I wrenched away. What would happen when we left this coffee house, would that be it? Would I spend my life wondering where he was, an awful "what if" haunting me?

"It's getting dark." He nodded at the window. "I would never normally spend so long here, especially on a Thursday. I should have had four coffees in all this time, yet I've had one. Huh." He fixed me with a penetrating stare. "I'd like to drink coffee with you again."

My lips felt dry. I would drink any number of coffees with him. Fling myself at him. Do whatever he wanted. Here was a guy that seemed to want to spend time with me. Except ... "Where are you going on the date?"

The brown eyes turned mournful. "The Robin Hood. I don't usually have dinner as a first date; the idea of spending a couple of hours with someone hideous or boring terrifies me, but my friend–God Bless Her Soul–had already booked the table."

"Is that her name? God Bless Her Soul?" He shot me a disgusted look and I chuckled. "You could always talk about yourself." Calum did that very well. I used to find him charming but lately had become bored. Could it be that agreeable people talked very little about themselves, while the less agreeable talked as though they found themselves of unending fascination? I speculated as to what that meant, and found myself desperate to talk it over with this man I had fatefully bumped into.

"Talk about myself? How ghastly." He shuddered. "I find other people far more interesting. Like you." He peered at me." I'm trying to work out what's lurking in the depths of your sea-green eyes."

193

"I thought you could read my every expression."

"Expressions, yes. Eyes, no. Your eyes hide and reveal at the same time." As if to make a point, he leaned across the table and peered at me. "Part of me is tempted to come around there and kiss you on those pouty lips, just to see how you react."

I pretended not to have heard. I had no idea what to say to that. Well, I had a very good idea of what to say, but this was not the time or the place. He kept his gaze on me as I fiddled with my hair. It needed another cut, the layers were growing out.

Kiss, he'd said. This time I could not prevent the blush from rooting up my neck and all over my face. I must look like a stop sign. The need to escape and scrabble my thoughts back into line made me blurt, "Maybe we could meet here again next week. You could tell me all about the date, but I will buy the coffee."

He winked. "It's a date. Look at that, two dates in one week! I must be popular, after all."

We rose from our seats in unison. He was a good head taller. I imagined walking down the road with him, tucked into his shoulder. The yearning slammed into me so hard I fought for breath. Dizzy, I bent to grab my bag off the floor and as I came back up, I collided with his body.

He clasped me to him in a brief hug. "Thank you for spilling your coffee. You made my day." Then he bounded down the stairs, out of my sight. I sank into the chair for a few minutes and closed my eyes.

~ * ~

Calum rang me that evening, but I didn't answer. The third time, I flipped the phone onto the floor, tempted to crush it into the carpet. He rang all throughout the next day, and then the calls became more sporadic until they finally stopped. He appeared on my doorstep early Wednesday evening.

"Why don't you answer my calls?"

Calum smelled good. He always smelled good. For a moment, I weakened. He pushed past me and into my tiny kitchen. I watched him poke around my preparations, fascinated at how differently I saw him. In one single day, last Thursday, Calum had morphed from handsome hunk to egotist. How had I not seen this before?

"You cooking dinner for me, babe? Lasagne? You know I hate that."

My previous self would have mumbled an apology, scooped out the meat sauce into a pan and turned it into a ragout pasta sauce. I was not that person anymore. "I am not making dinner for you." I smiled sweetly. "I will not make dinner for you ever again."

He slammed his hand on the counter. "What the hell's the matter with you? I had to cancel the table at the Peacock because you refused to answer my calls, and now you're making dinner I hate."

I smiled. "I wasn't making dinner for you, and I'm quite sure the table didn't go to waste. I expect you took your pregnant girlfriend."

His mouth opened and closed like a fish.

"You're bleeding." I nodded towards his finger.

"Damn. Your stupid knives." He examined the cut. "You'll have to take me to the ER. I can't drive like this, and it looks like I need several stitches. This is all your fault."

I heaved a sigh, covered the half-assembled lasagna, and drove him to the ER. And saw *him*. The guy from the coffee house.

Horrified, I buried my head in the magazine. He could not see me here. Not with Calum. The doors opened, and I mumbled something about the loo and dashed out the entrance, almost colliding with a girl in a wheelchair.

I sat in the car shaking. My heart pounded so erratically, I thought I'd have a heart attack.

~ * ~

That night I barely slept. I dropped my head onto the pillow exhausted, and all I could think about was *him*. Funny how something, or someone, can be so real in one part of your life, yet when you are operating in another part of your life, to see that same person comes as a shock. Like a ghost.

Thoughts of him had consumed my waking moments and invaded my dreams. Sometimes I indulged the fantasies; other times, I pushed them so far I all but forgot him. When I awoke the following morning, I spent twice as long in the shower and agonised for an hour over what I should wear. I wanted to look sexy, yet not look as though I made an effort. Something suitable for work. Not the black skirt. To slip once would be misfortunate, to slip twice…well, as he had said, he would run far. Besides, I couldn't wear it. *I hadn't wanted to wash it.*

195

Since my early teens, if a good-looking boy had winked at me or given me a half-smile, I had instantly put him on a pedestal and worshipped him from afar. If one of these guys actually spoke to me, I'd turn into a puddle of mumbly goo.

I made a face at myself in the mirror. The mistake was putting Calum on a pedestal, thinking he could do no wrong. So enchanted by his apparent acceptance of me, of my very being, I had been blind to the real Calum.

The eyeliner smudged. Ugh, beautiful. Great big smear on my upper eyelid. Well, at least it matched the twin pools of sleeplessness beneath my eyes. I cleaned my eyelid and then took care with the new mascara I had bought. It was supposed to give the effect of false lashes. Not that I had ever worn false lashes. I did have some idea of what the mascara should do for my woefully short lashes, but it took three layers before I was even slightly impressed.

About to add a fourth coating, I paused, hand arrested in mid-air. I wasn't preparing myself for Calum, but for a guy who had seen me at my hellishly-embarrassed, coffee-splattered worst. And he *still* wanted to talk to me. My self-esteem, long since bashed into a hole, bloomed like a desert flower. In the mirror, I watched my back straighten, my posture improve and my whole face lighten. I looked younger. Incredible what a boost of self-confidence could do to the appearance. I thought about the presentation I had to give that morning and mimed it to my reflection, fascinated. The mascara wand caught the mirror and smeared black paint in a long streaky line. Gah. I put it away and scrubbed the glass.

I tugged my figure-hugging grey trousers on and examined my cream blouse. The design of it concealed my belly, while the neckline plunged in a way that made me feel sexy. Would he like it? Would he even be there? Enough! This guy was a friend and nothing more. Platonic zing. Did such a thing exist?

I finished work late. With no time to check my appearance, I parked the car and managed to find a space near the coffee house. Heavy clouds threatened rain. I'd left my umbrella at home so I ran to the coffee house, telling myself it was because I didn't want to get wet.

Inside, a steam-fogged mass of humanity and noise enveloped me. Normally I hated claustrophobic coffee, but today was different. Feeling bold, I ordered two cappuccinos. Confident I wouldn't trip over my trousers, I carried the tray up the stairs. Light-headed with anticipation, I gazed around the crowded room.

Sofas all taken. Shame. The idea of sitting wedged next to him tickled my nerve endings. I squinted through to the other room.

Not there. I checked around the corner. No.

Disappointment rocked me. He forgot. He didn't want to come.

I stood there, numb, staring at nothing. Was there something wrong with me? I might not be skinny or beautiful or rich, but I had some worth. Didn't I?

Someone jostled my elbow and I blinked to see two teenage girls push past me with their mocha-latte-caramello-raspberry-besprinkled beverages. Well, I didn't know that for sure but they smelled fruity and sweet. They whispered to each other and one turned to peer at me, her cerulean eyes vivid in a face otherwise starkly bland.

Pity. I hated pity.

I would not be pitied. I was a successful, motivated purveyor of organic cleaning products and good at my job. No matter that my dream was to run a pet sanctuary. So what, that this one man had not bothered to turn up to have coffee. He was not obligated.

A table next to the wall freed up as a man a few years older than me shoved back his chair and got up. His neat, shoulder-length dark hair hung in clean, thick locks. Nothing worse than a man with long, thin hair that hung in greasy hanks and thinned to points at the ends.

I frowned, trying to work out where I had seen this guy before. He caught me looking and indicated the table with a smile and a nod. Plastering a look on my face that said it was perfectly normal to want two coffees, I weaved through the other tables and set the tray down. A spicy, lemony scent drifted towards me as Mr. Suit moved past. Mmm. "Thank you so much, Mr—"

He'd gone. I craned over my shoulder to see a pretty brunette greet him with a lengthy smooch.

With a sigh, I sank into the coffin-shaped faux leather chair. If I put two together and lay down, I could pretend I was dead.

"Well, I have good news to share, and here you are looking glum!"

I shoved upright. Blue jeans, dark green tee with the slogan *Spooning leads to Forking*. His grin stretched from ear to ear. The smell of leather blew over as he dumped his jacket on the back of the chair. Then the meaning of his words penetrated my dense skull. Good news? My stomach roiled. I wanted to hear that his date had been a disaster, that he'd wished it were me sitting opposite him at a snug table for two hidden in the corner. I imagined him staring into my eyes, telling me I was the love of his life—

"Sorry I'm late." He wiggled his seat further from the gangly youth and his girlfriend seated behind. "We're short-staffed at the hospital, and I had to stay an extra three hours. I came straight here, couldn't bear the thought of disappointing you."

Unable to think of a decent retort, I pushed the rapidly cooling coffee towards him. "So, tell me your good news. How was your blind date?"

He leaned forward and steepled his fingers. "Let's see. Becca is beautiful, amusing, eats more than a lettuce leaf at dinner and she loves Grey's Anatomy."

I swallowed too hastily. A little went down the wrong way and I coughed, banging my chest. "Grey's Anatomy? You like Grey's Anatomy?"

He sorted through the different sugars and sweeteners I had collected and picked the brown sugar. "Of course I like Grey's Anatomy. I am an ER doctor at the hospital. The whole show has me in stitches."

"Haha." Cross for some reason, I said, "I hate Grey's Anatomy."

He set his cup down so hard coffee sloshed over the side. "What?"

I pointed to the mess and grinned, delighted. "You spilled."

"Your fault, though." He gave a crooked smile and held out his hand. "Napkins, please."

I handed him the couple I had and got up for more while he mopped.

"You hate coffee, yet you drink it," he said thoughtfully as I returned. "You hate Grey's Anatomy, so do you watch it?"

I cleaned the saucer. Our hands collided as we reached for more napkins. I froze. My mouth went dry. "Only when there's nothing else on." Calum hated the show, so I had lost the plot a long time ago.

He drew a quick finger along the length of my hand. "I find it very hard to believe you dislike Grey's Anatomy." He dumped the wet napkins on the tray. "Every girl I know has the hots for Dr. McDreamy.'

"Well, I'm not like every other girl you know." My heart pounded like I had run around the block.

"Clearly, you are not like every other girl." His eyes gleamed. "And neither is Becca."

Damn. I had forgotten about her. "So she likes Grey's Anatomy and had a good appetite. Sounds like your twin."

"Now, now, now." He snatched my second sugar before I had time to open it. "I've been around women long enough to understand when they are hiding an insult within the depths of a compliment. You should hear the things nurses I work with say. One reason I never date any of them."

I stuck my hand out, palm up. "Give it back. Like I told you, I'm not like the other women you know."

"Hmm. Perhaps I shall test you." He swung the packet between his finger and thumb to persuade the sugar to the bottom, tore it and dumped it into my cappuccino.

"Thank you." I spooned up froth and sugar before it melted and crunched the grains between my teeth. "Go ahead. Test me."

"Let's see." The cushioned fabric squeaked as he sat back. "You're a brunette with red tones in your hair. I can see you wear contact lenses and I reckon you were teased at school for wearing glasses."

A lead weight sank in my belly. "Why are you describing me? I know what I look like."

He leapt out of his chair and scraped it close to mine. "Ah. But do you know that your hazel eyes have green flecks in them that catch the light, and that tiny, oval mole near the corner of your eye just makes a man want to kiss it?"

This was poking me in a very raw place. Tears threatened. He was too close, but the wall prevented me from moving the chair further to the side. I scooted back as far as I could in my coffin seat. "Nobody ever kissed my mole."

Disbelief and a hint of sadness shadowed his eyes. Sensitive to my disquiet, he withdrew a little. "Do you date?"

"It's been a long time." I refused to think of Calum. He didn't know how to date or woo a woman. Woo. I liked that word. It conjured up images of knights and their ladies and handkerchiefs. Romance.

He drained half his cup in one slug. "Tell me about your last date."

"Persistent, aren't you? Why don't you tell me about Becca, instead?"

"Touchy subject for you. I wonder why." He squinted at me over the rim of his coffee. "I will find out, you know." With his gaze locked onto mine, he said, "Becca is blonde, green-eyed and curvaceous. A bit like you. Curvaceous, I mean."

"Some would say pudgy," I muttered.

He set his cup on the saucer with a clack. "You are not pudgy. Pudgy

199

is…is…" He beckoned me near and whispered, "Do you see that fine lady over there on other side of the room, next to the window where we sat last week?"

The lady, around sixty, had grey hair cut in a bob that bounced around her plump cheeks. Completely the wrong hairstyle for her round face. She kept her bag on her lap, as if to conceal the rolls of fat that stretched her blouse. Calum had always taken great delight in pointing out overweight women, nudging me to indicate why I shouldn't eat chocolate. I used to irritate him by immediately poking around in my bag for the M&M's I kept there. A bag had laid unopened for an entire week now.

A young mother and her son walked through the room, blocking our view of the lady. "I think she looks comfortable," I commented. "Like a grandmother should."

His gaze roved over me, lingering where the top button of my cream blouse preserved my modesty. My cheeks grew hot, and I fought the urge to check if it had come undone. I had come undone. He affected me like nobody else ever had. I sipped more coffee, cross with the perverseness of life. If I had met him two weeks ago, maybe he would not have agreed to the blind date. Heck, maybe he would have gone with me. I scowled at my coffee. I needed something stronger.

Rain pelted against the windows. The inside of the coffee house had turned from a public meeting point to something much more intimate as we sat side-by-side, both involved in our own thoughts. I scooped up the remaining foam around the edge of the cup and wondered what he was thinking. His face was turned away toward the other occupants of the room, so I leaned forward to catch his profile.

A long nose. Lower lip fuller than the upper. His eyes, or rather eye, fascinated me. Instead of staying still as though looking inward, his gaze danced all over the room, alighting first on this person, then that object. I don't know if he *saw* anything.

People clattered up the stairs and pushed past our table, wet jackets and umbrellas leaving an aroma of wet wool and a trail of water droplets behind.

"Are you going to see Becca again?"

He shifted in his chair and studied me, eyes gleaming. "Are you jealous?"

"Of Becca? No. Of you? Maybe, if Becca is as wonderful as you say."

All sorts of expressions flitted across his face. Confusion. Surprise. Disbelief. I struggled not to laugh.

"You...you're not...no, of course you're not." He pulled at his lip. "Are you?"

"No! But it was worth it to see your face."

He gave me a long, slow smile. "My turn. Tell me about your last date."

I mulled this over. Should I mention my last proper date, or the last time Calum had turned up at my place to stay the night?

He squinted at me. "That long?"

I decided. "Two weeks ago."

"And? How was it?" He wiggled his eyebrows.

"He talked about himself the whole time." It was true, I realised.

"I hope that was your only date with him."

"We had a few dates, but then I met somebody else." I stood to go, fumbling with my bag to keep my face down. My purple cardigan fell from the back of the chair, and he picked it up and held it for me to shrug into.

"Same time next week? Then you can tell me all about this new man of yours."

His breath warmed a spot just below my earlobe. I shivered. "I have a meeting next Thursday."

"All day?"

I chuckled and shook my head. "No. I must travel to Sheffield, and I won't be back until late."

"Sheffield?" He looked appalled. "That's hundreds of miles. You're not going to do that in a day, there and back?"

"No, I'll stay in a hotel the night before."

"Which hotel?" He winked. "You will need someone to carry your suitcase up the stairs."

I prodded him gently in the chest to make him move out of the way. "I am not one of those women who need a giant suitcase for one night."

"I remember." He indicated for me to precede him down the stairs. "You're different from all the other women I know."

~ * ~

I did not realise that not seeing him for two weeks meant barely eating, barely sleeping...and an odd silence in my life. Somehow, I got through my meeting with our best customer, despite my momentary lapse of attention. With my hands tight around the steering wheel, the drive back from Sheffield passed in a blur of images and snatches of remembered conversation. I hardly know how I got home.

There was a queue in the coffee house. I edged my way in and placed my order.

"You've lost weight."

His voice, disgruntled and faintly reproving, drifted over my head. I smoothed the fabric of my favourite clingy dress, one I had not fit into for over two years. Butterflies knotted my stomach. I could feel the warmth of his body. My skin bumped all over. The temptation to press myself into him overwhelmed me. I dared not turn. "I forget to eat when I travel."

"Then I must travel with you. As a doctor, it's my duty to prevent people from dying."

I burst out laughing. "I won't die because I lost a little excess weight. Excess weight," I emphasised.

I took the tray with our coffees and started up the stairs, convinced his eyes were glued to my bottom. I gave an extra wiggle. "When I'm on the road, I can't stand the thought of pre-wrapped sandwiches or a quick greasy burger or..." I reached the top and turned.

He was not behind me. A lanky kid stood two steps down. Mortified that he was still staring at where my bottom had been, I glared at him and moved aside. The kid, a young guy in his mid to late teens, flushed and skittered off to his buddies in the corner. A second later, I heard a roar of laughter. I sucked in my belly as far as I could, straightened my shoulders and pretended I was a supermodel.

I peered down the stairs. Where was he? Had he taken fright at my vividly flowered dress and then taken flight?

He appeared at the bottom, waving a bag of mini muffins. "I thought you needed these."

"I happen to be quite pleased with my current physical state," I called.

Another snort of laughter from the kiddie corner. Enough. Ignoring the stares of three pimply youths, I set the tray down on our usual table near the window and then rummaged in my bag. Surely there must be one still in here from way back when. Ah ha.

I marched over to the pimply table and threw an ancient condom packet at the boy who had ogled my backside. "You dropped this on the stairs." I stalked back to my table, amid protests of innocence and roars of laughter.

One sugar in my coffee this time. I fingered the packet thoughtfully and wondered if I dare attempt cold turkey. It would mean enduring the taste of coffee, though, and I wasn't ready for that quite yet.

"What were you doing over there?" He plonked himself down. "Decided I'm too old for you or something?"

"Or something." I grinned when he tut-tutted.

"Muffin?" He opened the bag and wafted it under my nose.

They smelled good. Double chocolate chip or vanilla and raspberry. Cruel. With a great effort, I shook my head.

He pulled a face. "If this is the effect I have on you, I must stop seeing you, or else you'll disappear entirely."

"Not much chance of that." I poked my stomach. One roll when I sat. Not too bad. I had never been one of those women who had a flat belly, especially when seated. It had been the bane of my life when I was younger; now I knew better. Where was the fun in maintaining a flat belly? I liked chocolate and cake and ice cream.

"Ben and Jerry's?"

I shot him a suspicious look. "How did you know?"

He whistled a short tune before answering. "Well, if a woman is thinking about her weight—as you clearly were—then she will also likely be thinking about where she can cut back. Which naturally leads to chocolate and ice cream. So, how was your meeting?"

Well, that was a non sequitur if ever there was one. "You want to talk about work?"

He rolled his eyes. "No, I don't really want to talk about work, but it occurs to me that I have no idea what you do. For all I know, you could be the nasty boss I never see, my electricity meter reader, or worse, work for the tax office."

"Tax office?" I spluttered and grabbed a napkin to wipe my chin. "I have no idea how to read electricity meters, and I doubt I'm your boss. I would have fired you by now."

His face took on a hurt expression. "I happen to be a very good doctor."

I lifted my spoon out of the cup and stared at the drops of coffee dripping from it. Dripping drops. Almost sounded like a curse. DRIPPING

DROPS.

The Suit with the long hair passed by our table and gave me a brief smile. The same citrus scent. Today, though, it made my nose wrinkle.

I inhaled the nutty aroma from my cup and swallowed some coffee. Like more caffeine would help my skittering heartbeat, but at least I was with a doctor.

"Speaking of doctoring," he went on, "I had a guy come in the ER the other week with a bleeding hand. He'd cut himself on a kitchen knife. Said he'd come with his girlfriend but she'd abandoned him at the hospital. In his hour of need."

I almost dropped the cup. My hands tightened around it instead, the warmth comforting. It was about time I told him about Calum. Besides, I had split with him that Thursday when I saw him with the girl whose name I refuse to mention.

"You will laugh." He popped a chocolate mini-muffin in his mouth and winked. "Seeing as you're off chocolate, you won't mind if I eat them. Anyway, this guy droned on about how his girlfriend forced him to eat his least favourite meal and had accused him of sleeping with another woman. He seemed to find his woes of paramount interest. I nearly fell asleep."

I hid my face behind my cup.

"Fortunately," he went on, "a screaming kid came in and I fled. The only reason I mention it is because he sounded similar to the guy you dated. The one who talked only of himself. Seem to be more of those guys around than I thought." He pursed his lips and then prodded my bare knee. "I thought you'd find it amusing, yet you're frowning. You only had a couple of dates with the jerk, right?"

I sighed. "His name's Calum. I'm not with him anymore, but we were together for two years."

He drained his coffee and shoved another muffin in his mouth. Exposed under his scrutiny, I rummaged in my bag for my lip balm.

"Two years constitutes a lot more than a few dates. Calum seemed to think you were still his girlfriend two weeks ago in the hospital."

"He tends to ignore what's not convenient for him." I smeared balm over my lips and dropped it back in the bag. "I was a convenience for him, only I was too stupid to see it."

He snapped his fingers. "That's why you had that look on your face the first time we met. Something happened that day, didn't it?"

"I saw him with someone else. A supposed friend of mine. She must have been at least eight months pregnant." I stared out the window, rage and pain burning like acid in my belly. Calum had rubbed her bump. He had never shown me such affection. "If I had told you about Calum, would you still have wanted to meet me for coffee the week after we met?"

"Of course." He toyed with the spoon, twirling it like a baton between his fingers. "I like you. I think we can be good friends, and it's better to clear these things up first. Why do you think I told you I had a blind date? It wasn't just to get a reaction; it was to let you know where you stood."

"And where do I stand now?"

"Oh, you're not standing, you're sitting." He sucked in a breath. "I would say pretty comfortably, too."

I sipped coffee, trying to work out whether he spoke literally or figuratively. Maybe both.

He chuckled. "I wish I had known that guy was your boyfriend. I could have had a good laugh at his expense in the hospital. Told him he had blood poisoning and was dying."

My smile widened. "Calum would have insisted you cut off a limb or something."

He gathered cups and debris onto the tray. "I would have told him the truth, eventually. You never know, it may have changed him for the better." The clinking stopped. "What on earth were you doing with him, anyway? You're a dreamer, and he seems more nightmare than dream. The kind of guy that always blames others when something goes wrong, or wants everything his way." He scowled. "Do you have some kind of masochistic desire to live in misery? Is that why you chose to be with someone who makes you unhappy?"

My immediate reaction was to laugh off his words, yet something clicked. "Maybe." I rubbed my finger. It no longer felt naked without a ring. So convinced Calum would propose, I had gone to a jeweller and tried on diamond rings. My favourite was still a simple solitaire but I knew, deep in that place where truth lies, that Calum would have wanted a huge, ostentatious monstrosity.

A weight lifted from my shoulders. I no longer had to please him, no longer had to wear clothes I hated or cook food only he liked. I was free. My shoulders relaxed into the back of the seat, easing an ache I hadn't noticed before.

I glanced over and wondered. How much of my inner circumspection had he seen?

A satisfied smile quirked the corners of his mouth. "Tell me how you met," he ordered. "I need to understand your head in this."

I pulled my skirt down as far as it would go, prepared to humble myself. "Guys have never fallen over themselves for my attention. So when this handsome guy in a bar asked me out on a date, I was horrified and delighted at the same time. Horrified because I thought at first he had mistaken me for one of his harem of females, delighted when he spent the rest of the evening by my side and afterwards drove me home."

"You had no idea he was cheating on you?"

I rubbed the back of my neck. "There were odd things, I suppose, like when he changed the password on his phone and didn't give me the new one." I took a breath. "I chose to overlook these because I thought he was what I wanted. I thought he might change, thought I should make more of an effort. I was lazy, I suppose. Didn't want to upset the applecart."

He pegged his nose with his fingers. "Not even when they're all rotten and stinking?"

"Dig down far enough and you might find one that is still good."

He nodded understandingly. "How far did you dig?"

"Not very far—I guess I couldn't stand the smell." I gave a half laugh and blinked back tears. "You must think me stupid. A fool."

He shook his head. "Calum is the fool. He couldn't see the fabulous girl in front of him. Well, his loss is my gain. I have a spare room if you need somewhere to stay." He gave me a sideways look. "I might be a doctor, but I cannot promise to heal the heart. Do you have a pen?"

I dug in my bag again. "Here. I don't need anywhere to stay. I appreciate the offer but I have my own place, tiny though it may be."

He handed me a scrap of paper. *Sidney.* He hadn't told me his name until now. The phone number blurred. Just as well I wasn't standing; my entire life now spun around me. Hope bloomed. My feet itched to dance; my soul opened a shutter and began to sing.

I extracted an old receipt from my bag and wrote my number down on the back and handed it to him. "You see, I do have a phone." I stood up.

He blocked my path and tipped my chin up with a finger. "You look happy, free," he said softly. "I've never seen your eyes so luminous." With an embarrassed laugh, he shook his head. "Just as well you don't want to move in with me, I might not let you leave. Well after that, I'm starving. How about pizza?"

The smile budded in the pit of my stomach and grew, spreading through every fibre of my being. As we descended the stairs, I said, "What about Becca?"

He stepped up to me, his body close yet not touching. "Would you like me to invite her, too?"

~ * ~

The following Thursday, we were back in the coffee house.

I needed it today. Tea was all very well for breakfast, but the extra kick the caffeine and sugar provided would help stir me from the sludges of a cocktail overhang. Hangover. Whatever.

Our window table was free but still dirty. I slunk in the chair and lifted the cup, hoping the aroma alone would work wonders.

A whisper of a kiss floated past my ear. I shivered.

"Exceptional."

Puzzled, I watched him down half the contents of his cup. "The coffee always tastes the same and I forewent the muffins, so what's exceptional?"

His eyes lit up with amusement. "You are."

I kept my face neutral while my body hummed. "I am?"

"Of course. I have never enjoyed an evening more. We should do it again, sometime." Then he looked surprised. "Oh that's right, we did. Last night."

Last night had been our second dinner date, and afterwards we had walked for hours along the beach. Best night of my life. However, Saturday night? "You spent the entire evening on Saturday dissecting my personality."

A smile wound across his face. "And last night you dissected mine. With a little less success, I'll admit, but it made for great entertainment." He eyed my short skirt. "I can't believe you turned down the decadent fudge cake. This Saturday, come to my house and I will make the most calorific dinner and dessert for you. I need to get you back to your target weight."

"Cal-horrific," I corrected. "Besides, I have reached my target weight, thank you." I had not been interested in chocolate or cake or ice cream for several weeks.

"All right then, *my* target weight." He scooted out from behind the table and shot downstairs, returning a minute later with a slice of death-by-chocolate cake. Waving it under my nose and flashing his fingers in a supposedly hypnotic manner, he purred, "You want it. You know you do. It's healthy. Your poor, deprived, depleted fat cells are starving."

I pushed it away. "They can go on starving. I have no intention of returning to cuddly."

He pouted. "Not even for me?"

"Nope."

"So I just have to accept you as you are, now?"

"Yep."

He tapped a finger on his lips and thought about this. "Do you promise not to get any thinner?"

I laughed. "Calum always had the opposite complaint."

"Like I told you, Calum is a fool." He finished his coffee. "So, now that you are a free woman, do you accept my invitation to dinner at my house on Saturday?"

~ * ~

We broke our habit and met on Sunday morning for coffee. The place was crowded so we stood at the bar. Just as well. This would be a very short coffee. I was annoyed and glared at him icily. "You invited Becca."

He shifted sideways and leaned his elbow on the bar. His eyes gleamed. "Don't forget Lauren, or God Bless Her Soul. I invited her, too."

I stepped on his foot, grinding my heel in. "You invited three women, and then sat there and laughed while two of them tried to outdo each other in securing your attention."

"And the last slice of cake." He chuckled. "Oh, come on, you have to admit it was hilarious."

"For you, maybe. For me it was like being with Calum all over again."

"Except you knew my attention was firmly fixed on you. I saw your lips twitch more than once." He put his lips close to my ear. "Becca and Lauren were an entertaining sideshow and much needed, else I would have jumped on you and ripped that sexy red dress all the way off."

Tingles shot from my ear all the way to the centre of my being. I removed my foot from his. He shifted so that the length of his body touched mine. Fire sparked through my veins.

"You see what I mean?" He kissed my ear lobe. "This is why we meet in public places."

I wanted him to kiss me all over. I didn't care that people pressed past us on their way upstairs to find a seat. I didn't care that the barista nudged her friend and grinned.

His gaze dropped to my lips. All noise seemed to fade into the background, yet become a loud hum at the same time. I closed my eyes as his lips caressed mine. The warmth of his body tantalised my seeking hands, and I tugged his t-shirt out of his trousers. Hands pulled me tight against him. For a long moment, there was nothing but the sense of belonging, the promise of oneness. Then coolness, the clink of cups and the loud hiss of steam.

He drew back. "You see?"

~ * ~

We snagged the sofa upstairs next time. Hollering in triumph, I parked my bottom and slid over to make room for him.

He landed practically on top of me.

"Give me some space!' I shoved at him.

"Not on your life." He squidged up tight. "What if some elderly woman entered in dire need of a seat?" Arranging his arm behind me, he pulled me into his shoulder and patted the space next to him. "I have been thoughtful in leaving said space. You should thank me."

I put a hand on his knee and slowly stroked upwards. "Your consideration is my gratification."

His hand enclosed mine and held it firmly in place. "If you have the slightest idea of what would happen should you continue, I beseech you to stop. Listen." He touched his forehead to mine. "I have a question to ask you that I will never ask any other woman."

I stilled. Hope and fear rushed through in equal measure. It was too soon. It was not soon enough. "Are you sure you want to risk such a question on me?" I feigned interest in the Snoopy cartoon on the sugar bag. At least, it looked like Snoopy.

"Of course." He removed the packet from my fingers and dumped its contents into my coffee.

"I didn't really want that."

"Tush, of course you did." He poked me in the side. "I cannot have you disappearing altogether. I wish for something to see when you are *in* the altogether."

I tensed. "What do you mean? I'm not moving in with you, not yet. It's too soon, and although I'm over Calum, I don't want to look like a bed-hopping slu—"

"We're not teenagers anymore." He relaxed against the cushions. "We know what we want, so why not reach for it? I have something that might help you decide."

A small, dark blue box. He set it on the table and pushed it towards me. I touched it with my little finger. A maelstrom of emotions whirled inside me. A few weeks ago, I had been desperately hoping Calum would propose. I had never expected a proposal from a completely different man. One who had been a stranger until a month ago.

He linked his hands behind his head, enjoying my reaction. "It's not an engagement ring, you know."

I slapped his knee. "It had better not be. If I'm not ready to move in, I'm definitely not ready for that kind of commitment."

"I don't believe you, but never mind. Open it."

A diamond ring. A beautiful solitaire. The exact one I had been eyeing in the shop weeks ago. The air whooshed out of my lungs as though someone just punched me in the gut, albeit a painless punch. Did he know? Had he seen me? I stared at it, wondering if he was playing a huge, elaborate joke on me. You know, let's tease the sad girl who tries on rings alone in the jewellery shop. If I didn't know he worked at the hospital, I might have believed it. As it was, I shot a look at him. Although outwardly calm, the fingers of his left hand fiddled with a hole in the chair fabric. I managed to speak. "It's stunning. This isn't an engagement ring?"

"Try it on."

"Which finger?"

He sighed and shook his head. "The thumb. No, you dipstick, here, let me."

"That's the ring finger."

"Of course. It's. A. Ring."

I snorted with laughter. "What is this, if it's not an engagement ring?"

"Consider it a contractual ring." He stirred more sugar into my coffee and handed it to me. "You are under contract to consider me as a life partner."

I sipped, taking all this in. "And if, three months hence, we decide we do not suit?"

"You can keep the ring." He twined his fingers with mine. "But I'm willing to bet that in three months you will be walking down the aisle toward me. There is one proviso," and he held up a finger, "I will only wed you if you feed your fat. I do not want a skinny wife." He shuddered.

"Three months isn't long."

He scowled. "It's a lifetime. I tell you what, I promise not to breathe the word 'commitment' or talk about moving in until the three months are up. In the meantime, we'll continue to drink coffee and ..." He took my hand and planted a kiss on the palm. "I shall woo you. How about it?"

He said woo. I agreed. Why not? I had nothing to lose.

Three months later

He was there before me. No coffee on the table though. I set the tray down with a clatter, nerves getting the better of me. Coffee spilt. "You're here and you didn't get the coffees in?"

"Nope. Thought you would do it. I was right." He stuck his thumb in the direction of the mess and grinned. "Maybe I should have gotten them. Half of mine is now a moat around the cup."

I swatted at him with a napkin. "You can have mine."

He emptied a sachet into my coffee and raised an eyebrow when I reached for a second one. "Dare I hope this means you've decided thin is boring?"

I tore open the bag and waited a millisecond before dumping it in. It would give me the fortitude I needed today. "Call it an experiment."

"An experiment?"

"Mmm. If I don't like it, then I have succeeded."

"In liking coffee."

"No, in adapting my dislike of coffee." With a deep breath, I reached inside my bag and withdrew the blue box. "I have an answer for you."

"Shh. Don't tell me yet." He opened the box and removed the ring, holding it up to the sunlight falling through the window. "You know, I bought this the day I met you. Found it in a shop down the road. I wasn't looking, or even thinking about marriage, but I found myself in the jeweller's handing over my life savings." He took my hand. "Well, not quite, but it felt like it. It also felt...wonderful." He waited until I looked up. "I never asked you before," he said. "Maybe I should have. Charlotte, will you marry me?"

Joy surged through me. I had made my decision three months ago but not said anything for fear he might change his own mind. "I can't promise to put weight on."

His finger glided up my arm to tickle the hollow in my collarbone. "There's more than one way to ensure you get fat. Rest assured, I will do my utmost. How does Barbados sound?"

I leaned over and kissed him on the lips. "Perfect. How does 'yes' sound?"

"Perfect."

THE END

About the Author

Louise Redmann grew up by the sea in England, spent some time in the USA where she fell in love with the deserts, and now lives in Switzerland with her husband and two boys. When not chasing after the boys or teaching English, she spends many a happy hour daydreaming. Currently editing her first novel and writing her second, she also enjoys dabbling in short stories, flash fiction and vignettes.

Connect with Louise at:
https://louiseredmann.com/
https://louiseredmann.wordpress.com/
Twitter@louiseredmann
https://www.facebook.com/louise.redmann

LOVE WEAVERS

By

Katie Stephens

Dedicated to daughter Kate and future son-in-law Karl,
celebrating his proposal to her on May 8, 2015.
Love you both!

Chapter One

Lancaster, Lancashire County, UK: present day

"Grant!" Hannah barreled through the front door of the art gallery, allowing the heavy oak to slam behind her. She slid to a stop when she spied the owner at his desk, deep in conversation with a middle-aged woman, obviously rich—judging by the Prada and Vera Wang—and obviously buying. Hannah made the latter deduction by the quick frown Grant sent her way, as well as the shooing motion of his hand when the woman glanced up.

She nodded obediently and wandered across the marble floor where Grant had set up Glimmer Man's mirrors. Leaning forward to examine her favorite piece, Hannah pushed away annoyance at its location between De La Garza's oil landscapes and Schmidt's sculptures. Their fellow artists at the gallery had earned high acclaim in the latest edition of Lancaster's quarterly tourist journal with their pieces.

She had to admit Glimmer Man could be considered an artistic genius, too. If she stood directly in the center of the mirror, the frame caught her dark-haired, hazel-eyed reflection hundreds of times. Brilliant. She searched for the tiny card mounted on the wall. *Beauty Multiplied. $9400.*

"Wow," she whispered. Her eyes went to the other mirrored pieces. "Grant jacked up the prices. I will not be intimidated. I—"

"Hey, Hannah. How goes it?"

Great. Glimmer Man himself. Hannah resisted the urge to roll or, even worse, close her eyes. *Mirror, mirror on the wall, Al can see me best of all.* She glanced at his reflection. "Hey."

Alvin Watkins raised an eyebrow. "That's it? No disparaging remarks? No 'How did a muscle-bound guy like you have the dexterity to handle small delicate pieces?'"

"Yeah, well." Hannah turned to face him. "I'm impressed."

Alvin put a hand to his chest and staggered backwards in a parody of a heart attack. "What? Do my ears deceive me? The amazingly perfect, and soon to be successful, Hannah Mackenzie actually *likes* my work? Okay, that's it. I've died and gone to heaven." He dramatically collapsed onto the nearest chair, one of many strategically placed throughout the room. "You can take me away now. My work here is done."

Hannah bit back a smile. Friends and rivals since high school in upstate New York, their competitiveness stayed alive and well and resided at Grant's art gallery. The famous British curator had snatched them both on graduation day from the Art Institute, luring them across the Atlantic with promises of studio space and a hefty clientele. The new situation worked well for Hannah—her maternal grandmother lived forty miles east of Lancaster in Clitheroe.

Over the years, Alvin had transformed from a short, skinny kid with thick, black glasses into a muscular, blond hunk with contact lens-enhanced sapphire eyes. Although she couldn't tell him because he'd laugh hysterically and she would die of embarrassment, Hannah adored him either way. She remarked on many occasions that he should meet with potential woman buyers before Grant did. Alvin wasn't amused. Deep down inside, Hannah knew his amazing talent didn't need that kind of push.

And there it was. The green-eyed monster once again rose to the forefront. The one that nudged her every single time they vied for the same client. That red haze that covered her vision when he got a sale ... and she didn't. She tamped the monster down hard. Glimmer Man had his talent with mirrors, and she had hers with jewelry.

She took a deep breath and smiled, allowing it to actually reach her eyes. "Very good, Alvin."

And that sounded like the guy in the stupid chipmunk song, only he was talking about chipmunk Simon, not chipmunk Alvin. Hannah stifled a giggle.

Alvin, the real man, cocked his head. "What are you thinking about now? You've got that wicked 'I'm-going-to-screw-with-Alvin' grin on your face. You're scaring me, Hannah." He leapt out of the chair and grabbed her arm, dragging her away from his exhibit and closer to her jewelry display. "You're not going to do anything to my stuff, are you?"

Hannah put on the brakes, stopping in the middle of the open-space gallery. She stared at him. "Do you really think I'd do something to your work?" she asked in a low voice. "Wow."

That he even entertained the notion devastated her. The green-eyed monster had left the room, only to be replaced by a cold, grey cloud of disappointment.

"No." He rubbed his hands up and down her arms, pulling her towards him into a hug. "Of course not. I thought we were just playing around."

She firmed her trembling lip and pulled back, forcing a twinkle in her eye. "Gotcha."

He searched her face for a moment and then chuckled, apparently satisfied with her deception. "Brat."

Hannah offered a cheeky grin and turned to Grant, whose customer was making her stately way out the front door. The owner did a little happy dance, a sure sign he had been the recipient of a big sale. Hannah was about to do one of her own when Grant swept past her and slapped Alvin on the back.

"Congrats, man. My friend, Sarah Emerson, took the *Aphrodite*." Grant resumed his dance on a larger scale, including Alvin in an arm swinging, he-man rendition of a Scottish reel.

Hannah moved back to avoid being stepped on and then shrieked when the two men exuberantly swung her into the dance. Grant pulled her close enough to whisper in her ear. "And ... she took the emerald key."

Hannah's eyes widened. "What?" Alvin grabbed her and swung her away from Grant. "What did you say?" she called over her shoulder.

By contract, Grant had total autonomy to sell anything his half-dozen sponsored artists crafted in the back studios of the gallery. He provided the place; they created art. He marketed and sold the finished pieces. Everyone

217

split the profits, with a generous percentage going to the man who brought in the clients.

Grant skipped—as much as a grown man who weighed over two hundred pounds could skip—back to his desk. "You heard me. One person, two sales, ten o'clock in the morning, and we've hit our mark for the day. Anyone want to celebrate by closing down early?"

Hannah and Alvin slowed to catch their breath and beamed at their friend, arms around each other in perfect accord. "Seriously?" Alvin asked.

"No, he's not." Desiree, Grant's wife and general manager, poked her head around the corner of her office at the back of the gallery. "We have three more appointments today and our artists," she pointed towards the workroom, "have work to do." Short and elegantly Bohemian, Desiree kept them all in line. "We'll have dinner together tonight. Capesh?"

Chapter Two

Clitheroe, Lancashire County, England: 1543

Wynter dabbed the soft bristle brush into a tiny jar, half-filled with golden dust. Her hand shook a little as she said the incantation and stroked the jeweled copper key.

> *O wise Guardian soft and strong,*
> *Maintain protection, to her belong,*
> *Insure within your charge and cares,*
> *Expose the heart of he that dares.*
> *There is no harm to come or worse,*
> *Secure and safe without a curse.*

A tiny stab of guilt pierced her chest. Not exactly the magick Lord Theodric expected, she supposed. But Wynter loved her queen and mistrusted the lord who vied for the woman's hand. Unless her magick mislead her, she could see through the charade to his true desires; he did not love the queen. That became more apparent with each of his visits to secure her jewelry, purportedly for their ruler.

She examined the piece in the light. About six inches in length, copper wire twisted intricately around its form. Caged amethysts in a delicate shade of purple dotted the bow. Wynter added a holder piece at the top, so the wearer could adjoin it to her girdle. But she knew the queen would want to wear this near her breast, as a token of her loyalty to the man she imagined she loved.

And by doing so, the incantation would do its work.

A flash of light caught the corner of her eye, but she knew better than to turn her head and look at it directly. She had tried before, but the apparition only disappeared. Wynter found if she kept her eyes averted, the specter would stay.

For years, Wynter had observed her mother and grandmother each speak with something *other*, although Wynter could never see anyone or anything. She had been told when the time came, she would entertain her own guest. Wynter smiled at the thought. One day, Goddess willing, she would be enigmatic to her own children and grandchildren.

Woman, witch or ghost? Wynter had no clue what visited whenever she worked a piece. The spirit exuded no malice, just a curiosity—as if it wished to enjoy whatever she created too. Perhaps one day she could devise a spell to keep it, and they would converse.

Cat jumped to the window ledge, releasing an annoyed hiss just as the sound of horses thundered over the hill. She placed the key carefully in a soft leather pouch and turned her head. The apparition in the corner disappeared.

She quickly put her tools into the barely-visible niche in the wall before gathering her skirts to step outside. If spied through the open window, the expensive tools might give Lord Theodric's men reason to enter her domain. The spells on the cottage made quite sure they would never leave again. She didn't relish explaining *that* to Theodric.

With a quick whisper, Wynter altered her appearance to what they expected from a witch. Her straight shoulders rounded. Tiny wrinkles—not too many—carved into her smooth skin. Soft facial features strengthened into crags, her lips thinned and her piercing blue eyes became grey. Even her gown cooperated, dulling with age and seemingly countless washings.

Three men pulled their horses up, dust flying in their haste. Two dismounted.

"Show me," the remaining one demanded.

Wynter shuffled to his side and held up the pouch, all the while keeping a wary eye on the other two men. Lord Theodric opened the pouch and dropped the key into his gloved hand. He turned it, lifted it to the sky and squinted at the stones. Finally, he grunted.

"Did you magick it? 'Tis better than I expected." He secured it in his leather shoulder bag and spurred his horse into a turn. "Pay her," he instructed his men, "then catch up. I want to get to Clitheroe Castle soon after midday." He allowed his horse to complete the circle until he faced her again. Controlling the stallion, he bent low over the animal's neck.

"What did you do to your appearance, witch? You look different from the last time I saw you. Perhaps a bath is needed." He winked.

Wynter listened to his laughter echoing through the hills after the three men left. She imagined he thought he outsmarted the witch.

Think again, my lord.

~ * ~

Clitheroe Castle

A grin still played around his mouth when Theodric dismissed his men two hours later. He strode through the open front door of the small castle he occupied, by the queen's regard, and nodded to the servant.

"Bring me an ale, then I don't wish to be disturbed until dinner."

"Yes, my lord." The man turned to a side table and poured from a ready pitcher. "Shall I take it up myself?"

"No." Theodric pulled off his cloak and exchanged it for the tankard. He drained half of it and took the stairs two at a time, anxious to be alone. He didn't think twice about the servant. Adrian was the only one he employed as such, and he trusted the man implicitly.

Once inside his apartments, he sealed the door with a word. The heavy tapestries over the windows already clung together, not allowing even a small ray of light to escape into the room. He snapped his fingers and two candles, situated on either side of a covered easel, flared to life.

Theodric drained the tankard and set it on a sideboard. He crossed the room and pulled the cloth down, revealing a full-length mirror. Unlike others, this one's uncommonly smooth surface reflected a master's magick. His.

He pulled out the key Wynter had made and grinned, running his thumb over her work. Did the witch really think he hadn't seen through her feeble attempt to age herself? He tapped the key lightly on the corner of the glass. Instantly, Theodric's reflection disappeared, and he beheld another person in a brightly lit room, engrossed in a task he couldn't identify.

"I have the key," he said.

The reflection wavered for a moment then stilled again as the beautiful silver-haired woman looked up, her face softening when she saw him. "Good."

Chapter Three

Hannah rubbed her thumb along the length of the key her grandmother sent months ago, feeling the magic within its form. The patina of the old copper glowed a beautiful greenish-blue, almost teal, forming a perfect backdrop for the three amethysts woven within it. She had convinced herself that touching it helped her create her designs.

Alvin would laugh at her.

She set the key in its velvet case and began working the copper on her bench.

Hannah had used the basic design to create five keys, all with different stones and weaving patterns. If those generated enough interest—especially after the sale today—she could work off the commissions. Right now, she wanted to craft one identical to the original.

Desiree poked her head in.

"Ready for dinner?"

"What?" Hannah pushed her hair out of her eyes and glanced at the clock. She didn't realize how much time had passed. She listened intently, but her stomach stayed silent.

"Dinner," Desiree repeated.

"Oh. No, I'm fine." She gestured to the box. "I want to work on this a bit more."

Hannah held her breath as Desiree stepped over to the workbench and put out a finger to touch the old key. She quickly offered a pair of white cotton gloves, similar to the ones covering her own hands.

Desiree shook her head. "That's okay. You've told me often enough that I shouldn't touch, no matter how tempting." She leaned against the wall and crossed her arms. "I can't believe you're not hungry. But you artists are always working on your own schedule, so I suppose us mere mortals must forgive you."

"Is Glimmer Man going?"

Desiree laughed. "Are you daft? A sale *and* a free dinner in one day? Alvin wouldn't pass on that one." She inclined her head towards the key. "I'm surprised you are."

"Tell you what." Hannah decided to be sociable. "Where are you going—the tavern? I can join you there in about an hour."

"We'll be at The Hanging Tree, and I'll even order you a meat pie. The chef makes it from scratch for you anyway." She paused on her way out. "I won't get you a pint, because I know you Americans drink them cold. Later, luv."

"Thanks, Desiree," Hannah said to the closed door, already intent on the curvature of the bit ward.

It wasn't right. She checked the original. No matter how she turned the wire, it wouldn't follow the same curve. What had the artist done to form this part?

Hannah went to the door and eased it open a crack. No noises came from the front of the gallery, but that wasn't unusual this time of night. Her workroom faced south, situated at the back of the building. The rooms Grant and Desiree offered to their current artists were spacious, well lit, soundproof—and away from the actual gallery to keep wandering guests out.

Gripping the old key, she slipped her cell phone into her back pocket and made her way to the gallery's showroom. The overhead lights were off, but the security night-lights glowed. She stopped in front of Alvin's *Beauty Multiplied*. For weeks, this particular mirror had propped up a wall at the very back of his studio, somewhat lost throughout the sheer number of pieces cluttering the room. She had to give him credit—he was a prolific artist. Where she had two or three pieces ready for sale at any time, Alvin had dozens.

This one amazing creation, hidden in plain sight, turned out to be perfect for her needs. Hannah stood directly in front of the full-length mirror. She lifted the ancient key, held it against the glass and recited the verse her grandmother taught her in high school.

Katie Stephens

Guardian of all, hear my plea
Safeguard those who count on thee.
Take me to my sister dear
The one whose heart knows I am here.
No harm to those, I pray to you,
Who seek your wisdom, great and true.

The mirror shimmered and then burst in a flash of lightning. Hannah didn't flinch at the optical illusion; it happened every time. The surface of the glass rippled and slowly settled, like water in a pond, until Hannah could see the room in the glass. It was always the same setting: a one-room cottage brightly lit by several lamps. Heavy drapes pulled to the side of an open window allowed the sun to slant on a workbench covered with small tools. Spools of fine metals with different diameters hung on the wall, within easy reach of the woman sitting there. Several open boxes held uncut stones. On one side, a small grinder waited for feet to urge it into a spin. To the left of the bench, on the other side of the room, a small bed nestled against the wall. A black pot steamed over the fireplace; Hannah imagined she could smell the aroma of the contents.

The urge to step forward assailed her, but her grandmother had warned her to ignore it. "Look for what you seek," G-ma said, "but do not attempt to enter." Often, Hannah imagined the woman on the other side wished to interact, but it never happened.

The woman raised a key to the light—identical to the one Hannah held secure on the mirror—and inspected it. Hannah marveled at the beauty of the newly formed copper and leaned forward to examine the detail.

Without warning, a cat jumped to the open sill, interrupting their scrutiny. The woman placed the key in a leather pouch and glanced across the room. When she met Hannah's eyes, the scene disappeared.

"What are you doing?"

Hannah let out a small scream of surprise and tripped over her own feet as she spun around. The precious key flew out of her hand, skidding across the marble floor. Alvin stopped the slide with his shoe and extracted a white folded handkerchief from his front pocket. He crouched to scoop it up.

She fought to gain her balance without touching or falling into Alvin's

224

exhibit. Devoid of any grace at all, she tiptoed out of the area, glaring at him.

"What are you doing sneaking up on me?" Hannah heard the snark in her voice but couldn't control it. She hadn't thought anyone would be returning to the gallery.

Alvin rose. "I told Grant and Desiree that you probably lost track of time," he said mildly, holding up two bags. "They went home. I brought you a meat pie and a couple of brews."

Damn the man. Hannah's anger and embarrassment drained away. At least he didn't say anything about her touching his expensive mirror. "Thanks." She held out her hand. "My key, please?"

He held it up to the dim overhead light, the gesture so similar to the woman in the mirror that Hannah's heart thumped. "Beautiful," he said before handing it back along with the food. "By the way, what were you doing with my mirror?"

Busted.

Chapter Four

Wynter traversed the length of the castle's throne room, accompanied by four honor guardsmen. The full skirt of her white gown swayed with each step; a jeweled headdress secured the dark contrast of her hair from too much exuberance in the eyes of the court. She gazed straight ahead, yet her ears couldn't help but register the whisperings of the other occupants. Lords and servants alike on either side of the procession shrank back a bit, reluctant to feel even the breath of the witch passing.

When she came within ten feet of the throne, Wynter sank into a full curtsy and held the pose.

"Wynter! Approach."

Wynter raised her head to see the queen motion to her grumbling court and advisors. Gaining her feet, she folded her hands together and watched them retreat. A warm breeze blew through the open windows, fluttering tapestries against the stone wall. Once the last guard closed the tremendous oak doors, the queen dropped her haughty demeanor and leaped to her feet.

"Wynter, how are you? It's been much too long since you last visited me."

The two women met at the steps and embraced.

"Aurelia, my queen, I am well. You look beautiful, as always. How goes the running of our country?"

Arm in arm, they entered the queen's apartments through a door behind the throne and settled in the padded chairs next to the fireplace. Aurelia pretended to pout. "How is it you never ask how your queen fares?"

Wynter raised an eyebrow. "You feel fine, but your courses run too

226

strong. I have a potion for you that will help."

"I don't know if I like having a witch in my queendom."

"I could leave—" Wynter teased and half-rose from her chair.

Aurelia leaned forward to put her hand on Wynter's. "I do wish for you to leave … your cottage." She paused. "And move here, into my castle."

Wynter frowned. "Why? We've known each other since we were children. You know it's not my preference to be in the castle." She sat back and cast a thread into the queen's mind. "You worry about Theodric."

"Somewhat." Aurelia shrugged. "He is what he is. No more and no less."

"Have you any clue to his intentions? He strikes me as too …" She paused, searching for a word. " … Arrogant, too strong. He'll smother you."

"Or all that arrogance and strength might keep this kingdom safe."

Wynter rose to pace in front of the fire. "What about love?"

Aurelia laughed, an enchanting sound like the tinkle of bells that filled the room, making Wynter smile. "Stay here and make a man love me."

"You don't need me to make someone love you, my queen."

Aurelia put out a hand when Wynter paced close. "No, but I need you to talk sense into my advisors. Please."

Wynter bowed her head. "Of course. You need only to command me."

~ * ~

Busy selecting the herbs she needed for a potion, Wynter barely registered the heavy footsteps crunching on the gravel in the conservatory. She didn't have to look up from her task, though, to know who approached. His scent engulfed the area, even stronger than the fragrance of the plants.

"I have another commission for you."

She pinched off a leaf and took a steadying breath. "You recognize me? I'm surprised you approach me here."

"I would know you anywhere, in any guise." Theodric touched a tiny flower from the plant and bent his head to inhale the fragrance. "I went to your cottage three times. It was only when I mentioned your absence to our queen that she revealed your presence."

In the month she had been here, she kept herself busy looking after her queen's needs. The conservatory thrived under her watchful eye. She spent her days mixing elixir, and her nights polishing stones for her jewelry. And she kept her ear to the ground for news of the men who desired the royal hand in marriage. Theodric had just returned to the castle in the past day or two. He was on the prowl. She could feel it.

Wynter watched him inspect her plants. She had to admit he was a pleasure to the eye: tall and muscular, yet with enough scars to claim a warrior's title. He surprised her with his soft touch on the flower. Still bent over, he turned his head to stare at her.

Something went through her, coursed through her body like a bolt of lightning. She couldn't tell whether it was good or evil and took a step back.

"What do you want?" His presence unsettled her and Wynter wasn't stupid enough to deny it. Her mind told her to take another step away, but her body refused the command and stayed.

He straightened. The same finger he used to touch the flower now slid lightly across her cheek. He smiled.

Only when Wynter took a deep breath did she realize she had been holding it. And that annoyed her. She picked up her basket and swept down the aisle to her workbench, leaving Theodric to follow as he pleased. *Damn him!*

Wynter threw a portion of two plants into the stone mortar, crushing them together with a violence that revealed her inner turmoil. She calmed herself and stayed her hand as he strolled past. Her eyes closed as his presence again overwhelmed her. *What in the name of the Goddess?* He threw off pheromones as if he were ready to mate that very moment. And her witch embraced it. She bit her tongue hard to break his thrall.

"You said you wished to commission another piece. What do you want this time?"

"I wish for a lot of things, my lady, but today I want you to design me a snare."

"A what?" Wynter faced him, very aware of his close proximity. She silently vowed not to let him intimidate her. She frowned. Intimidate her? No man could do that. Ever. What was wrong with her?

He paced away and she could breathe again.

"Are you a wizard?" she blurted out. His head swung toward her, eyes narrowed. Wynter immediately searched her memory for a spell to undo the words, but her mind remained blank.

Then Theodric threw his head back and roared with laughter.

After a few moments, Wynter had an urge to join him. Although her lips twitched, she tamped down the impulse and returned to her work. "It wasn't that amusing."

He collapsed onto her stool and propped his chin on his hand. "Yes, it was. I wonder why you would think I dabble in witchcraft."

She glanced at him. The broad smile and twinkle in his eyes transformed him from the man she loathed into ... something more. As if he read her thoughts, he cupped the back of her neck and tugged until his parted lips touched hers.

Neither closed their eyes. After a long moment, he eased away. His hand lightly caressed her throat, and then he drew his thumb along her lower lip.

"I've wondered what it would be like," he murmured, "to kiss a witch." He grinned and cocked his head to the side. "When you don't make yourself appear as a hag, I quite like it."

His flippancy broke the spell for Wynter. "Don't get used to it," she retorted and pulled away.

Wynter didn't understand what just happened. How did he know she had changed her appearance? She still didn't trust him, yet he made it difficult to resist his charms. It didn't make sense at all, since he wished to impress the queen, not her. Maybe he had obtained a spell from a wizard, one that made him palatable to the opposite sex. That had to be it.

Satisfied with her deductions, she allowed her mouth to curve up. "You said you wanted a snare. For what?"

"To capture the lady of my dreams."

"You mean the queen?"

"Can you design something for me? I need it soon." He reached out and swept his fingers lightly across her hand.

With his touch, Wynter's vision blurred. She could already see the piece. A necklace, worked with exquisitely thin copper, forming a spider's web. The spider herself would hang from the bottom, carrying a precious jewel. She blinked and the image disappeared, but the seed of urgency remained. Shivers crept up and down her spine. She silently vowed to devise a spell to protect the queen.

"Give me three days."

Chapter Five

Lancaster: present day

Hannah juggled her phone and the grocery bags on the walk home. "Hi, G-ma," she said when her grandmother answered.

"Hannah! It's lovely to hear your voice. When are you coming to Clitheroe to visit me?"

"I can't this weekend. I'm working on a key design, but it's just not coming together."

Her grandmother laughed. "You were always single-minded, even as a little girl. I remember your mother calling me and complaining that you could never multi-task."

"I *can* multi-task, just not when it comes to my jewelry. Question, G-ma?"

"Yes, dear?"

Hannah reached the entrance to her apartment building. Situated in the middle of downtown, the old row houses brought charm and a sense of shared community to the area. Instead of one family occupying each house, a developer had renovated the entire block to include three flats per unit. Across the tree-lined street, a small cafe on one corner and pizzeria on the other offered take-out meals.

Instead of a triple-juggle to include a key search, she set the groceries down on the small landing and sat on the top step. "Um, it concerns the mirror."

Even without seeing her grandmother, she felt a wave of renewed interest through the airborne signal. "What is it you need to know? Did you forget the verse?"

"You can say 'spell.' I won't freak out on you like I did in ninth grade when you told me I was a witch." She huffed out a breath, unsure how to

231

go on. "Sorry."

"Hannah, it's okay to ask questions. Don't be afraid."

"If I'm not afraid of seeing a medieval scene in a mirror that *Alvin* made, G-ma, trust me, I'm good."

"Renaissance scene, dear. Alvin may have made the mirror but you—and what's inside of you—bring the vision forward. You know, Alvin has secrets too. You should actually sit down and talk to him."

Hannah huffed out a laugh. "Oh, I like that, G-ma. The conversation will go something like this: "Hi Alvin. My art is inspired by jewelry that my *witchy* grandmother obtained from her *witchy* ancestors centuries ago. Can you feel the sorcery?"

"Sorcery is a good word. Witchcraft is better."

G-ma's previous statement finally clicked into Hannah's consciousness. "Wait a minute. You said Alvin has secrets too. Does this have anything to do with the mirror? That's why I called. Grant put the mirror in the gallery. It's up for sale."

"Hmm. Slow down. Is that the only mirror of his you can access to see the past?"

Hannah nodded as if her grandmother could see the gesture. She bit her lip, thinking. "Do you think there are other mirrors in Alvin's studio that I can use?"

"Did you hear what I said about Alvin?"

With her foot, she pushed a pebble across the second step until it fell over the lip, delaying her answer as long as possible.

"Hannah? Did you hear—"

"Yes," she interrupted. "Alvin and I should talk." She winced. If she heard the pout in her voice, her grandmother couldn't miss it.

Her grandmother sighed. "Honey, your mother left your teaching to my care because that's the way it's always been done in our family. I know you've been busy with your art and haven't had as much time to devote to our craft. You're still young, and I'm a patient woman. You'll tell me when you're ready to discover more, both about yourself, your friend and his … amazing mirrors. "

With those words, like someone flipped a switch, Hannah felt a need to return to her studio. She wanted to leave the groceries on the stoop, walk away.

But there was something … here. She stood, searched up and down the now empty street and even glanced at the neighbors' open windows. Nothing. Nothing moved but a spider spinning her web between the light fixture and the railing, preparing for a busy night of moths and mosquitoes. Hannah inched closer and watched the sunlight shimmer on the delicate strands in the slight breeze.

"G-ma, can you tell me the name of the woman in the mirror?"

Her grandmother didn't hesitate. "Wynter, with a 'y.' Oh, and look through your mail. You should have received a package from us today."

Hannah glanced through the locked glass door. Sure enough, a small package was on the table next to the mailboxes. "You and … Wynter? Or you and Alvin?"

"Isn't that what I said? Love you. Come see me soon."

The phone went dead, leaving Hannah staring at the box. *Wynter.*

~ * ~

"Hannah, come take a food break."

"Don't annoy me, Glimmer Man. I'm working."

Hannah took another length of ultra thin wire and wove it back and forth between the anchoring stems. She grasped a narrow metal pick, using it to gently push the wire down, completing a row.

Alvin sauntered to her side. "Wow. That's an incredible spider web. I like the Steampunk look. You've got a lot of detail going on here."

She stretched the kinks out of her back and hands. "It's coming along." Peering through a twelve-inch magnifier, she soldered both ends and clipped the wire. "One more row and I can place the gears and the spider on it. See?" She motioned to her right, where the preliminary pieces she had worked were finished and ready to mount.

He bent close. "Incredible. What is it, exactly?"

Most artists would have been annoyed by the question, but she knew Alvin well enough to understand he looked beyond the obvious. He delved into the *reason* behind the creation.

She glanced for the umpteenth time at the box that had sat on the top left corner of her workbench for over two weeks. She had only removed the outer wrapping of the package from her grandmother, and the black velvet now enticed her with a subconscious *open me—open me* chant. The extreme pull of whatever nestled inside brought out her stubborn streak.

233

She refused to open it until she finished the piece on her bench.

"It's a snare." The words tumbled out of her mouth before she could think.

"A what?" Alvin pulled up a nearby stool, a sure sign he was intrigued.

"A snare." Hannah put her chin on her doubled-up fists and contemplated the piece attached firmly in the jeweler's clamps. "That's apropos, don't you think? It's a collar designed to encircle a woman's throat, used in the Renaissance as a sign of possession. And a trap—how better to catch your prey than with a spider's web?"

"Prey? I'm not sure I like the sound of that." Alvin reached for a pair of stretchy white gloves. "May I?"

Hannah nodded. His big hands caressing the delicate spider made a beautiful contrast. He examined it from all sides before setting it back down.

"You do amazing work, Hannah. We should plan to do something together. You game?" His words were benign, but the intense look in his eyes created another contrast.

"Maybe." *God, yes.* "Listen, I can finish this later. You want to grab a pizza or something?"

Alvin grinned like a kid in a toyshop. "Ah, a woman after my own heart. And to prove how much I appreciate you, I'll buy." He rose from the stool and offered her a chivalrous bow.

"Charmed sir, I am sure." Hannah turned off the soldering iron and set it carefully out of the way, so she could cover her work. She hesitated a moment while her hand hovered over the box, unsure whether she should take it with her or leave it.

"What's in that?" Alvin must have noticed her uncertainty.

Hannah made up her mind. "I have no clue," she said cheerfully. "No clue at all."

Alvin stuck his head into Grant's office as they walked past. "We're heading out now. Do you need anything else tonight?"

Grant stretched his arms over his head and twisted in his chair. "No. I'm waiting on one more client. He should be here before closing time. Then Des and I will do Chinese take-out and make passionate love all night long."

Hannah grabbed Alvin's hand and pulled him away from the door. "Ewww. That's just TMI, Grant."

Alvin laughed. "Too much information. Agreed. Come on. There's a new place I want to try." He didn't let go of her as they strolled out the door and through the downtown streets.

It felt good to touch him. They argued good-naturedly, each pointing out the merits of different pizza restaurants. Hannah urged him toward the one she loved—Angel's, across the street from her flat. She didn't know if that was an unconscious attempt to have him close to her home, but she didn't care. She decided tonight she'd just let go and have fun.

Maybe she would even take G-ma's advice and have that chat.

Chapter Six

Lancaster Castle: 1543

"What are you doing? I haven't seen or heard from my counselor for a while."

Wynter felt Aurelia's hand on her shoulder. She bent further over the sheet of parchment covering the middle of the workbench, cut herbs strewn and dying on both sides.

"A commission for Lord Theodric. You probably shouldn't be looking at it, for I fear it is for you."

"Fear?"

"It's a snare. See?" She leaned back and pointed to the picture. "It's a trap for ... marriage, I suppose." Wynter contemplated the web. It was turning out better than she even imagined it. She could cast the copper by tomorrow. Over the past few days, the longing for Theodric's approval gnawed deep inside her. She shook her head. It was a commission. Period. That it was for her queen ... well, she'll deal with that when the time came.

"It's beautiful, Wynter. If he doesn't accept it, I will."

Wynter flushed with pride and trepidation. She felt the pull of the object even without a spell. That worried her.

"Can you tear yourself away to walk with me in the garden? It's a beautiful day, and I have need of your advice."

Wynter didn't want to go. She wanted to finish the drawing. "Of course, my lady." She stood but couldn't make her feet move as she stared at the parchment. Her heart beat faster; it felt as if it would burst out of her chest and take flight. Sweat poured down her face and between her breasts. She wiped her palms on her skirt.

Snatching up the parchment, Aurelia placed it face down on the table. Instantly, Wynter felt the weight release her from its grasp. She gasped for

236

air.

"Are you all right, Wynter? What happened?"

Wynter shook her head. She took the queen's hand and quickly led her out of the conservatory and into the fresh air. "It's a spell. It has to be. I knew Theodric could not be trusted. He came a couple of days ago with this commission. I instantly knew what he wanted—but there was something unusual, different. Aurelia, I know we haven't talked about this much, but can you tell me your thoughts of him?"

They strolled the dirt paths of the garden, arm in arm, the fragrance of roses permeating the air. Here and there, a gardener clipped the dead and dying flowers to encourage greater growth, or cut the long stems to decorate the hall. Colors of every hue filled the eye.

"I don't know, Wynter. There are so many vying for my hand. If I thought of each one, I wouldn't be able to take care of other, more important things."

Wynter stopped and examined the other woman. Tall and elegant, the queen dressed as befitted her station in a sapphire blue gown. Her blonde hair fell loose down her back, an indication of her unwed state. Wynter assumed her marital status related more to the untimely death of her parents, the previous royals, rather than reluctance on Aurelia's part.

"You do wish to marry, don't you?"

"Of course. When the time is right."

Wynter smiled. "That might be forever at your pace. Has any caught your eye at all?"

The queen took her arm and resumed their stroll. Every few steps she bent to bury her nose in a flower, inhaling deeply. "Yes, there is one."

Wynter waited. The sun disappeared behind a cloud and glowed again. "Well? Shall you tell me?"

The queen hesitated slightly. "No, I think not. You'd put a spell on him."

Wynter's mouth dropped open.

"Oh, not in a bad way," Aurelia assured her. "Only in a way you would assume was the best for me. Am I not right?"

Reluctantly, Wynter nodded.

"It's all right. I do understand. You've been taking care of me for a long time, Wynter. But in this, even your magick has its limitations."

"True, my lady. But there are ways to cast the spells—"

"So they don't come back to haunt you. Yes, I know. But in this, I want nothing to do with spells and magick. I want the man to come to me, open and honest, and I will judge him for what he is."

A spear of guilt pierced Wynter's chest. "What if he appears to be something he's not?"

Aurelia inclined her head. "Highly possible. But that is life, is it not?"

"My queen, I would protect you from fraud and heartache."

"I know you would, but this is not necessary. I came to you because I want to show you what I received a few days ago." Aurelia pulled an item from her pocket and put it in Wynter's hands. "One of yours?"

Wynter stared at the key she had turned over to Lord Theodric a month ago. So he had given it to her. If Aurelia wore it, the incantation should do its work. The queen will see into the man's true heart. So much for the queen's insistence of no magick. She forced a smile and a light tone.

"Yes, it is mine. Will you wear it?"

"That depends. Did you put a love spell on it?"

"No, I did not put a *love* spell on this key," Wynter answered, careful to speak the exact truth.

Aurelia nodded as she took the key back. "My handmaiden is looking for the perfect chain. I'll have it on at dinner tonight." She turned it over and over. "I'm happy to know it is made by your hand. It will protect me whether I will it or not."

"Yes, my queen." She paused. "And the man you received this from?"

"He won't be at dinner. He is away gathering more gifts for me, or so he said. We shall see." She guided them towards the conservatory. "We both have work. I'll leave you to it and expect you to dine with me later." Her nose wrinkled. "Bathed and freshly dressed, if you don't mind. You've been at your task for three straight days."

Chapter Seven

Lancaster: present day

Half a pepperoni pizza and three pints should have mellowed Hannah into a good night's sleep, but all she could do was stare at the ceiling. She tossed and turned for an hour with her stomach churning before she gave up and pulled on her sweats.

Ten minutes later, she used her key to enter through the back door of the studio. The restlessness and sense of foreboding evaporated the instant she uncovered the web. She breathed out a relieved sigh. The swarm of butterflies, beating to escape her insides, hadn't affected her budding relationship with Alvin.

Hannah examined the piece for flaws. None at all. A tiny *hallelujah* popped into her brain, and she glanced in triumph at the gift G-ma had sent.

And gawked at the empty spot where the box should have been.

Her eyes swept the entire workbench, to no avail. The gnawing in the pit of her stomach returned with a vengeance. She searched under papers and in containers while a quick succession of events from the evening flew through her mind, like a movie on four times fast-forward.

Alvin stopped by at eight.

They left to eat.

It took at least an hour to agree on a place.

Another hour before the pizza was ready.

Midnight had come and gone before Hannah got home and into bed.

Did she move the box without thinking? No. She swept her hand slowly over the empty place. No magic vibrated. That left ...

Grant.

He never closed the gallery before nine o'clock during the week. She pulled out her cell phone.

"Hello?" Grant's voice sounded more alarmed than annoyed. "Hannah? What's wrong? Did the gallery burn down?"

Thank the Goddess for caller ID.

"Where's the box, Grant?"

"Huh?"

"The black-velvet box from my workbench." Other alternatives popped into her head: a thief, the after-hours cleaning crew, Alvin. Nope, she wasn't going there. Not after the amazing evening they just spent together.

"Oh, that one. I sold it."

Hannah tried to speak but nothing came out of her open mouth. She sank onto the stool.

Grant yawned loudly. "Remember my friend, the one who bought the emerald key? Her husband came in and wanted another piece from your collection. He saw the necklace you were working on and fell in love with it. Really nice, by the way, Hannah."

"Gahhhh ..."

"What's that? Oh, anyway, I accidentally knocked the box to the floor, and lo and behold, a finished piece exactly like the one you had on your workbench! Charles purchased it on the spot. Get to bed, girl. It's three o'clock in the morning." He yawned again. "We'll talk commission tomorrow."

Hannah dropped the silent phone on the table. Another web necklace? "G-ma will be so pissed," she said to the empty room.

After ten minutes of pacing, and an inner debate on the merits of waking her grandmother or letting sleeping elderly ladies lie, her phone rang. She didn't have to peer at the faceplate. She swiped to answer after the first ring and listened.

"You lost it."

"Umm, more or less, G-ma. Grant ..."

"If you had opened the box, you would have seen the value of the necklace inside and then taken appropriate action to protect it. Correct?"

"Yes, ma'am," Hannah said meekly.

"Have you spoken to Alvin yet? Never mind," G-ma interrupted herself. "I know you haven't."

She heard G-ma breathing lightly for the next few minutes. Hannah knew better than to interrupt.

"All right, here's what we do. You contact Wynter; tell her not to let the necklace out of her sight. I'll call Alvin, explain everything and have him meet you at the gallery. He can help."

"What do you mean, explain everything? How is Alvin going to help with this?" In the short silence that followed, Hannah's imagination went wild. She huffed out a breath. "Just tell me, G-ma."

"Your Alvin has been working with me since you two started at the gallery a few years ago."

"Working with you? You mean, with witchcraft?"

"Yes, dear."

Hannah's mind whirled. "He's a witch?"

"Well, men prefer the term *wizard* to *witch*." Another pause. "I told you to talk to him."

"He knows about me?" She couldn't catch her breath. All those years she knew him, wanted him. He probably read her mind and felt sorry for her.

"Yes. Talk to him, Hannah. Only you two can fix things now."

Chapter Eight

Lancaster Castle: 1543

Wynter pushed away from the workbench and stretched. The web was nearly complete. Intricate in form, with worked metal adornments in silver and burnished gold, the delicate scrollwork glistened in the late morning light. She recited a spell with each weave of the wire, convinced the strong pull meant someone else had cast a different, blacker magick upon it than hers.

> *O dear Guardian wise and bold*
> *Maintain protection, strength behold.*
> *Allow this web to trap and clutch*
> *Keep them safe within your touch.*
> *I weave no harm as you decree*
> *As I am, so must it be.*

She had not seen Theodric since he commissioned the piece. Yet even in his absence, he haunted her mind. A sense of urgency to finish the piece before he returned ate at her. Every waking moment found her working on the piece—for him—no matter who the recipient would be. His scent lingered in the room; sensual waves teased her senses.

It thrilled her. It annoyed her.

Oddly enough, Aurelia left her alone. After their garden walk, she ceased to require Wynter's presence at meals. Her handmaiden never came for potions, only to deliver food. The other advisors no longer pounded on her door; they tended to avoid her anyway. The quiet was both welcome and unsettling.

Now that she thought of it, she had been at odds and ends with her feelings for quite a while. Ever since Theodric came to visit the workroom and commission the snare, her mind tangled from one extreme to another. Not a good sign at all.

A flash of light out of the corner of her eye announced her phantom's appearance. She really had no time for this, but her curiosity demanded satisfaction.

Wynter made the first move. "Will you speak to me today?"

The apparition shimmered, as if shifting. "Yes." The woman sounded more determined than acquiescent.

"Tell me your name so we may be comfortable with each other."

"Hannah MacKenzie."

"Hannah. What a beautiful name. I am Wynter." She started to swivel but stopped herself. "I can't behold you fully. Your image has always disappeared in the past when I try."

"Oh, wait. I have a spell for that."

Wynter brows lifted. How intriguing. She heard a rustling and then Hannah's voice, slow and clear.

> *Sacred Guardian, listen well*
> *Help me work this mirror spell.*
> *Keep me clear in this pressed glass*
> *Allow my ancestor true access.*
> *No curse or harm shall come from me*
> *As I will, I promise thee.*

Wynter winced at the horrible rendition of the spell, yet noted the words. She faced her great-great-great … whatever descendent. From her experiences with her own grandmother, this woman could be centuries into the future.

"We really must discuss your spell-wording abilities. But the Goddess apparently listens when you speak, so I should be grateful." The woman could have been her twin sister. They had the same dark hair, hazel eyes and similar coloring, but Hannah appeared to be older.

Hannah cocked her head. "Does that mean we'll have many more conversations in the future?"

"If you wish it." She snapped her fingers as a name popped into her head. "Gwen."

"That's my G-ma. Grandmother. How did you know?"

"I remember listening to my grandmother speak to a clanswoman by that name. But every time I looked, the woman disappeared. My grandmother told me she was of my blood but not for me, and I'll have my own to confer with when I get older."

Hannah smiled. "That sounds exactly like something my grandmother would say. I spent a lot of time in art school. I had a late start to the family business."

"You went to school? For art?" Wynter's attention waned. "You're here for a specific reason." She glanced over her shoulder. "And I want to get back to ..."

"The necklace."

Wynter narrowed her eyes. This witch had numerous surprises. "Yes."

Hannah nodded. "I have a lot of questions for you, but G-ma said I must hurry."

"Such a strange name you call your relative. The sound is disrespectful."

"Not at all." Hannah cleared her throat. "We—*I* have a problem. It concerns your necklace. I'm making one, too. I've lost yours, the one you're working on right now. G-ma says if I don't get it back, it might affect things in your time period as well as mine. She keeps talking about 'completing the circle.'"

Wynter thought over Hannah's words and dismissed them. "I see." She had no time to deal with another witch, one from the future *and* untrained. She'll take care of things here, as she always did. "Well, I'm sure your ... G-ma ... will be able to help you."

"But—"

Wynter glanced at the web and instantly forgot everything else. Her hand caressed a precious stone, its warmth awaiting a final resting place between the legs of the spider. Her lips moved.

O dear Guardian, wise and bold ...

Chapter Nine

Hannah backed away from the mirror, stunned. Her ancestor was a bit of a witchy snob. She strode back to her studio, plugged in the soldering iron and began putting the necklace together. Her hands flew through the motions; she knew exactly where each piece fit.

At this point, she wasn't sure she wanted to talk to Wynter again. The woman seemed intrigued at first, and G-ma would probably insist she give it another try. But something had distracted Wynter's attention enough to totally shrug off their shared problem.

Hannah held up the necklace. Done. Now for the chain. She crimped it on, performed one final inspection and rummaged in the cabinet for a case.

Talking to someone from hundreds of years ago was pretty cool, right? Hannah imagined that someone of her flesh and blood would feel the same, not dismiss her out of hand. She nestled the web on the black velvet and snapped the lid shut. What could be more important than—

Hannah froze. Than the necklace. Of course.

She strode across the room and pulled open the back door. Alvin stood motionless on the other side, eyes wide, one hand upraised to knock.

"Don't get all crazy," Hannah said. "I heard your car. What's in the package?" She hated the sound of her voice, clipped and angry.

"Your grandmother said to bring a mirror gift for the exchange?"

He sounded uncertain. Hannah suspected his hesitancy concerned the topic of conversation he had with G-ma, rather than the actual middle-of-the-night wake-up call.

"Fine." This time, for security, Hannah opened the large safe in the back corner of the studio and placed her necklace on a shelf. "Let me grab

Grant's records and keys so we can retrieve the other necklace." She strode out the door, Alvin dogging her footsteps.

"Your grandmother told me you lost it. Can't you replace it with the one you're making?"

She glared at him over her shoulder. "I didn't lose it, and no, I can't replace it with mine. According to G-ma, they're both part of a circle, some great plan," she put air quotes around the two words, "you and I have to figure out. We should be happy Grant and the Emerson's are practically family, otherwise we couldn't pull off the switch with your enchanted mirror." She waited for him to notice her emphasis.

Alvin checked his watch. "We have about two hours of darkness left. Do you have the spell?"

She stopped without warning and swung around. Alvin backpedaled to avoid a collision. "What? You didn't bring your wizard wand?" She poked a finger into his chest. "How long have you been working with G-ma?" She poked again. "How long have you known you were a wizard and *didn't*." Poke. "*Tell*." Poke. "*Me*."

He grabbed her finger before she could stab him with it again. "Whoa. Just to make things perfectly clear, I didn't know the extent of your powers until your grandmother called and explained what had happened. So that works both ways, Hannah. Plus, she said we were supposed to talk the other day?"

The man had a point. She resisted the urge to growl. Pulling her finger out of his grasp, she continued down the hall. "She's a sneak, isn't she? After all this is over, the three of us are going to sit down for a long talk." She rummaged through the papers from Grant's inbox without waiting for him to answer. "Here it is."

"Hannah." Alvin dropped his package on the desk and stepped up behind her, effectively imprisoning her against the desk. He put his hands on her shoulders.

She wanted to tell him this wasn't the time. She wanted to ask him if he felt the connection between them without their magic—or because of it. She wanted to kiss him and know that he wanted it, too. Reluctantly, she obeyed the pressure of his hands and turned.

And melted when his hands rubbed lightly up and down her arms.

"I don't want you angry with me, Hannah. My world's not right if you're upset." His face took on the appearance of a whipped puppy.

Hannah narrowed her eyes.

Before she could respond, he shook his head. His mouth quirked into a half-grin. "Sorry. I didn't mean to do that. I have a lack of control around you, Hannah. I think of something and it happens."

"Really? So you thought to make me feel sorry for you?"

"To make you not mad at me. I figured everybody loves a puppy when they're down." He widened his eyes and cocked his head to the side.

Hannah couldn't help it. She laughed.

Before she could blink, Alvin had his mouth on hers. His arms surrounded her, pulling her close.

By the Goddess. Hannah didn't know why that expression popped into her head, but she didn't care. She closed her eyes and poured herself into the kiss.

When they parted, Alvin's forehead touched hers. "Wow," he whispered. "And the reason we've never done this before?"

"No clue."

As she angled her head for another kiss, Hannah felt the equivalent of a slap on the back of her head. When his eyelids popped open, she realized Alvin felt it too.

"Your grandmother." He gave her a quick peck and moved away. "We definitely need to talk. Think she's getting a kick out of this?"

Hannah nodded. "Oh, yeah. Let's get this done, and then we'll deal with everything else." She picked up Grant's keys and reached into her pocket. "Here's the spell. I'll drive while you try to make it better. Someone told me I'm not very good at it."

In the car, Alvin read the words out loud.

> *Beloved guardian, hear me well*
> *Lend your strength to help this spell.*
> *Guide our passage soft and fast*
> *Help us find the item past.*
> *A gift we leave as a trade*
> *By our word, no harm conveyed.*

~ * ~

At ten minutes to six in the morning, Hannah stood in front of *Beauty*

247

Multiplied with the necklace in her left hand. Alvin stepped next to her; she met his eyes in the dozens of reflections as his hand snaked down to encompass hers.

"G-ma?"

"She'll be here."

She expected him to reach into his pocket for his cell phone and make a video call. Instead, he laid his palm flat on the surface of the mirror. Her grandmother appeared to one side like a flickering, translucent life form straight out of the latest episode of Star Trek.

Hannah gasped. "How did you do that?"

He laughed. "Secret wizard stuff. Ask your grandmother."

G-ma shook her head. "We don't have time right now. Do you have the necklace?"

Hannah held up the one she had made.

"That's not the original." G-ma frowned.

"You said the magic is inside of me, didn't you?" Hannah didn't wait for an answer. "We drove to Blackpool and retrieved—"

"Stole," Alvin interjected.

Hannah sighed. "*Stole* Wynter's necklace from Charles Emerson, Alvin did his wizardry thing and returned the necklace to the past. I need to do the same with mine, so the circle is complete, right?"

"It sounds as if you two finally talked and made some decisions. But there's something missing. I just can't put my finger on it. Did you leave a gift in its place?"

Alvin nodded. "A small handheld mirror. It's enchanted, so the Emerson's will think that's what they bought from Grant last night."

"G-ma. I thought you said we were running out of time. Have you changed your mind?"

"No. Not at all." She paced away. "Be silent a moment, and let me think."

Hannah stifled a snort when Alvin hummed the Jeopardy theme under his breath. "Shh. You'll get us both in trouble," she whispered.

"Worth it to get in trouble with you, Hannah Mackenzie."

She dropped her eyes, afraid to look at him. His voice was too soft, too enticing, his hand too warm. The man wove his own kind of spell around her.

"What do you want, Alvin?" she murmured.

When he didn't answer, Hannah's gaze cut back to the mirror. He watched her grandmother, a slight smile dancing around his mouth. If he ever looked at *her* that way ...

She couldn't pinpoint the exact moment his eyes went from G-ma to her. Everything literally stopped. Her breath, her heart. *Time.*

When the world began again, his smile had grown wider. *Holy mother ...*

"I hate to interrupt this tender moment, children." G-ma's brisk voice acted like the sound of a gong in an otherwise silent room—hard and jarring, yet soothing in the echo. "I know what we missed. It's Grant. One of you," she stared pointedly at Alvin, "will have to correct the paperwork. I'll leave his handling to you." As if in slow motion, she shimmered to face Hannah. "Do you have the spell?"

"Yes," she croaked and then cleared her throat, concentrating once again on the task at hand. "Yes. Everyone ready?"

Alvin squeezed her hand and nodded. G-ma raised both her ghostly arms into the air; Hannah saw her lips move. Probably praying. She touched the necklace to the mirror.

Guardian that lives within the dale,
Protect our goal so we won't fail.
Allow this gift to timely leap
Into the warden's hand to keep.
No harm shall come, nor any strife,
A promise kept upon my life.

Anticipating the split second between shimmer and flash, Hannah tossed the necklace like a Frisbee through the glass. Straight into an upraised hand on the other side.

Chapter Ten

Clitheroe Castle: 1543

Theodric opened his fist as soon as the three spirits disappeared. The old woman, Gwen, he knew well. He assumed the other two were the now grown children she spoke of so often. The new generation, she called them.

The necklace seemed the exact replica of the one Wynter had crafted by his request. He opened the trunk set in the back corner of the pavilion and took out a small bag. Pulling on the drawstring, he tipped the jewel into his palm before comparing the two pieces side by side. He felt the pull of magick in Wynter's creation, weaker in the other. He shrugged. He'd take care of it. There would be sufficient magick when he finished. It was enough they appeared identical.

He contemplated the spell spoken by the young witch. Warden. He liked the name, for he fully intended to take control of *his* witch, as well as guide the descendants. At least Gwen agreed the circle of power should not be broken, which is why she planted Wynter's artistic seed within the conception of her granddaughter. The boy's presence and abilities strengthened the bond. Theodric looked forward to the day he would tell Alvin of his own blood descent and role within the circle.

"Theo! Are you ready to ride? The day grows late and our people are restless!"

Ambrose sounded anxious to get to Lancaster and for once, Theodric didn't blame him. He tucked both necklaces securely in the pouch.

"On my way, cousin," he called back. "On my way."

~ * ~

Lancaster Castle

The instant she had packed away the finished necklace a fortnight ago,

Wynter felt more herself again. Gone were the longings for Theodric, the memory of his kiss. His scent evaporated, and she spent most of her time close to the queen, intent on keeping the advisors aware of her presence and protection.

One afternoon, a courier announced a large entourage due to arrive at the castle. Giddy as young girls, Aurelia and Wynter ran upstairs to the top of the ramparts, anxious to see new faces. They peered into the late afternoon sun, searching for a pennant.

"There!" Aurelia pointed and then grasped the key that rested on her bodice.

She didn't recognize the pennant, but the queen's gesture wasn't lost on Wynter. As the column rode closer, she searched for Theodric and then squinted again, stunned. He rode at the very front, conversing with another man, both covered in helmetless armor. That meant the rest of the men were … his. Wynter saw women and children well guarded on all sides by scores of warriors. He had brought his entire household.

She waited for the familiar ache in her chest, present whenever he came to mind. Perhaps the months of absence had finally broken his hold on her. Then Theodric looked up, as if he knew her thoughts. Even from that distance, their eyes met. Her heart fell deep into the pit of her stomach and then leapt back again, beating hard.

By the Goddess.

"Look, Wynter. My future husband is here. Would you relay my command to ready the castle for guests?"

Wynter glanced at Aurelia. A smile curved the queen's lips, but her flushed cheeks and the sparkle in her eyes belied her calm exterior. Wynter's throat closed; she could not utter a sound. Before Aurelia noticed, she embraced her queen and stepped away, bowing low.

By the time she blindly made her way to the bottom of the stairs, she had decided to immediately return to her cottage in Clitheroe. No magick or potion on earth could help her now. Quickly, she relayed the queen's orders and ran to pack her things. Aurelia would forgive her for leaving without permission. She would be occupied with Theodric and his people.

Wynter tried for over an hour to escape the castle, but servant after servant detained her for instructions, "my lady this" and "my lady that." She finally exploded, "I am *not* a lady, I am a *witch*!"

251

Wynter swung around at the slow clapping that sounded from across the room.

"True words, my dear." Theodric chuckled and inclined his head in her direction. "You see, Ambrose? I did tell you we had a witch in residence. She's delightful once you get to know her."

She ground her teeth. "You seem to forget I am not here on any person's command except my own."

He crossed the room, hand extended, and smiled when she hid her fists behind her back. "I would never forget. Come. I have someone I wish for you to meet." He waited patiently for her to comply.

She could no more deny him than she could breathe. Despair ate at her, knowing he belonged to another, but she obeyed by placing her hand in his. The instant they touched, she almost pulled away. It felt so *right*. His fingers closed around hers as he drew her across the room.

"Wynter, this is my cousin Ambrose. He wanted to meet you before our audience with the queen."

The man equaled Theodric in height and coloring; he even sported the same twinkling eyes and slight smirk around his generous mouth. However, he was dressed completely in black, in opposition to the normal greens and browns of Theodric's wardrobe.

Ambrose claimed her hand from Theodric. He charmed her with a slight bow and a kiss on her knuckles, but he wasn't his cousin. "You are as beautiful as Theo told me."

Wynter almost snorted before she realized the man offered her a genuine compliment. "Thank you, sir." She remembered her manners and curtsied in return. "However, I would think your cousin should speak to you of his *bride*, rather than the resident witch." She faced Theodric. "And you, my lord. You have been gone many weeks, which doesn't bode well for you. The queen has been anxious but silent."

"What? My name has not been bandied about in my absence?" He grinned at Ambrose. "I am devastated."

Wynter rolled her eyes, bobbed another curtsy to them both and swung away. "I'm sure the queen will make up for it once you are in her presence, for she said *nothing* while you were gone. Just played with that key I created for you." She *had* to leave quickly, unsure how much more time she could tolerate in his presence without throwing herself in his arms. She cursed under her breath.

"Ah, but I am not finished with you, my dear." Theodric moved in front of her and walked backwards when she didn't halt. "You have something for me?"

That stopped her. The snare. Without thinking, she put a hand on the satchel attached to her girdle. His eyes followed the movement, and she swore they lit up in anticipation.

He had been gone for so long she hoped he would forget about the necklace. As much as she hated to admit it, her great-great-great ... descendent, Hannah Mackenzie, had been right. The necklace *was* gone. She had wasted too much time searching for it while she packed. Now the only man in the world she wished to avoid trapped her in this room.

She stalled. "We never talked price, my lord," she said slowly, allowing her lips to curve upwards. Her mind raced, trying to think of an excuse to explain the jewel's disappearance.

He stepped closer, until only a breath could come between them, and bent his head to her ear. His whisper sent shivers down her spine. "Minx. Trust me, we will talk price but not here and now." He eased away as Ambrose joined them. "Show me, Wynter," he demanded.

When he spoke to her that way, when he was that close, Wynter forgot about everything—forgot about his forthcoming proposal, forgot that the queen held the key to his heart, literally, through *Wynter's* spell. Forgot that the necklace was missing.

She offered him the empty box.

Wynter waited for Theodric's anger to explode. When both men smiled and nodded, she seized the open case out of their hands. The necklace!

Ambrose bowed low to her. "It's exquisite, Wynter. Theo told me much about your work, but his words didn't do it justice. I hope you allow me to commission other pieces as well." He plucked it out of the box. "Please, may I hold it up to you?"

Still stunned, Wynter balked. "Um, that is not a wise thing to do, sir. It's made specifically for one woman, and it would be bad luck for anyone else to wear it." She glanced at Theodric. He watched his cousin, silent.

"One woman?" Ambrose circled her and she turned, trying to keep pace with him, so he couldn't place it around her neck. He stopped and cocked his head in question.

As she took a breath to answer, Wynter saw a blur swing in front of her and something heavy struck her throat.

She tried to turn, to bat it away, but it was too late. Theodric closed the clasp with an audible snap. The spider nestled between her breasts; the snare set. She twisted to look at Theodric.

"What have you done?" she cried.

~ * ~

Wynter spent an entire hour attempting to remove the necklace, reciting spell after spell to break through the snare. Impossible. What game was Theodric playing? Why had the necklace disappeared and then reappeared when he touched the box? What kind of magick did the man possess?

She finally gave up trying to answer the riddles when a servant came to fetch her to dinner—an intimate affair in Aurelia's apartments rather than the great hall.

Aurelia paid no attention to Theodric at all, instead keeping her gaze and conversation with Ambrose. Wynter supposed it was only polite. After all—he *was* a king in his own right, a tidbit of information both men had failed to convey to her earlier in the evening.

However, Wynter believed the queen's constant caressing of Theodric's pendant, in front of Ambrose, a bit tasteless. She wondered what Theodric thought about it. He ignored the queen in turn and kept his attention on Wynter.

After servants cleared the last of the food, Lord Theodric grasped her hand and pulled her from the table, bowing a "by your leave" to the royals. Head spinning with all that had transpired, Wynter had no will to protest. Once past the door, he guided her to a shadowed area between the torches. He gently pushed her against the wall and leaned forward, hands flat on either side of her head. Just before their lips met, she averted her head.

"Don't."

He put his hand softly on her throat, over the necklace. "Why not? I think I've made my claim fairly obvious." His eyes glittered in the dim light.

She huffed out a laugh. "Oh, you didn't need the necklace to stake any claim, my lord. Trust me on that. But how can you play with two women the way you do? One a queen, and one a ... a *witch*. Do you not fear the consequences of your actions?"

He chuckled and nuzzled at her neck. She lifted her head to give him better access to the sensitive skin. Wynter wasn't sure if the necklace took away her strength to deny him, or if she just used it as an excuse to gain what she truly wanted.

"Does this feel as if I'm worried?" He lifted his head. "I know what I'm getting into, Wynter. You've beguiled me as much as this necklace has snared you."

Her fingers traced the contours of his face. "You didn't need the necklace, Theodric. You had me the first time you approached my cottage. Although I denied your charms with every breath I took." This time, she brought their lips together.

A thought crossed her mind. "What of Aurelia?"

He shrugged. "What of the queen? I gave the gifts to her in Ambrose's name. As we speak, he's probably proposing to her. They suit, don't you think? I believe Ambrose and Aurelia will have their hands full with each other."

"What? Why didn't you tell me?" Wynter tried to push him away, a difficult task since his body pressed fully against hers. He allowed her a few inches before she stilled, her mind racing. "You have magick of your own, don't you? You countered mine."

He drew her near again. "Does that upset you? You're not disappointed in the outcome, are you, my witch? That day, at your cottage, when you tried to hide your true self from me ..." He trailed his lips across her cheeks and forehead.

"What about it?" she mumbled, turning her head so his mouth met hers.

"Hmmm. Tell me more about not needing the necklace to bind you to me."

Wynter laughed. "You are impossible, my lord."

"But you love that about me, do you not?" He leaned back a bit to search her eyes. "Will you wed me, Wynter? Do you believe I will treasure and cherish you all my days? I want children with you, boys who will be wizardly lords and girls who will be lady witches. I want to spend eternity with you."

Wynter felt the spell of the snare working through her body as he said the words and realized the web worked both ways.

Before she could answer, the door next to them burst open. Aurelia and Ambrose rushed into the hallway, hand in hand. "Wynter! You'll never guess what just happened!"

Around the queen's neck lay an identical web. The one she had crafted.

Everything fell into place. Earlier, when Ambrose took the necklace from Wynter, he always intended it to be for Aurelia, the queen he wooed from afar. Theodric, on the other hand, already had *Hannah's* necklace in his possession. A fine piece of magick she intended to discover from her soon-to-be betrothed.

She smirked and finally answered Theodric's question. "Yes, my lord. I foresee many, many daughters."

He groaned.

THE END

About the Author

If you discovered a sealed box with "Katie's memories" scribbled on the side, you'd find a lifetime of partially completed stories, plays and musicals. Katie Stephens has opened that box and writes both non-fiction and fiction, where she happily experiments with all genres. Although her grown children are scattered east and west across the country, she lives solidly in mid-America with two kitties and a husband who keeps asking when she's really going to retire.

Connect with Katie at:
Facebook https://www.facebook.com/KatieStephensAuthor
Twitter @standardishue
Website http://standardishue.com/
Email standardishue@gmail.com

A note from the publisher

Thanks to all of the authors who contributed their creative stories for our summer anthology, Propose To Me. Your voices shine through these stories and I am confident readers will enjoy every one of them.

And to the readers, thank you for supporting the authors and small press publishers.

Nancy Schumacher, Publisher

Melange Books LLC
www.melange-books.com

Satin Romance
www.satinromance.com

Fire and Ice for Young Adults
www.fireandiceya.com

www.ingramcontent.com/pod-product-compliance
Lightning Source LLC
Chambersburg PA
CBHW031941260626
47157CB00016B/1092